Iain Hollingshead is a journalist at the *Daily Telegraph*, and has also written for the *Guardian*, the *Sunday Times* and *GQ*. In 2007 he co-authored a musical, *Blair on Broadway,* which transferred to the West End the following year. He is also the editor of *Am I Alone in Thinking…?*, a bestselling collection of unpublished letters to the *Daily Telegraph*. He is 29 years old and lives in London. *Beta Male* is his second novel.

www.iainhollingshead.co.uk

To Phil, James, Fez, Rick and Tom

Complete masculinity and stupidity
are often indistinguishable.
H. L. Mencken

Chapter One

It all started, appropriately enough, at a wedding.

Like most people between the age of twenty-eight and thirty-five, the rhythm of my calendar year is ruled by the predictability of the marrying classes. In January, people get engaged, the less imaginative among them on New Year's Eve, encouraged by the dictatorial timekeeping of a sixteenth-century Pope to make the ultimate, timely resolution: this year, they slur, I shall lose weight, drink less, give up smoking, change jobs and yes, marry that girl I took out the joint mortgage with a few years back. Others wait until they go skiing later in the month, sufficiently taken, perhaps, by the panda eyes, peeling nose and balaclava-clad beauty of their beloved to decide to spend every other skiing holiday together for the rest of their lives. The laggards leave it until the middle of February, so horrified by the prospect of trying to get through another Valentine's Day of hints and significant looks without a serious row that they too throw in the towel and pledge to make an honest woman of their scowling girlfriend.

Then Facebook statuses can be updated, walls congratulated, groups created. Former lovers finally give up 'poking' someone else's fiancée. Back in the real world, everyone scrambles over the guest list and the all-important 'save the date' fridge magnet. Are we first round or first refusal? Bride, groom or maybes? Suddenly, we show a frantic interest in getting the future Colvilles round for dinner. *Such a nice couple. They never make you feel like a gooseberry. I've always fancied his sister.* Sometimes – in a roundabout way, for we are British, after all – we even try to get the information from the horse's mouth. *Have you set a date yet? Where are you going to have it?* Or, most shamelessly and transparently indirect of all: *Are you planning a big wedding?* Arguments over the date itself can turn violent, especially if you've chosen a bumper year. Keep the date free, we're told. That date? No, this one. Sally's got that date already. She reserved it as soon as she got engaged *last year* and her mother has ALREADY BOOKED THE MARQUEE.

There then follows a few months of peace and quiet, punctuated only by unseasonable March nuptials of surprised-looking girls with five-month bumps and highly traditional fathers.

The real fun, however, doesn't start until the stag and hen season, the John the Baptist of the wedding season itself. Some people enjoy being lectured by a little toe-rag on his gap year, brandishing a paintball gun as if it were part of his anatomy. Others get a genuine kick out of an expensive holiday they can't remember, doing things they hate, accompanied by people they wouldn't like even if they did know them. I am not one of those people.

And then, finally, it's the summer: the sound of leather on willow, the smell of freshly cut grass and the rumbustious clatter of £20,000 parties that have a forty per cent chance of ending in divorce. My favourite time of year. As you may have guessed, I am an old-fashioned romantic and there's nothing I like more than a good wedding.

*

On the 'day it all started', right in the middle of the wedding season, I was woken by Alan, which is a fairly unpromising way for anyone to start a day. Alan is, by some margin, the youngest of three brothers – it is widely assumed that Alan's rather forceful mother desperately wanted a daughter and either tricked or bullied Alan's father into trying one last time. Alan was the result: an unfortunate name bestowed in the throes of revenge on an unfortunate boy who had the misfortune not to be a girl. Worse still, Alan looks like an Alan. If he had been particularly good at sport, he could have been Al. *Big Al. Al man.* If he had been artistic or creative, he might have got away with branding himself *Ali.* But as it happened, Alan was no good at sport or art. He grew up to be a short, slight, malco-ordinated philistine, who was quite good with numbers. So he became an accountant instead. Alan the accountant. Poor sod. And, perhaps worst of all, he also had the misfortune to be my flatmate.

'Wake up, you dozy tosser.'

'Go away, fuckface.'

'Big day today.'

I groaned and pulled the duvet a little higher. 'Not as big as your mum.'

Alan and I have known each other since we were five (his stick-thin mother was our primary school teacher), which is long enough to get away with affectionate abuse. I suppose it's our substitute for hugging and crying and giggling and eating chocolate and arguing over boys and stealing each other's clothes and synchronising menstrual cycles and competing over who can eat the fewest Ryvitas, then hugging and crying and giggling all over again, which is what girls who share flats do. Alan's long-term girlfriend – Jess, who actually *is* huge – just thinks we've never grown up. She might have a point, but it doesn't make me dislike her any less.

We got up, breakfasted on cold pizza left over from the previous evening, and took Alan's rusty old car – partly because I don't own one, partly because Lisa's parents live in the arse end of Arseville. And on the way, Alan attempted to 'talk'.

'So, how are you feeling?'

'I am feeling too hot,' I said, turning on the car's air conditioning.

'No, how are you *feeling*?' he repeated.

'Oh, how I am *feeling*? I'm *feeling* you should shut up and concentrate on the driving.'

Alan looked momentarily hurt, making me feel momentarily bad. Then he caught Jess's eye in the rear view mirror and ploughed on regardless. When you catch Jess's eye, you tend to do what it tells you to do.

'I mean, Lisa… '

'Lisa what?'

'Lisa, you know… '

'Yes, I know Lisa.'

Alan tried, and failed, not to look exasperated. Poor little Alan; he was always looking slightly exasperated by something: by me, by his mother, by his overweight girlfriend, by his job, by his bullying boss Amanda, by life in general. He pushed his glasses back up his nose, sat up straighter so he could peer more convincingly over the steering wheel and let out a long-suffering sigh. 'All I'm trying to say, Sam, is that it was a relatively long time for you guys so I know how you must be feeling. I mean, I remember what it was like with Matt and Sophie when… '

Alan droned on in his good-intentioned way, but I didn't really care what he was trying to say, or just how empathetically he attempted to say it. The truth was that today my ex-girlfriend was getting married to some rich bastard she'd met at work and, on reflection, I probably shouldn't have accepted the invitation. Alan and I had had an intense debate about it the moment the thick, expensive card had landed on the doorstep six Saturdays previously, its every detail – from the calligraphed address on the envelope ('Sam Hunt Esq.'), to its precise timing, to the embossed third-person wording of the invitation itself – cloyingly correct.

She'd only invited me to be polite, Alan had said. I couldn't possibly go. I'd only been asked in the expectation that I would say no. To avoid any awkwardness, I would be expected to make an excuse about a prior engagement, a family summer holiday perhaps, and politely decline. This was *the done thing*. Well, perhaps this was the done thing, I'd told Alan, scrawling on a sheet of Basildon Bond and thrusting it under his nose. He'd read it out loud: 'Sam Hunt thanks Mrs Geoffrey Parker for her kind invitation to the marriage of her daughter. Incidentally, while he's at it, he'd also like to thank Mrs Geoffrey Parker for letting him sleep with said daughter for eight of the last forty-eight months, even though Mrs Geoffrey Parker never thought Sam Hunt was good enough for said daughter. Unfortunately, due to this latter point, Sam Hunt feels it would be the done thing for him to decline the invitation due to a prior engagement he is just about to invent.'

'You're a tosser,' Alan had said, accurately, screwing up my last sheet of writing paper, which meant I had to send an electronic reply instead to lisawedding1@hotmail.co.uk, a nod to modernity which was certainly *not* the done thing. It would have had Mrs Geoffrey Parker writhing in agony (although not as much, I suppose, as if she'd had to choose lisawedding2@hotmail.co.uk).

But I'd accepted, all the same – partly out of sheer perversity, partly because I was still friends with Lisa and thought I could handle it, partly because my best mates would be there and I didn't want to miss out. Anyway, as I've already said, I like weddings. The difference between a cynic and a sentimentalist is measured only by success.

'You going to be okay?' asked Alan as we finally pulled up in front of the church after a torturous twenty minutes getting lost in country lanes and attempting to read the tiny Google map on the back of the invitation while Jess shrieked at us from the back.

'Yes.' I smiled at him. 'I'm going to be just fine.'

And I was just fine, at first. I managed not to snort when we entered the church and an usher I'd never met accosted me with an Order of Service on which the letters 'L' and 'T' had been unattractively entwined to resemble some sort of GCSE geometry question. I held my peace when Alan stamped jocularly on my foot during the bit where the vicar asked if anyone knew of any lawful impediment why Lisa Amelia should not be joined to Timothy James. I even succeeded in keeping a straight face while Lisa's elder sister – a harlot of a girl, if ever there was one – read a Bible passage about chastity. At least we were spared Khalil Gibran. And immediately after the service, I was greatly cheered by the look on Alan's face as Jess successfully jostled for the bouquet.

The beginning of the reception was 'just fine', too. I smiled graciously when Lisa thanked me in her absent-minded way for the generous wedding present, recalling the set of £3.99 tablemats that Alan and I had rushed to buy online the moment the list was announced. I made friends with the waitresses and persuaded them it would be easier for them just to leave the bottle with me. I even had an enjoyable catch-up with Lisa's father, Geoffrey, in which he did his best to put me at my ease.

'Hello, Sam. How is the acting going?'

'Oh, you know. Bit quiet at the moment. Thinking about sacking my agent. Holding out for the next Bond vacancy. That sort of thing.'

He laughed. 'Will I have seen you in anything recently?'

'Not unless you've watched Greek television on holiday at 3am and were particularly taken by a credit card advert.'

Geoffrey smiled sadly. 'Oh, dear, Sam. It doesn't sound like much of a way to make a living. Maybe you should settle down yourself some time. Give up the Peter Pan act.' He turned to intercept someone making his way across the lawn in tails – his own, to judge by the cut. 'Oh, now, have you met Timothy, my new son-in-law? Works with Lisa in her bank.'

'Worked *for* Lisa, actually,' corrected Timothy. 'I married the boss. And then I quit and went back to university. Good timing, really. Bankers aren't exactly flavour of the decade. Haw haw.'

Timothy and I made inconsequential small talk until 'breakfast' was announced at 5pm, giving me plenty of time for an important internal debate about whether or not I'd be able to beat him in a fight (conclusion: yes, he had a weak chin). But in retrospect – in as far as you can be sure of anything in retrospect – this was probably the moment that the idea first took root in my subconscious. Lisa now worked in a bank? Lisa was filthy rich? Her husband had worked *for* her? He'd left to do what he wanted to do?

We'll come back to that later. More important at that precise moment was the seating plan. To avoid the embarrassment of numbering the tables – and thereby creating the impression of some sort of hierarchy – the geometrically entwined Lisa and Timothy had taken the considerably more embarrassing decision to give the tables names of English counties instead. My table, 'Rutland', was, I noted, the furthest from the top table in the marquee and comprised ten people: my three oldest friends, Alan, Matt and Ed; the achingly trendy young vicar (I think he was called something like David, or *Dave*) who'd married the couple; his dull, plain wife; and four other born-again Christian girls who apparently knew Lisa's younger sister from university.

Lisa had obviously decided that if I was going to be stubborn enough to come to her wedding, then she could at least ensure I wouldn't get laid.

Sitting on a table with religious people at a wedding does, however, have its advantages, as I soon found out. Even if Jesus can't pop up to turn the water into wine, you can be sure that there will be more for the rest of you to get stuck into. And stuck in the four of us got, talking, perhaps a little rudely, over the heads of the others, who were too polite to say if they thought it strange for four people in their late twenties to have stayed in touch since primary school.

We'd never made any new friends since, Matt used to joke. It's a dangerous world of strangers out there, Ed would say. I'm too old to make new friends now, Alan liked to quip. But the truth was we liked each other; we knew each other – better than we knew our own families, even. Some unmarried people find themselves stuck with their leftover friends. We were lucky enough to have stayed in touch with the ones we actually liked. We felt like brothers who would never fall out, who could always pick up where we left off, who would never lose touch even if we didn't see each other for a while. And these days we didn't get to see each other nearly as much as we wanted. Work got in the way – for the others at least. Girlfriends, distance, travel – all created obstacles. Matt was a not-very-good doctor who kept getting placements he didn't want in crap parts of the country. Ed had quit his inner-city school due to stress and gone off to TEFL abroad for a while, before coming back to teach in London and moving in with his girlfriend, Tara. Meanwhile, Alan and I kept the home fires burning in our tiny north London flat, which the others would come and trash whenever they could (and whenever Jess, who didn't seem to like any of us very much, wasn't around).

But still, it wasn't the same; it wasn't the same as it used to be – at the same series of small schools in Reading, at university together in Manchester, and then in London, predictably, like the rest of the graduate world, in the glory days when all four of us had shared a cheap house next to a drug den in Brixton. It wasn't how we'd imagined. And now we were almost thirty and hangovers took two days to clear and our parents were retiring and growing old and our other friends were marrying and breeding and getting fixed-rate mortgages and promotions at work and going on smug holidays with other smug couples.

Now was the end of the beginning of our adult lives and I, for one, was terrified.

'Are you thinking of getting married, Sam?' asked the trendy vicar, pouncing on the tiniest of pauses in conversation. Given that I'd just finished telling Matt about the casting director I'd attempted, and failed, to seduce in a desperate bid to get a part in a fringe musical on £50 per week, it was a somewhat naïve question to ask.

'I don't know,' I said, even though I did. 'It's just that I've been to so many bloody weddings that it can be difficult to get excited about them any more. White weddings, black-tie weddings, Scottish weddings, second weddings, winter weddings, Catholic weddings, happy-clappy weddings, Jewish weddings, civil weddings, gay weddings, Hindu weddings that go on for several weeks, weddings in hotels, weddings in people's gardens, weddings abroad, weddings on beaches... ' I broke off to take a swig of wine and stroke the knee of a girl called Mary sitting next to me. 'I mean, all those hymns and in-laws and seating plans and first dances and speeches and cakes and bands that think they can play The Beatles and "champagne" that's not quite champagne... Seriously, why are people so keen on getting married? Why does our generation even bother any more? You'd have thought that, in the twenty-first century, we'd have grown out of it, along with black and white television, slavery and religion.'

The vicar and the born-agains winced. I ignored them. I had an audience for the first time in months and I was on something of a roll.

'Honestly,' I continued, 'what's the big appeal? Years ago, people got married because it was the done thing to do. You chose a girl who didn't look like the back end of a bus, wooed her, said polite things to her father and then settled down to raise children together. It was the only way to get on in life –'

'It was the only way to have sex,' interrupted Matt.

'It still is, for us,' said Mary, removing my hand from her knee.

'But why do the rest of us carry on with the charade?' I continued. 'We have friends, we have guilt-free sex, occasionally. Some of us have jobs. Why do we kid ourselves that we can really choose a partner for life? We're not swans, after all. I might be a completely different person by the time I'm forty.'

'I hope you're a completely different person by the time you're forty,' said Ed.

'Forty is a very long way off for me, Ed.'

'How so? You're twenty-nine, like the rest of us. In fact, you're a few months older than the rest of us.'

'Age isn't linear. You, Ed, have a long-term girlfriend and a mortgage. That makes you at least thirty-three. I have neither, so am still twenty-two at heart.'

'Lisa is Sam's ex-girlfriend,' Alan informed the rest of the table.

'Ah, that explains it,' said the trendy vicar.

'That explains what?'

'That explains why you're rather anti-marriage today.'

'I'm not anti-marriage, today any more than any other day. I rather enjoy other people's weddings, as it happens. Attending the funeral for their sex lives is often surprisingly entertaining. No, I just think that marriage should be recognised for the convenient sham that it is. You guys think it symbolises some sort of mystical union between Jesus and his Church, which has to be the biggest pile of bollocks I've ever heard. "Christ is the bridegroom, the Church is his bride and Christians marry each other to try and get closer to God." I mean, come on: talk about three in a marriage. And we heathens aren't much better, either, pretending to be religious for a few months – sorry, vicar, but do you really think you're going to see Lisa again now the Alpha course you made her go on is over? – so we can get married in church with some of our favourite childhood hymns and a reading from Corinthians.

'Why can't we just be honest and say that our choice of partner is decided by a crap little game of musical chairs? At some point in our late twenties or early thirties, blokes think that they might as well settle down with the girl they're with – the better-suited one they were going out with before becomes a victim of unfortunate timing – and have babies before her biological clock starts ticking any faster, the rows turn more violent and she runs off with someone else. After all, that best female friend we respected too much to risk asking out is now engaged, and so are most of our friends. And it would be nice to have children at a similar time to our friends so we can send them to the same school and take them on joint holidays with their agnostic godparents we no longer like, but have to stay in touch with "for the sake of the children". Plus, Granny would like to attend a wedding of a grandchild before she dies and the parents are getting broody about becoming grandparents themselves, so hell, let's put a ring on her finger, get her to the church on time and waltz off together into the sunset.'

Ed cheered sarcastically. 'Bravo, Sam. A fine little monologue. You should be on the stage, you know.'

'Encore,' cried Alan. 'Our lovely dining companions have seldom encountered such a chivalrously attractive catch.'

'With all due respect to our virgin friends, it is not them that I'm trying to catch.'

'Thank God,' said one.

'Literally,' said another.

'So who is fisherman Sam after?' asked the trendy vicar, chuckling contentedly at his piscine pun.

'Fisherman Sam has absolutely no idea,' I said, untruthfully, for in some dark, dank recess of my brain an irresistible scheme was just beginning to take shape.

Chapter Two

It's not easy living with Sam. Actually, it's not easy doing anything with Sam — particularly accompanying him to weddings — but we'll come back to that later. Let's start with the difficulties of sharing a flat with a work-shy would-be actor. Like most young(ish) people in London, I have a proper job — not a very interesting one, admittedly: I am an accountant — but a proper job nonetheless, with proper gym membership, proper pension, proper colleagues and, above all, proper hours. That means I have to go to bed and get up at a proper time. Every morning I have to wash and shave. Every evening I have to iron a shirt and ensure I have the requisite number of matching socks for the following day. It is a routine that is entirely anathema to Sam.

Sam, in fact, is opposed to any sort of routine at all. Some days he's out temping, waitering, tutoring or — rarely these days — auditioning. Others, he just sits morosely in the flat in his pants watching daytime television. You might have thought he'd find time in his busy schedule to tidy up once in a while or perform a few simple, selfless tasks, such as buying more dishwasher tablets or replacing the toothpaste he's stolen from my sink. You might have hoped to return occasionally to a flat that is not even messier than the one you left. But no: this, too, is beyond him.

I can often go an entire week in our cramped flat without seeing Sam. In the morning, when I leave, he is normally still asleep, although I do occasionally get to have breakfast with a girl who has stayed over in his bed. Then, in the evenings, I'm often at Jess's or she's at mine and Sam vanishes out on the town with his thespian friends, living on British Thespian Time.

Sometimes he's good enough to bring these friends back at 3am – particularly when I have an important meeting the next day – and play loud, naked drinking games in the sitting room. Picking one's way across the detritus the following morning is like an intriguing game of Cluedo, as you note a discarded belt here, an empty bottle there, and try to work out what crimes have taken place since you went to bed.

And yet – if I'm honest – I still love the stupid prat. Unfortunately, it's almost impossible not to. Even those girls at Lisa's wedding forgave him his extraordinarily insensitive rant. Ed might have sneered sarcastically that Sam was a 'chivalrously attractive catch', but one of the Christians, at least, thought so. Mary, I think she was called: a holy name for a girl exhibiting distinctly unholy behaviour. Sam spent most of the pudding course telling her about the void in his life, which he sensed could only be filled by religion, or at least by a religious girl, before whisking her off to the dance floor and spending the night with her in Mrs Geoffrey Parker's marital bed. 'Rutland' was not an entirely inappropriate name for our table.

I wish I knew how he gets away with it. In fact, I do know how he gets away with it: Sam has charm by the bucketload. And not the kind of superficial, smarmy charm that a certain type of insecure, middle-aged secretary finds attractive, or the brown-nosing flattery of an ambitious graduate trainee, but the genuine charisma of someone you can't help but like. Everyone likes Sam – often despite themselves – because he makes them feel likeable, because they want him to like them back, because he exudes such a Tiggerish enthusiasm for life. Quite simply, he makes life more interesting. He's fairly good-looking, too, I suppose, in his way – above average height, messy hair, an infectious, lopsided grin – and every woman with a pulse fancies him. Even my mum, who doesn't seem to like anyone very much, has a secret crush on him.

I don't deny that he can be a complete tosser. He often is. But as far as Matt, Ed and I are concerned, he's *our* tosser. He's also very loyal, which counts for a lot. The lynchpin of our little group, it's always Sam who worries the most about losing touch with Matt and Ed; always Sam who goes out of his way to get everyone together. Maybe it stems from losing his mother when he was very young. Sam's not close to his dad – he barely ever mentions him, in fact, and he took an engineering job abroad soon after Sam left home. Sam's an only child, so the rest of us are like a dysfunctional family to him.

Our friendship came about by accident more than anything else, after discovering on our first day at primary school that we lived on the same street in Reading. I remember Matt and Sam pelting me and Ed with pebbles on the walk home. Naturally and temperamentally, we still divide much the same way: Sam and Matt are the outgoing ones; Ed and I more reserved. They do a lot better with women in the short term; Ed and I have had rather more stable relationships. The group isn't without its tensions, of course. Sam is entirely oblivious of the extent to which Ed resents his self-assurance. Matt and I rub along fine together, but don't really share confidences. And yet somehow, we all get on best as a four, everyone complementing everyone else.

Sam and I, who are probably the least similar, are also the closest. He's much cooler than me. He's certainly 'lived' much more than me. When the four of us shared a flat in a crummy part of Brixton straight after university, Ed brought a large map of London one day and hung it in the kitchen. Soon afterwards drawing pins started appearing in random places on the map.

'What do they represent?' I asked Ed.

'Well, the blue ones show where our other friends live.'

'Nice. And the pink ones?'

'They mark where Sam has had sex.'

Within five years Sam had colonised most of Brixton, Herne Hill, Clapham, Wandsworth and Fulham with Ed's little pink dots. He pretended to be embarrassed about it, but Ed kept on pinning away, in awe, as ever, of Sam's success. Matt, who's always been a little bit too competitive for his own good, then started adding red dots of his own. Sam was just starting on Finsbury Park when he met Lisa and the map suddenly vanished into a drawer.

If Ed had kept a similar map for me, I reflected, it would have had just one lonely pink pin, for Jess, in Borough.

Despite our different temperaments, though, Sam has always included me, always stood up for me. Sure, I don't like the way he picks on my name. What's wrong with being called Alan? It's not as if I couldn't make puerile jokes about him being called Sam Hunt. But he's essentially a good person. I wouldn't trust Sam with anyone else's girlfriend, but I'd certainly trust him with mine.

That said, Jess doesn't think much of Sam – a feeling I fear might be reciprocated. She mocks me sometimes for having two lovers, which just shows how little she understands male friendships. Maybe she's just jealous she doesn't have an equivalent Sam of her own. She also thinks he's a talented wastrel, which is probably true, and a misogynist, which is definitely untrue. If anything, Sam likes women too much. Certainly, he's never cheated on anyone. He's never deliberately led anyone on. He actually deludes himself far more than he deludes the willing victims he sleeps with. I've seen him genuinely surprised that he has, yet again, fallen head-over-heels in a fortnight and grown bored a week later.

Sam's problem is simple: he thinks too much. Take his tirade at his ex-girlfriend Lisa's wedding as an example. All I could think was, *Thank God Jess isn't on our table*. Jess is a terrifyingly clever barrister. She would have torn Sam's head off. And mine, too, probably, by association. I mean, sure, you can be all cynical and clever about why people get married. You can shock vicars by using rude words. But where does that get you? Nowhere.

I prefer not to analyse. Analysis can be saved for the spreadsheets in the office. Marriage is just something you do, a stage you reach, like learning to drive or getting your first job or buying a flat. You get married and then you have to grow up and see a little less of your childhood friends. You certainly have to stop living with them. It's awkward when you earn a lot more than them.

I was planning on buying a flat with Jess soon. She's been nagging me about it for ages, but I'd prefer it if the initiative came from me. Then I thought we'd get engaged – maybe when we went skiing next year – and settle down to start a family. It would make my parents happy, I think, to see their final son married. My mum has never been that keen on Jess but hopefully she's given up holding out for anyone else by now. And, in any case, she's broodier about having more grand-children than most mothers are the first time round. As for me, I feel quietly content about the prospect – not heart-racing, adrenaline-pumping mad with excitement – but quietly content. And that is much more important.

'If you marry, you will regret it,' wrote Kierkegaard. 'If you do not marry, you will also regret it.' But I can't imagine ever regretting getting married because, you see, I *am* a swan, and I think Jess is, too. She is intelligent, beautiful and kind (and not nearly as fat as I know Sam likes to make out). I *want* to spend the rest of my life with one person. I *want* to go out for an evening and not endure the terrible stress of not knowing what will happen. I want never to have to lunge at vacant air again.

Ultimately, then, I have a simple, old-fashioned idea of marriage: I will choose the girl, I will ask her and I will support her.

At least, that is what I thought. That is how I imagined it until, two weeks after Lisa's wedding, I ironed my shirt – my Thursday shirt – picked out a pair of Thursday socks and went to work in the expectation that everything would be the same when I came home again, just as I like it.

But it wasn't. It was all horribly different.

Chapter Three

Different people have different criteria by which they judge a successful wedding. When Matt's elder sisters got married a year apart, I'm told his mum simply counted the thank-you letters afterwards and declared that daughter one's wedding had beaten daughter two's by a factor of eighty-nine to fifty-four. His dad preferred daughter two's, though, because it cost £1,237.57 less and he didn't have to prompt that set of in-laws to go halves.

Personally, I like to judge an evening on how much carnage I've caused. On that basis, at least, Lisa's wedding was a roaring success.

'Are you proud of yourself, Sam?' Alan had asked on a rather awkward journey home.

'Of course.'

'I think Alan was being sarcastic,' added Jess, helpfully. I don't think I had risen much in her estimation over the previous twenty-four hours.

But what wasn't there to be proud about? The best man mentioned me in his speech – at least I assume he intended a dig in my direction when he said how glad Lisa's family were that she had, *at last,* found a suitable life-long partner in Timothy. After the speeches had finished, Matt and I embarked on a bet to see who could dance with every woman in the room first; a bet which I celebrated, gloriously, by giving him the finger over the shoulder of Timothy's waltzing 96-year-old grandmother as Matt attempted to make up lost ground by dancing with two toddler bridesmaids at the same time.

Then there was the Christian girl, Mary, with whom I spent an amusingly heathen few hours in Mrs Geoffrey Parker's bed before Mrs Geoffrey Parker herself decided that she would quite like to sleep in it, although probably rather less acrobatically, with Mr Geoffrey Parker and, understandably, threw us out. This, apparently, was all my fault, so Mary drove off in a self-righteous huff – it was fine for her; all she had to do was say sorry and she'd still go to heaven – to her friend's house nearby, leaving me with dubious mobile reception and precious little battery as I tried to remember which B&B the other three had booked themselves into (I couldn't afford a room so had decided to take my chances at the wedding – I find it helps focus the mind). Matt always sleeps with his phone on silent, Ed had passed out and, when I finally got through to Alan, Jess yanked his mobile away to tell me, rather harshly I thought, that I had got myself into this mess so I could get myself out of it as well. Taking the initiative, then, I settled down in the dog's basket – a rather apt metaphor – until the deceptively docile-looking Labrador padded in from the drawing room and decided he wanted his basket to himself, leaving me to steal half his blankets and settle down in the hammock in the garden instead.

The 'proud' incident to which I think Alan was referring occurred the following morning when I emerged from the bottom of my ex-girlfriend's parents' garden, still clad in my rented morning dress, its jacket lightly dusted with leaves and dog hair, and found myself in the middle of an apologetic lunch party for all the people in the village who hadn't been invited the evening before. Mrs Geoffrey Parker hastily showed me out, her firm goodbye more of an *adieu* than an *au revoir*.

All in all, then, it was a highly successful wedding. Life is short; you have to chase the anecdote. One day, when you're slowly fermenting in an old people's home, calling the matron by your aunt's name and dribbling liberally into your soup of no identifiable origin, it would be nice to have something amusing to look back on before you lose your memory altogether and your grubby little grandchildren finally get their hands on your money.

*

The only problem with attending such a fun wedding is that the aftermath always feels so depressing. Timothy James and Lisa Amelia were flying off somewhere warm to have lots of rampant honeymoon sex, while I returned to the dodgier part of Islington, where it was raining, and tried to block out the sound of Alan and Jess shagging on the other side of our flat's thin walls.

Summer, though, is meant to be one of the happier times of year, especially if you are professionally unemployed. And, after this wedding, at least I had an immediate escape route to look forward to: my annual fourteen-hour, £1 Megabus trip to the Edinburgh Fringe, where I hoped to be able to take my mind off things.

The truth was that Lisa's wedding had worried me more than I'd realised. It wasn't just that Mr Geoffrey Parker had reminded me I was turning thirty and still hadn't made anything of my life. I was an optimist. Something would turn up. It wasn't even the obvious reason that my ex had married someone else – that didn't bother me much either. No, it was more what Lisa's marriage symbolised. I'd been to lots of weddings before, but this was the first one involving someone who had actually meant something to me. Was this it, then? The start of the rot? Had the first domino in the line fallen? And if so, who was next? Ed? Matt? *Alan?* I wasn't sure I could cope if Alan got married. I would be moved out of the cheap, subsidised flat owned by his wealthy, childless uncle, the loathsome Jess would be winched in and I would die alone on a street corner, urchins stealing my tattered rags, rats gnawing my face and the police struggling to identify the remains of an unloved soul.

I'm not being melodramatic. I'd seen Jess's face when she caught that bouquet. She was a determined woman and I knew what she wanted. She wanted Alan away from us and there would be nothing he could do about it. I've seen it happen before. Friends get married and then they vanish — however much they protest they won't — into Marriage-Land, a small country like Lichtenstein or Andorra, which no one who isn't married can ever find. You can't get a visa to visit Marriage-Land, even if you want to. They do things differently there. The customs are strange, the language alien. They have 'dinner parties', 'weekends in the country' and, eventually, small alien creatures called 'children'.

I hoped Edinburgh would be a good place to get away from all this. I've always loved the Fringe. During the day you can wander around the city, soaking up the atmosphere created by the street entertainers and resolutely refusing to pay them any money when they embark on their speeches to a crowd of confused Japanese tourists about how they have 'suffered for their art'. I have suffered for *my* art. No one wants to pay me for it. When any of my friends come to watch my plays, they probably suffer for my art, too.

In the afternoon, if the mood takes you, you can watch someone eat their own penis while standing on their head and playing the ukulele. If you're feeling more serious you can catch the latest production of *Othello,* re-interpreted by an avant-garde company of blind Latvian dwarves. My favourite activity, though, is to wander among the students on the Royal Mile, occasionally approaching the stressed, red-eyed producers and asking them how much money they've lost so far on their festival jaunt.

'My advice to you is to become a lawyer instead,' I said, only half-jokingly, to one student producer-cum-actor on this trip.

'Oh, I fully intend to,' he said, entirely seriously. 'I just thought it would make my CV look more rounded when I apply for my City internship next summer if I could show that I've worked creatively in a team while managing a limited budget for the benefit of that team. Then, of course, there are the concomitant marketing skills I've added to my skills basket... '

Twats constitute a relatively large sub-species of the performers in Edinburgh, but at least most of the twats at the Fringe are interesting ones. You might not have a great deal in common with someone who eats his own penis while standing on his head and playing the ukulele, but you'll probably have something interesting to talk about. It definitely beats going to Alan's office summer party, as I did earlier this year. Were it not for an intriguing half hour with Amanda, Alan's rather frisky boss, it would have been a total washout.

The most fun thing about the Fringe is, of course, the evening, when all the best partying takes place in a series of large, interconnected marquees called the Spiegeltent. I can still remember clearly the first time I went there, as an eighteen-year-old; it was as if I had wandered out of the normal, mundane world into something magical. Swing bands played on raised, misty stages. Girls in bright dresses twirled below. Champagne corks popped. Cigarettes, or something stronger, flickered like glow worms in the dark. Everywhere there were beautiful, smiling people; the gentle, murmured undercurrent of a festive atmosphere which occasionally burst into louder, more raucous approval when a band started a song we recognised or finished a set we'd particularly enjoyed; the sights, the sounds, the smells, even, of people having a good time.

This, I thought, *is where I belong.*

That, at least, was how I felt the first eleven times I went there. This year – exactly a week after Lisa's wedding – was very different indeed.

It was the final day of my trip and I'd spent a pleasant enough afternoon torturing students before meeting up with my old friend Claire in the evening and taking her out for dinner – or, to be more accurate, letting her take me out for dinner. Claire is something called a management consultant, although she appears neither to manage nor consult anything or anyone. Still, she has more chance of her credit card being accepted than I do. Her dad used to play football with my dad so we first met when I was ten and she was eight, lost touch, met again at drama school (which she came to briefly after studying finance at university) and have been good friends ever since. She gets on very well with the others, too.

Claire and I had 'a moment' once, of course. Which male and female friends haven't had a moment? But ours was mercifully brief and almost entirely without consequence. It lasted about thirty seconds; a lustless half-minute of drunken snogging at our drama school's Christmas party before collapsing into giggles, each telling the other that their technique was dreadful. It was about as romantic as I'd imagine (not that I have imagined it) kissing Alan or Matt or Ed would be.

If anything, Claire and I became even better friends afterwards because we'd got that awkward will-we-won't-we? moment out of the way early on. We'd try to set each other up with our friends while always joking that we'd marry one another if we hadn't found anyone else by thirty-five. Our friendship often felt like a proper relationship, but without the responsibility, the angst, the guilt trips, the phone calls, the annoying friends, the expensive presents and the sex which starts disappointingly, becomes briefly exciting and then fades into infrequent, bored familiarity. And before I'm accused of misogyny, that point about the boring, familiar sex was first made by Claire, not me. She's a realist – an amusing, filthy, cynical, kind-hearted realist – and that's why we hit it off.

This particular evening we were getting on well as usual, catching up on the gossip from Lisa's wedding (Lisa had never liked Claire, whom she'd viewed as a threat, so hadn't invited her) and discussing which one of our friends would be next. Claire, who had always had something of a soft spot for Ed, thought he and Tara would be engaged and married within a year. My money was on Alan.

'What about you?' I asked. 'When are you going to vanish, never to be seen again?'

Claire laughed. She looked pretty when she laughed – her round face flushing slightly, her dark blonde, now sensibly-styled hair bobbing around as she threw her head back. I still didn't fancy her, though.

'I'm a young career woman, Sam,' she replied. 'Why would I want to settle down now?'

'Because you're twenty-seven,' I said, pouring her another glass of wine. 'Therefore you're a rapidly declining asset who should cash in now before gravity takes its toll, no one fancies you any more and you're too old and barren to have any children.'

An elderly couple at the neighbouring table looked a little shocked and motioned to the waiter to bring their bill. They didn't know that it would take far more than this to upset Claire. She leaned closer and whispered, loudly, so that most of the restaurant had no choice but to listen: 'That's where you're wrong, Sam. As a modern woman of twenty-seven, I'll be in the prime of my life for at least the next five years. I can go out with younger, more virile men or I can enjoy being the plaything of a rich, bald and charming sugar-daddy in his fifties. Or I can simply choose to be single. Either way, I have at least another half-decade of living selfishly, dangerously, and doing exactly what I please. Only later, much later, will I start thinking about finding a suitable lifelong partner – someone kind who's good father material; a nice beta male who won't stray, after all the wild but unsuitable alpha types I've been having my fun with – and we'll settle down and live happily ever after.'

I patted her patronisingly on the hand. 'Well done, my dear. Well done. You are in the vanguard of the new wave of feminism. Mary Wollstonecraft and Simone de Beauvoir would be proud of you. Right now they're eating chocolate in heaven together, watching *Sex and the City* and quietly high-fiving each other's podgy palms. You should indeed have your cake and eat it.' I pulled her pudding towards me and took a bite. 'Although not too much, or the rich, bald and charming sugar daddies might trade you in for a younger, slimmer model.'

Claire pulled her pudding back. There was a brief tug-of-war, which she won. 'You can be as patronising as you like,' she said. 'But if I were you, I'd worry about yourself, not me.'

I looked at her quizzically. I rarely worried about myself for long.

'Yes,' she continued, 'I suppose you can be charming when you make an effort. And I admit I've sat opposite uglier people at the dinner table. You've worked your way through most of my friends, the less discreet of whom report back favourably. And I have no doubt that, on the rare occasions you are involved in a play, you have a decent chance with whichever gullible, insecure actress has just left drama school and is filling the "fit girl" slot in the cast. But what do you really have to offer any of these people long-term? You're not a nubile twenty-one-year-old any more. You're almost thirty. And even if you do age well, as men tend to, you won't have that gravitas which is the main attraction of powerful, older men. You will just be a nice-looking fiftysomething with a not very good job who was once an attractive but fairly unmemorable actor. Someone *with* potential is very attractive. Someone who wasted it, well… ' She shook her head, mock-sadly. 'Not so much.' She leant forward and took her opportunity to return the patronising hand-pat. 'My dear Sam, you fall between two stools: the wild and the dependable. You are stuck in the middle. You're going nowhere faster than you realise. And my advice to you is to cash in now before gravity takes its toll, no one fancies you any more, and you're too poor, tired and infertile to have any children.'

Claire leant back triumphantly in her seat, knowing full well that she had just added to her pudding tug-of-war victory. It wasn't much of a surprise, to be honest. Claire always won these play arguments because she was prepared to go one step further than you would dare. Her conversation rarely played by the rules.

Not that I minded. Or not that I pretended to mind. I could take a joke – our entire friendship was based on jokes at each other's expense – but the problem was that I couldn't help becoming increasingly sensitive about my acting. However much anyone tries to pretend the opposite, the truth is that if you haven't made it in acting by thirty, you are unlikely ever to make it. And when I say make it, I don't necessarily mean becoming the latest sub-Bourne action hero or playing the lead giraffe in *The Lion King*. I mean merely making a decent, honest living as a jobbing actor. Acting is a young person's game – you need to be young to put up with the travelling, the strange hours and the assistant director's STDs – and few make it to the top of the career pyramid. Decent parts only exist for a tiny number of stars; there are thousands of people coming out of drama schools every year eager to foist their talent on the world. Ten years later most of them are foisting their talents on a photocopier.

So it was all very well for Claire to mock me for my lack of work. *She* had fallen off at the very bottom of the pyramid. *She* had flunked out of drama school after only a year. *She* had taken the easy option of a secure job. What did she know about anything, anyway?

Help, I thought, as Claire paid the bill. *First my worries about losing my friends, and now this. What has happened to happy-go-lucky Sam?*

My poor mood wasn't improved when, during our walk to the Spiegeltent, Claire mentioned in passing that one of our friends from drama school, Chris Peck, had just been accepted to play the lead in the Old Vic's touring production of *Hamlet*. Chris was a good guy – we'd acted together, got drunk together, even slept with the same girl twenty-four hours apart without knowing it – but in that moment I could have murdered the little fuck. Of all the lies spouted backstage – and there are many – the biggest one is: 'I'm *so* pleased for you.' No one is ever pleased for anyone else in acting. You're jealous, you're bitter and, quite frankly, you'd like them to fall over during rehearsals and break their neck so you can go on and break a leg.

Your tutors warn you about rejection at drama school. Actors get told 'no' as often as naughty toddlers. Acting, they tell you, is like going to four interviews per week for a job for which you're entirely unsuited before you even walk in the door. But you can't get too sensitive about it or you'd start to question your looks, your abilities, your personality – your entire self – until you crumbled into a mess of insecurities. So you console yourself that you didn't have 'the right look'; that they were looking for someone a bit younger, a bit stronger, a bit more intense. You'd never tell yourself the truth, which is that they were looking for someone a bit better.

Jealousy. That's what they should really warn you about at drama school. Chris? He and I had exactly the same 'look'. And now he was playing Hamlet? I could fucking play Hamlet, too. I can do tortured and moody and suicidal. I was born to play Hamlet. Worse, I had auditioned to play the little fuck of a Dane. And the fatuous fuck of a casting director hadn't even fucking recalled me. *Fuck. Fuck. Fuck.*

I was in a fairly atomic mood, then, by the time Claire and I finally arrived at the Spiegeltent around midnight. I was too old for this rubbish; too old to be wandering around the Fringe with a bunch of student pricks who treated acting like hobby. This was meant to be my career, my life, but everything that was once beautiful seemed fake. The bands were still wreathed in mist, but the effect looked as tacky as their dreadful cover versions sounded. Corks still popped, but they came from bottles of stale, fizzy white wine. Girls twirled around in cheap dresses from charity shops. A cigarette burnt the back of my hand as we pushed through the crowds. This was a fake world full of fake people faking it for a shadow of a living. Not a new revelation, but, for the first time, I really hated it; all of it. I hated it because I wanted it so much and couldn't get it. I hated it because I had failed and it was easier to hate the acting world itself than my own failure within it.

Claire went off with some other friends and I could feel myself spiralling helplessly downwards into a dark, dangerous place I didn't want to be. I made a half-hearted attempt to talk to an attractive BBC comedy producer from Leeds called Vicki, or maybe Vicky, but my heart wasn't really in it. I kept on making darker and darker jokes until she started to shift uncomfortably and glance over my shoulder for an escape route. There's always an escape route when you hang out with thesps. There's always something else that glitters.

Vicki, or Vicky, eventually managed to escape and I meandered aimlessly through the crowds, ignoring the curses and stares as I knocked over a drink or pushed my way through the middle of a group. What were all these people doing here, anyway? What crap were they talking? Who did they think they were? I felt old and pointless and drunk and angry. I needed a target.

I walked around a corner, clutching a plastic glass of lukewarm Guinness, and spotted Claire talking to the annoying student actor with the bulging skill basket I had wound up a few days previously. She rolled her eyes at me over his shoulder. My spirits lifted. Perhaps we could have a bit of fun.

'Jeremy,' I said, offering a hand. 'How nice to see you again.'

He took it, warily. I held it for a little longer than was strictly necessary.

'I see you've met my girlfriend.' I gave his hand a little stroke with my thumb. 'We're always interested in meeting new people.'

Claire slipped her arm around my back. 'Oh, yes,' she purred, playing along. 'We're very open minded, Sam and I.'

Jeremy withdrew his hand rapidly, his face an ominous

mixture of embarrassment and anger. He was a big bloke. 'Why would you want to do a thing like that?'

'I was joking,' I said.

'Why?'

'Why was I joking? Oh, I don't know, Jeremy. Maybe because life can be a little boring and it's fun to jazz it up a little. Maybe I was just doing a bit of *acting*. Or perhaps I just thought you'd be easy to wind up.'

It was the wrong thing to say. Jeremy *was* easy to wind up. He pushed me roughly in the chest. I staggered backwards a few steps.

Claire tried to intervene. 'Now, come on, guys. Let's not be stupid. We're sorry about the joke, okay? We were only messing around.'

Jeremy rounded on her. 'You're sorry? Not as sorry as he'll be when I've messed around with him. I thought you and I were getting somewhere. Is he really your boyfriend? Or was that made up, too? You're not all that, you know, but you could still do a lot better than – '

I swung a punch – the first punch of my life – at Jeremy. It connected with his broad, stupid jaw, making a satisfying clunk. 'Never speak to her like that again,' I said.

He roared, like a wounded public-school bear, and shaped up to come back at me.

'Before we start, it's only fair I warn you,' I said, desperately looking around for an escape route. 'During my time at drama school, I passed my diploma in armed and unarmed stage combat with distinction. I can carry a plastic gun in a convincing James Bond pose. I am well versed in swordplay and jousting. And I have mastered a series of intricate and gymnastic hand-to-hand combat moves which will only result in your defeat.'

Jeremy guffawed. 'Maybe, dickhead. But I bet they didn't teach you this at drama school.' He swung his foot forward, his hard, right boot heading towards my nether regions. He fought like Claire debated. But I'd seen it coming and leapt gymnastically to one side in the tuck position. I rose to my feet again, my face muddied by the puddle I'd landed in.

'You fight like a girl,' I said.

By now a little crowd had formed, intrigued by the real-life drama unfolding in front of their eyes. I played to them. 'What's it going to be, Jezzer? Are you going to kick and scratch and bite and squeal, or are you going to fight properly? Are you going to run away or are you going to stand up to me like a man?'

Secretly, I hoped he would run away.

The crowd, on the other hand, knew what they wanted. 'Fight! Fight! Fight!' they chorused. Never underestimate the savage stupidity of a group of drunken Brits.

Jeremy looked fairly savage, too, standing there in his stripy pink shirt with his nostrils flared and his shoulders heaving. Then he suddenly slumped, attempted a half-smile and offered a hand to shake. 'Let's forget it,' he said.

The crowd booed. I hushed them. 'It's a noble gesture. And I accept your surrender, Jeremy.'

As I stretched out my hand to meet his, Jeremy swung with his left and caught me across the temple. I punched back, weakly, connecting only with air, and fell to the ground. The last thing I remember was Claire's face looming, concerned, over me, the stars above Edinburgh dancing in a halo around her head. She looked like an angel.

'Sam,' she said, 'I could have kissed you just then.' And I think I could have kissed her, too. I think I wanted to kiss her. But I couldn't. I didn't. For at that moment, a wave of nausea swept over me and I rolled over, vomited and passed out.

Curtain.

Chapter Four

'You punched a guy?'

'Several times.'

'And he went down?'

'He went down and he stayed down. Seriously, mate, if you think this black eye is impressive, you should see his.'

I was back in my flat in London with Matt, giving him an edited version of my time in Edinburgh. It was a Thursday afternoon in August and neither of us had much to do. Most of the firms that normally took on temps were employing keen, cheap university students instead. I'd had to resort to working occasional early morning shifts in a coffee bar in Camden and applying for a fifth credit card, which was granted with surprising ease – ironically, the only company which had ever refused to give me credit was the parent firm of the Greek card I'd once done a TV advert for. Maybe they knew just how likely actors were to default on their debt.

Matt was also in limbo, kicking his heels in London while still waiting to hear whether or not he had a job for the next six months. It didn't augur well. Last time their postings had been decided his then girlfriend had been shoved off to a dead-end urology position in the Scottish Highlands and he'd been given paediatrics in Devon. They'd split up on the second weekend after realising that even meeting halfway took twelve hours and cost £100 each.

'Modernising Medical Careers', the government had called it. 'More like Mutilating Medical Careers,' Matt had said on more than one occasion. He was right, too. The government spent hundreds of thousands of pounds training these bright young people and then couldn't even find decent employment for them at the end. No wonder they were all thinking of doing something else.

'So what kind of male does Claire think you are?' continued Matt.

'What?'

'That conversation you had in the restaurant in Edinburgh. Does Claire think you're an alpha or a beta? Are you "wild and unsuitable"? Or "kind, good father material"?'

'God knows. Neither, probably. I imagine a true alpha male to be a City trader who gets up at 5am, kicks his lithe intern out of bed, stands under a cold shower listening to "Eye of the Tiger", runs to work, makes a million pounds before his protein-shake lunch, loses a million in the afternoon, snorts his bodyweight in coke in the evening, sleeps for three hours – two of them with another intern – and then spends his weekends playing rugby with the Territorial Army.' I gestured at Alan's dressing gown, which I was still wearing at two in the afternoon. 'I don't think I'm an alpha male.'

'And yet you're not much of a beta, either, by Claire's reckoning,' said Matt. 'You're not even a safe, solid marriage bet.'

'Thanks.'

'So, if you're a fading almost-alpha stroke never-to-be-beta, what does that make you?'

'The third letter of the Greek alphabet, I suppose.'

'Whatever that is.'

'Gamma.'

Matt laughed. 'That's it. Sam Hunt. The Gamma male.'

'Thanks.'

Somehow, no one ever minds too much getting a ribbing from Matt. He's solid, decent and utterly dependable; a man's man without being too boorishly blokey; a natural, caring doctor who's never too worthy. Every guy likes Matt, and every bloody girl wants to jump him. He has that kind of strong open face and short hair you associate with South Africans or

Australians. He still plays rugby or football every weekend. He slept with so many girls at university that his nickname was Metronome Matt. He's taller, blonder, trimmer and squarer-jawed than me. If he wasn't so nice, he would be an absolute dick.

It's always been difficult for the rest of us to compete with him. You're in a bar. A girl starts chatting to both of you.

'*What do you guys do for a living?*'

'*Well, last week, I pretended to be someone else for £50 per week in an empty theatre above a pub.*'

'*Hmm, and you?*'

'*Me? I saved four babies' lives before lunch.*'

'*Okay, see you, Sam, I'm off to bed with blond George Clooney here.*'

But nothing had been going that well for Matt either recently, and I cared deeply about it. It's much easier being ambitious on behalf of your friends than it is on your own account. In any case, you're unlikely to get jealous if they're not competing directly with you. It wasn't as if I wanted to be a doctor. I couldn't even get a non-speaking part as a dead extra on *Holby City*.

That afternoon, things took a significant turn for the worse when Matt's mobile rang and he was rejected for the last of his potential jobs. There were now three options open to him: wait another year and re-apply; go abroad and become a doctor there; or give up medicine altogether. As none of them seemed very appealing at that particular moment, we took the fourth, more short-term option and opened the emergency crate of beer I kept hidden from Alan in a cupboard above my bed.

A few hours later, at some point between the second airing of *Neighbours* and the first of *Hollyoaks*, the doorbell rang. We opened the door to find Ed standing in the pouring rain, looking even more bedraggled than usual. Poor guy; he really wasn't aging that well, I thought. Too thin on top; too fat around the middle. Ginger, ballooning *and* balding. We'd been amusing ourselves recently cutting out Belgravia Trichological

Centre adverts and leaving them around the flat he shared with his girlfriend. The previous week he'd finally snapped and told us he didn't find it funny any more.

It was only when I looked more closely that I realised Ed's eyes were as wet and as red as his remaining hair.

'Ed, what the hell's happened?' asked Matt, bringing him inside and offering him one of Alan's accountant-weekend-wear jumpers.

'Tara,' he said, simply.

We didn't have to ask many more questions. Tara was one of those monkey-women who never let go of one branch until they have their hands securely attached to another. Ed was never going to break up with her and she knew it. So she'd strung him along until she found a replacement – a replacement, incidentally, that Matt and I had known about for a few months. After some debate, we'd decided not to tell Ed, in the vain hope that it would all sort itself out.

'She's run off with some lawyer bloke,' said Ed, sounding strangulated. 'Her partner and mentor at work or something. Twenty years older. Recently divorced.' He gave up and buried his head in his hands. 'What a fucking mess of a cliché.'

Matt and I didn't have to feign surprise. This lawyer bloke was news to us as well. We thought it was the banker bloke Tara was going to leave Ed for. You had to hand it to her. She'd been a busy little monkey.

'A mortgage… We had a bloody mortgage together.' Ed's words came out in fitful chokes. 'Four years… Four wasted bloody years.'

Matt and I looked at each other helplessly while Ed got it all out of his system. You can know someone most of your life and still not know what to do or say when they break down like that. I would probably walk in front of a lorry, if it meant saving Ed's life. But listening to him crying? No. It was a grief he would ultimately have to go through alone.

Led by Matt, whose one-time job had at least given him

some experience in dealing with difficult emotional situations, we both patted Ed awkwardly on the shoulder. Fortunately, Ed then saved us any further embarrassment by starting to laugh; a low, sorrowful chuckle that began quietly and gathered pace into full-blown hysterics.

'What is it?' I demanded. 'What's so bloody amusing?'

'It's the mortgage,' he said, his shoulders heaving through the sobs. 'I've just remembered that it's under Tara's name. So I'm not going to pay the four months' back-payments I currently owe her.'

Matt and I did our best to laugh along. We'd been hoping for something a little more amusing, to be honest. Mortgage jokes have never really hit my funny bone. I also felt it would be churlish to point out that repayment worries were probably the last thing on Tara's mind now that she was shagging her very wealthy boss. But for now, at least, none of that mattered. The important thing was that Ed had finally stopped crying.

I opened another beer and handed it to Ed.

'To Tara,' I said.

'The bloody slag,' said Ed, chinking cans.

'Tara the slag,' chorused Matt and I.

We slumped down on the sofa and decided to do the only sensible thing in the circumstances, which was to play a lot of Xbox and drink a great deal of beer.

'What a bunch of losers we are,' said Ed eventually, flinging down his controller after Matt had slotted another goal past his Argentinian keeper.

'Speak for yourself.'

'No, seriously, I'm speaking for all of us. Matt, you can't get a job. Sam, you can't even get a pretend job. And my girlfriend has just run off with her boss. We're all pushing thirty, none of us shows any sign of settling down, let alone "making it". We're still in touch with friends from primary school. And what do we have to show for anything? Nothing. You remember four-eyed Rob we used to play football with on Sundays? He's made a million already and got divorced. Twice. And what have we done? Diddly squat. We're a complete bunch of losers.'

'We're beta males,' said Matt.

'What?'

'Beta males. Sam and I were talking about it earlier. There are alphas, like Alan. Successful, dependable breadwinners. And then there are betas. Like us.'

'I'd rather be me than Alan,' I said.

'We'd all rather be you than Alan,' said Matt.

'Who says Alan is an alpha, anyway?' said Ed. 'Look how much Jess has got him under her thumb. We barely see him any more, thanks to her. I call that fairly beta, if you ask me.'

We all nodded encouragingly. It was good to see Ed distracted.

'Actually, I'd call most males beta these days,' continued Ed. 'Compared to all the alpha females like Jess, Tara and Claire, anyway. One barrister, one solicitor, one management consultant. We don't exactly measure up, do we? No, if you ask me, women have won the battle of the sexes. Hands down, across the board. They're better at school and better adjusted socially. They grow up quicker and go on to perform better at university. They're less likely to get mugged. They enter the workplace, where they get the best jobs because all the dinosaur male bosses fancy them – or at least they remind them of their daughters they never see because they work too hard – so they employ them at the expense of potentially better male graduates. And who can blame them? Everyone loves having pretty girls around in an office. Unfortunately, the pretty girls repay them by filing million-pound sexual harassment suits the moment someone so much as tells them their hair looks nice. Or alternatively, they wait until they're thirty-five, squeeze out a kid and demand six months' paid leave. If they marry well, they can choose to give up their jobs and potter around charity lunches. Or if they prefer, they can carry on working and everyone will think they're a heroine, even though they do sod-all work, knowing full well no one can sack them without HR screaming "discrimination". And then, just to cap it off, they live longer, having nagged their poor husbands into an early – '

I'd started an ironic, slow handclap three-quarters of the way through Ed's tirade. He'd grinned and got faster and faster, eventually giving up when Matt joined in, our rhythm becoming increasingly manic until it was one continuous line of applause.

'Excellent!' I cried. 'Tara has missed out on quite a catch with you, Ed. You are every inch the enlightened modern man.'

'I'm serious, Sam. I'm going to become a masculinist.'

'What the hell is that?'

'I don't know. I've just invented the word. But I'm going to be the male equivalent of a feminist. You'll see. All of 'em will see. I'm going to stand up for male rights.' Ed rose to his feet, as if about to address a grateful nation. 'I'll campaign to become the first Minister for Men. I'll write a book called *The Flat-Chested Eunuch*. I'll pitch a short and punchy column to *GQ* magazine – '

'Ed, aren't you becoming a little emotional?'

'No, leave him, Sam,' said Matt. 'He's got a point. An exaggerated point, admittedly, but a valid one. I've lost out on my last two jobs to female doctors. They're much better at the caring side of medicine. And Alan has to put up with Amanda, that dragon of a female boss who's a thousand times better at office politics than any of the men. He's always telling us how manipulative she is.' Matt broke off to take another swig of his beer and looked across at me. 'What's up, Sam? You're smiling inanely.'

The partial truth was that I had been experiencing a pleasant flashback to my encounter with the dragoneous Amanda at Alan's summer party. But that wasn't the only thing making me smile. 'I was just thinking how nice it is to have the three of us in the same room at the same time,' I told them. 'All of us together. Nearly all of us together, anyway. Talking rubbish. It feels like old times.'

'Yeah,' said Matt. 'You're right. It is nice.'

'So why does this have to end as we grow up?' I said. 'Why do I only get to see you two when something shit has happened? Or at weddings? Soon we'll be seeing each other once a year, or once every five years, or we'll just send Christmas presents to each other's children and never actually meet up at all. Tell me: why do we all end up vanishing into tiny, tight-knit family groups as we get older? Aren't friends supposed to be the new family for our generation? Even for men? *Especially* for men? Women have always had time to see their friends; men never have. But just look at how many people we stay in touch with now compared to our dads. They don't have four hundred friends online. They don't really keep up with people from their pasts. And it's their loss because you guys provide me with far more support than any girlfriend ever has. And more fun. And more freedom. So why would we want that to end? Why would we ever think that two people are enough these days for the rest of our lives? Or two plus two, two of whom are entirely dependent on the other two? Why does it have to be like that?'

'*Does* it have to be like that?' asked Matt.

I put my beer down. This was serious. 'Maybe not,' I said. 'You see, I've been thinking a little.'

The other two groaned.

I continued: 'You remember my views on holy matrimony, which I shared with you at Lisa's wedding?'

'Yes,' said Matt. 'They were very enlightening.'

'And enlightened,' said Ed.

'Don't take the piss,' I said. 'I mean this. Sharing those deeply held opinions about marriage helped seed an idea in my mind. I've been thinking about it ever since and have finally come to two conclusions, which I am ready to share with you.' I held up a finger to aid my demonstration. 'One. If we agree that marriage is a cynical sham, one logical option would be to have nothing to do with it. But although such a route might be fun and liberating for a while, the fun would never last. Friends will still vanish. Opportunities will slip away. Twentysomething girls won't want to sleep with you for ever. Neither, eventually, will thirtysomethings. You'll start going on holiday at Christmas to avoid being alone. You will never have children. You will die alone, prematurely, unloved and unfed. Therefore, I reject that option.'

'Great,' said Ed. 'What about the second option?'

'The alternative is to embrace the cynicism. If you reject the first logical conclusion, you're going to want to end up married anyway. You just have to do it on the right terms. My theory is that the reason we find it so difficult to settle down is that there is just too much choice out there for the modern man. You might hold a perfectly good blackjack hand with cards that add up to twenty. But it's still not perfect. She has a bit of hair on her upper lip. She's high-maintenance. The last one you went out with was more intelligent. So do you stick or twist? You're a man. You're competitive. You don't want twenty, you want the top prize. You want twenty-one, dammit. So you twist. Perhaps you'll be dealt an ace. Or maybe you'll fold and lose everything. But if you don't try another card, you'll always have to live with the niggling doubt that you could have done that little bit better.'

'Even if you think you have a twenty-one, she'll just run off with someone else,' said Ed, morosely.

'Or you'll want to re-invent the rules of the game and get another twenty-one because you're bored with the first one,' said Matt.

'Exactly,' I said, no longer sure that the metaphor still worked, but willing to gloss over it for the sake of making my point. I tried another one. 'Or imagine you're sitting at one of those sushi bars, watching the colour-coded dishes go round the conveyor belt. That conveyor belt is the dating scene. So do you gorge on lots of the cheap ones? Or wait for just one of the expensive ones?'

'The cheap ones, every time,' said Matt. 'I'm all about piling up the £1.20 "orange" girls.'

'I'd rather wait for a £5 grey,' said Ed.

'Okay,' I said. 'But what if someone steals your grey while you're waiting, Ed? Or Matt, what if you've over-gorged on oranges and don't have any space left for the perfect grey when it finally comes along? You see, there's no right answer because there's too much choice. We're doomed to be restless and unhappy either way. So what do we do? I'll tell you. We narrow down the decision-making process to a single criterion.'

'And what would that be?' asked Ed.

'Money,' I said.

'Why?' said Matt.

'Because, my slow-witted friends, money liberates. And if you're going to be trapped by marriage anyway, you might as well be trapped in the most liberated fashion. There are plenty of women now who have money, who earn it, who want to earn more of it. You guys have sat here all afternoon and prattled away about women running the world. Well, fine, they're welcome to the world. They're welcome to the world of work, at least. It's rubbish. But let's play them at their own game. As modern men, let's play the game that they have been playing against us for centuries. Let's find three girls who are ambitious, successful and, above all, very, very rich. And then let's marry them and become house-husbands. Just think — '

'We'll never have to do another day's work in our lives,' interrupted Matt, excitedly.

'Exactly! And I can act in my spare time without worrying about money.'

'We'll live on the same street.'

'We'll go to the pub during the day.'

'We won't have to lose touch with our friends.'

'I'll never have to look for a job I don't want.'

'I'll actually get to know my own kids.'

'I'll coach my son to play football for England.'

'All our friends will be jealous.'

Ed was just about to tell us what he thought of our scheme when a key turned in the front door and Alan walked in, as wet and as shaken as Ed had been four hours previously.

It was me who leapt forward first. 'Alan. What is it? What's happened?'

'Jess,' he said. 'It's Jess. We're getting married, I think.'

His face wasn't exactly the picture of a happy groom-to-be.

'What do you mean, "you think"?'

Alan surveyed the room of his drunk, oldest friends. 'Jess got down on one knee in front of my boss and asked me,' he said, reaching into his pocket and pulling out a hideously tacky piece of jewellery which we later discovered was called a 'male engagement ring'. 'It was the most emasculating moment of my whole bloody life.'

Chapter Five

For some reason you never really feel what you're supposed to when the big events in life happen. When my dad told me that my much-loved grandfather had died, my first thought was, *Will my parents get the nice table in the drawing room or will it go down my aunt's side of the family?* When I turned over my A-level economics paper, all I could think about was how easily I could screw up the rest of my life by writing 'Bollocks! Bollocks! Bollocks!' all over my essay. And when Jess got down on one knee and proposed outside the front door of my accountancy office, my knee-jerk reaction was that her cleavage looked very nice in that red top and that, whatever my answer, it might be the last time I ever saw her on her knees in front of me.

It was 6.30pm on a blustery Thursday in August in Embankment in central London. The sun was beginning to lose its warmth as storm clouds moved in from the south. Tourists ambled towards musicals in the West End. Commuters jostled to get to the Tube, or into the wine bars. Opposite my office a tramp was attempting to play a harmonica, sell the *Big Issue* and control his randy dog, all at the same time. A traffic helicopter buzzed overheard, competing with a constipated siren attempting to force its way through the rush-hour traffic on the Strand. But it was as if all this came to a stop. It was as if all this mass of machinery and humanity *knew* that something dreadful and embarrassing was about to take place. It was as if they were only there as extras in Jess's big scene, called upon to bear witness as she approached with a quiet, determined smile on her face and a box in her hands. As she sank to her knees and thrust it towards me, my brain pushed my initial, inappropriate thoughts to one side and my mouth began to form a silent, strangulated, prolonged, 'No'.

It was at that moment that I heard my boss behind me.

'Well, screw me sideways, Alan Muir, if this isn't what I think it is,' she bellowed. Amanda is in her mid-forties, a fading – if not faded – beauty, divorced, bitter, nosy, interfering, clever, terrifying, psychotic and always asking people to 'screw her sideways' or 'fuck her backwards' as a throwaway turn of phrase. Personally, I find the constant swearing a little offensive. The bellow continued: 'Are you really about to become Mr Jessica Gallagher in front of my very eyes?'

Inside an office Amanda's voice can break windows. Outside, well, the helicopter and the police car had competition. A little crowd gathered.

To her credit, Jess smiled her determined little smile and resolved to see it through. 'Alan Michael Muir,' she said, 'will you do me the honour of becoming my husband?'

I have never heard of any trusted authority – not a men's magazine, Nick Hornby, *Top Gear*, *The SAS Survival Handbook* – which tells you what to do in this sort of situation. I was on my own. Or at least, I wished I were on my own.

'Grow a pair of fucking balls, Alan, and say yes,' bellowed Amanda, evidently enjoying herself.

I wanted to say yes, of course. I looked down at my beautiful girlfriend, whom I certainly loved and probably wanted to marry, and thought just how much I wanted to say yes and make her happy. I looked around at the eager faces of the passers-by and thought how nice it would be to say yes and give them a pleasant vignette to share and remember in an otherwise forgettable Thursday. And I sensed Amanda behind me and thought how satisfying it would be to say yes and stop her constant, and somewhat crude, jibes in the office about 'popping the bloody question before my sperm count got any lower and Jessica Gallagher ended up barren'.

I really *wanted* to say yes. But more than that, I really wanted Jess to be answering yes to a question *I* had formulated, pondered and popped. That was the correct way to go about it.

So, instead of doing the right thing, swallowing my pride and nodding a straightforward affirmative, I attempted a clumsy compromise and fell to my knees in front of Jess, so that we looked like two amputees congratulating each other at the finish line of the five-metre Paralympic shuffle, and asked, in a meek, alien voice which sounded higher than hers, and certainly higher than Amanda's, 'Jessica Sarah, will you do me the honour of becoming my wife?'

It was meant to be romantic. Amanda guffawed, partly because my own knee-lunge had landed me in a muddy patch on the pavement. Someone in the crowd muttered audibly that Jess had asked first and therefore deserved an answer. Another siren made its way down the Strand.

Jess's face fell and I knew I'd done the wrong thing. 'Do you have a ring?' she asked, her jaw set a little more determinedly than before.

'Can't we go somewhere else to discuss this?'

'No,' said the crowd. Jess shook her head, agreeing with them, disagreeing with me.

'Well, as a matter of fact, I do have a ring.' I felt around in my back pocket and closed my thumb and forefinger around my car keyring. That would not do. 'But I've had it commissioned especially and it's not ready yet.'

Jess's stern face turned into a full-blown grin. With perfect timing, and a deft flick that made it look as though she had been practising, she opened the box with her thumb and proffered something I now know is called a male engagement ring. It was hideous: the gold too yellow; the pattern too ornate. Had she actually spent a barrister's monthly salary on this? It winked at me, mockingly, as it caught the light.

'Then, my lovely Alan, I think it only right that I should ask *you* if you would like to be my husband.'

'Yes,' I said, simply, for there was nothing else left to say. She had won.

The crowd clapped; a few tourists even whooped. Amanda snorted louder than all of them put together – a strange combination of disgust, contempt and jealousy – and walked towards the Tube. It started to rain.

I hauled Jess to her feet and took her away from this circus for a celebratory dinner on St Martin's Lane, at a restaurant I'd often walked past and admired but never actually plucked up the courage to enter. Once inside, however, the illusion instantly evaporated. The maître d' poured more scorn into his welcoming 'Sir' than Amanda manages in an entire offensive outburst. The disappointing food looked as if it had been priced by taking a sensible figure and adding a zero. We were seated, perhaps deliberately due to my muddy trouser leg, between the toilets and the kitchen, so that the swing door to the toilets caught Jess's chair leg every time it opened and the swing door to the kitchen caught me in the face. To add major insult to minor injury, the wine waiter approached our table, took one look at the ring I hadn't yet had the heart to remove from my finger and appeared to hesitate momentarily over whom to give the wine menu to.

'I'll choose the wine,' I said quickly.

'Of course, sir,' he said with a smile that made me want to stab him with his corkscrew. 'And so you shall.'

However hard I tried to remain cheerful, there was an atmosphere throughout dinner.

'What's wrong?' asked Jess, repeatedly.

'Nothing,' I said, a little more gruffly each time, until the main thing that was wrong was that she kept on asking me what was wrong. Nothing was wrong, really, if I was rational and honest. I loved the girl. I wanted to marry her, as you know. Her sweet and dramatic gesture was… well, sweet and dramatic. But I'm not sure that I was capable of being rational and honest at that moment. As far as I was concerned, *everything* was wrong.

The restaurant, the awkward bit of over-decorated metal on my finger, the fact that Amanda had seen everything. How would I survive in the office now? Amanda made life difficult for all her colleagues, but she seemed to single me out for particular abuse. She took far too much interest in my personal life for comfort. She was offensive about nearly all aspects of it. Perhaps it was because I didn't answer back. Perhaps it was because I was number two in her team and therefore the most immediate threat. Or it might even have been because I was one of the few people in the office who hadn't slept with her, despite a couple of thinly veiled advances. Amanda, it was widely thought, used sex to control people, but the truth was that no one really knew what motivated her. She could be pleasant one moment and horrendous the next. Office gossip put it down to a bad divorce that had left her with a lifelong mission to take her revenge on men. Yet she could be equally horrible to her female colleagues, ferreting around for any sign of weakness she could use to gain an advantage. Sometimes I think she just behaved as she did to amuse herself. And what fun she was going to have now with this latest bit of ammunition. *Hell, she had called me Mr Jessica Gallagher.* Is that what I was going to become? I didn't want to be Mr Jessica Gallagher. What was wrong with being called Mr Alan Muir?

Then I started thinking about my parents and what they'd say. Actually, I already knew what my mum would say, but my dad had always told me that Jess was a keeper, that I should ask her before it was too late. Yet even he would laugh if I told him how it had come about, and no son wants to be laughed at by his father.

Oh, fuck. What if Jess was so right-on that she'd already asked him for permission to marry his son?

Then there was Sam. His best-man's speech would be bad enough as it was, but if he had this extra bit of material...

Well, none of it bore thinking about.

I was so worked up by the time the bill arrived, I hadn't

realised I'd been on autopilot for the last two courses. When I'm angry, or distracted, I go quiet. Jess, of course, had noticed my pat responses to her increasingly enthusiastic monologues on mortgages and engagement parties and bathroom decorations, and eventually snapped at me again.

'Come on, Alan, tell me what's wrong.'

'Nothing.'

'You don't really mind that I asked you, do you? I thought you'd find it amusing. It's not as if we haven't talked about getting married before – '

The waiter, who had been hovering indiscreetly, eavesdropping on my misery, chose this moment to place the bill down on the table in front of us.

'I'll get it,' said Jess. 'My treat.'

'No, you bloody well won't,' I said, more loudly than I had intended. I gripped the table – I was on my feet and hadn't even realised I'd stood up – lowered my voice and spoke nonsensically at the confusing girl I loved: 'I have gone out to work today. I have hunted and I have gathered. Let me pay.'

Jess smiled gently, in a way that melted and enraged me simultaneously. 'Okay, Alan. As you like.'

But it hadn't been as I liked. Not one little bit. And although I knew I was man enough not to mind, although I knew I shouldn't have cared about the small details in the light of the bigger picture, I did care, deeply and fundamentally. And so when Jess asked if I was coming back to hers, or she to mine, I pretended that I was working on a big accounting deal and returned to the office, where I went to the gym for the first time in ten years, running like a madman on the treadmill until I collapsed.

Then I got a cab home so I could speak to Sam. In times like these, you have to rely on someone who will really understand.

Chapter Six

'You understand, don't you, Sam?' implored Alan after he'd finished telling us a completely incomprehensible, but highly entertaining, story about Jess proposing to him in a public place in front of Amanda.

'Of course,' I said, biting a beery lip and trying not to catch anyone else's eye. It had been a long afternoon and evening. 'It happens to all of us every day.'

'I understand that you'll never be able to show your face in public again,' sniggered Matt.

'I think it was very understanding of you to say "yes",' attempted Ed, before losing it and laughing as well. 'You're a twenty-first-century emasculated man, through and through.'

'Oh shut up, you pricks,' said Alan, still sweaty from the mini-marathon he'd run in the office. 'I'm not asking you to understand what happened, just how I feel about it.'

'Now, that much I do get,' said Ed, looking suddenly very dejected again. 'It's never easy when someone you love makes a decision without you.'

'What do you mean?'

Ed explained about Tara while Alan looked relieved to have something else to think about. After a minute or so the two of them had a little man-hug, unlucky and unsure in love respectively.

'What a pair of losers, eh?' snorted Matt, handing me another beer.

Neither Ed nor Alan felt the need to answer that.

'Still,' I said. 'At least some of us have got a solution for all this, haven't we, guys?'

'Speak for yourself,' said Ed.

'What?'

'It's a shit idea,' said Ed. 'It will never work. And even if it did, it would be demeaning to us as men.'

Ed explained my house-husband masterplan to Alan, whereupon he, too, declared that it was a ridiculous idea. 'If that's the alternative to swallowing my pride and saying "yes" to Jess's proposal, then I know which one I'd rather choose,' said Alan.

'We're not asking you to choose, you silly tit,' said Matt. 'You're one of the lucky ones – one of a very small, very lucky minority. Not only are you too dull, predictable and, probably, busy to look elsewhere, you also happen to have found someone you might actually want to spend the rest of your life with. Hell, I'd choose to marry Jess. Or at least, if I were as dull, predictable and busy as you, I'd choose to marry Jess.'

'Thanks,' said Alan.

'You're welcome. And you're welcome to Jess. She's not entirely ugly, she cooks quite well, she's bright enough but not too bright, her mother has aged fairly well, the rest of us can stand her, you seem to rub along okay without wanting to murder one another, at least in public, and she looks like she's better in bed than the last girl you went out with almost a decade ago.'

'Really, you're too kind.'

Actually, Matt really *was* too kind. There was no way any of us would want to marry Jess. Yeuch.

'All I'm saying, Alan,' continued Matt, 'is that you should have a little sympathy for the rest of us while you go about it. Not all of us are as dull and predictable as you.'

'Not all of us are as lucky as you,' chimed in Ed, toadyingly. Maybe he did actually like Jess, that great, big, friend-stealing whale of a barrister.

'And because we now have plenty of time on our hands, we can afford to be unpredictable and interesting,' said Matt.

'Well, we can't really *afford* to,' I said. 'Then again, we can't really afford not to. Imagine if we had time on our hands and we were also predictable and dull. Then we'd be losers twice over.'

'Exactly,' said Matt. 'This house-husband scheme is going to be our little hobby to pass the time.'

'*Your* little hobby,' said Ed.

'*Your* loss,' said Matt.

'Actually, it's really Alan's loss,' I said. 'He's going to look pretty stupid when Matt and I both manage to ask a girl to marry us before he does.'

Matt laughed. 'Yeah, let's have a bet,' he said. Matt loved his bets. The who-can-dance-with-everyone-first bet at Lisa's wedding aside, he usually won them.

'As if you guys could hold down a relationship for more than six months,' said Alan. 'I'd certainly bet against that. Anyway, Sam, I thought you hated the idea of marriage.'

'Oh, I do,' I replied. 'It's the most trapping, outdated societal more still in existence. Have I told you my theory?'

'Please,' groaned Ed. 'Not another one.'

'My theory,' I continued, 'is that, whenever you get suicidally bored of one stage of life, you move unquestioningly on to the next. You can't stand school so you go to university. You get bored with university so you get a job. Your job drives you mad so you get a girlfriend. You run out of things to say to your girlfriend so you marry her. You hate your marriage so you have children to take your mind off it. That doesn't work so you get divorced. Being divorced is lonely so you get married and start all over again. And then you die.' I shrugged. 'I suppose it's a progression of sorts. Anyway, Alan, as I've just been explaining to the others, it seems to be a fairly inevitable progression. And ultimately, probably better than the lonely alternatives. So what I really want to do is to show you just how easy it all is. You think you've found "the one" with Jess, don't you? But you can make anyone think they're the one. You can make anyone fall in love with you, if you really try. Just look at girls our age. They hit thirty, they panic and they can't wait to get married. Even the rich, supposedly liberated ones. Actually, *especially* the rich, liberated ones – they don't have time to meet anyone else. They're sizing you up as suitable father material to their as yet unborn children as soon as you open your mouth. So I tell you: when this scheme all works out – and work out, it will – Matt and I are going to be laughing almost as much as you guys are going to be kicking yourselves for not thinking of it earlier. Just you wait and see: finding an acceptable Mrs Sam Hunt is going to be a walk in the park.'

Alan smiled as if deep in thought and then reached for the BlackBerry he carried around in his jacket pocket like a yappy, Pekingese puppy in need of constant love and attention.

'Come on, Alan,' said Matt. 'Put your phone away. This is just getting interesting. Don't go back to the office now and pump a few more grams of iron. And definitely don't call Jess.'

But then Alan did something very unpredictable and un-Alan-like. 'I'm doing neither,' he said. 'I'm texting Jess to tell her that I'm still stuck in the office.'

'And why would you do that?' I asked.

'So I can take my mind off everything and hang out with you guys,' said Alan. 'Matt's right: this is just getting interesting.'

It is possible that I gave a small whoop of pleasure at this juncture. Maybe Jess would think this a dumpable offence and we'd have our Alan back. Matt took his expression of delight one step further and started swinging his arms round in the most bizarre fashion and chanting, 'You go, boy, you go, boy,' until Alan asked him if he had anything he wanted to share with us.

'Like what?' said Matt.

'Like the fact you appear to have turned into a raving homosexual,' said Alan.

'Better gay than married,' said Ed, laughing.

'And on what experience are you basing that analysis?' asked Alan.

'The unimpeachable armchair wisdom of never being likely to try either.'

We all laughed. *This was good*, I thought, *this was fun*. We still 'had it', we could still 'hang' together, we could still have conversations as immature as the ones twenty-five years ago, only with longer words.

'For the sake of fuck, Alan, would you please put your cunting BlackBerry away?'

I returned to the room with a jolt. You can always rely on Ed to ruin your nostalgic musings with an Anglo-Saxon interjection.

'Actually, Ed,' said Alan, peering over his BlackBerry and looking slightly wounded, 'I was trying to help you guys out. I am devising a spreadsheet.'

'Oh great,' said Matt, sarcastically. 'My life lacks spreadsheets.'

'Then it is all the poorer for it,' said Alan in what might, or might not, have been a joke. 'This, however, is not any normal spreadsheet. It's to help you guys out with your "kept man" scheme.'

'I thought you said it was a ridiculous scheme,' I said.

'It is,' said Alan. 'So you will need all the help you can get.'

We gathered round while Alan tapped away fluently on the tiny device, sending great blocks of text flying around the screen to reappear in other blocks, everything neatly arranged and colour-coded.

'Why do I have to be pink?' complained Ed.

'Shut up,' said Alan. 'This isn't *Reservoir Dogs*.'

'I thought you didn't want to be part of this, anyway, Ed,' said Matt.

As Alan typed and tapped and computed, he explained that the sheets represented our 'strengths and weaknesses', our 'threats and opportunities', our individual chances of success. He jabbed a finger at a blue patch of the tiny screen, obscuring most of it. 'Take Sam, for example. My "model" shows that acting is one of the strengths by which he will achieve his goals. His weakness is that he is very unlikely to be able to convince rich, successful women that he is an attractive catch on his own merits. But if he pretended to be something he isn't... Well, it might just work.'

'Wow, Alan. Thanks for that insight.'

Alan twiddled a button and Matt's spreadsheet appeared, highlighted in yellow. 'Matt's unique selling point, or USP, on the other hand, is that he is, or was, a doctor, and is therefore a caring, noble soul who can look after the children when they have colds and his wife is stuck in a board meeting.'

'You're not making this sound like much fun, are you?' I complained.

'My point is that Matt's best bet is to play the game straight,' said Alan. 'Career women looking for a suitable mate will love him. He's got charm candy written all over him. Just look at the spreadsheet. Excel never lies.'

He twiddled another button and the screen turned briefly pink for Ed, flickered three times and faded into nothing. 'Bloody battery,' said Alan, stuffing the machine back in his pocket.

'Oh, what a shame,' sneered Ed. 'I'll never get to find out what the oracle of Orange had in store for me.'

'All I was trying to illustrate,' said Alan, pushing his glasses back up his nose, 'is that you're going to need a proper plan for it to come off. You can't just waltz along and hope something falls into your laps.'

'It did for you,' said Matt.

'Well, I'm lucky, I suppose,' said Alan, looking bashful. 'And I don't hold out for perfection.'

'I'd love Jess to hear you say that,' I said.

'I don't think she'd be all that shocked,' said Alan. 'She'd probably say the same thing about me. We're both settlers, not fantasists. You know that stupid card metaphor you're always banging on about, Sam?'

'The blackjack one?' said Ed and Matt, almost simultaneously.

I frowned. Was I really that predictable?

'Exactly,' said Alan. 'In that daft metaphor, Jess is a twenty out of twenty-one. Or a nineteen, at least. So why torture myself looking for an improvement that doesn't exist? If I were to plot a graph representing my relationship with Jess, it might have fun on one axis and sacrifice on the other – '

'Ooooh, a graph,' sneered Matt. 'That's almost as much fun as a spreadsheet.'

'I could plot that graph,' continued Alan, 'and the fun would far outweigh the sacrifice. As long as that's the case, I think a relationship is healthy.'

Bollocks, I thought. *You're only saying that to make yourself feel better about being trapped and having to make so many sacrifices.*

'But as for the rest of you,' continued Alan, 'well, I support the institution of marriage. So I'm in favour of the fact you're taking a few proactive steps to find the right sort of partner, even if you are only doing it to take the piss out of me.' He held up a hand to stop our half-hearted protests. 'You're right: why leave such an important thing to chance? Why not devote as much time and resources to finding your lifelong partner as you do to your careers? On reflection, however, I wonder if you've properly thought through the way in which you're narrowing down your selection criteria.'

'On the basis of money, you mean?' asked Matt.

'It's not everything,' said Alan.

'That's easy for you to say,' said Matt, getting up and making his unsteady way to the kitchen to fetch some more beers. 'You've got it.' There was a crash as he slipped on the floor. 'And the rest of us don't,' he added from a prostrate position.

'Marry for money and you'll pay for it, every penny,' said Alan.

'And what the hell is that supposed to mean?' called out Matt, picking himself off the kitchen floor.

'It's what my grandfather always used to say.'

'And was he happy?' I asked.

'No, he was poor and miserable.'

'Then, with all due respect to his memory, your grandfather was an arse.'

'But what about "the one"?' said Ed, taking a beer from Matt and spilling it all over his trousers. 'It's not exactly a romantic scheme, is it?'

Matt put his large, handsome head in his hands. 'Dear God, Ed, you still believe in the concept of "the one"? After what Tara's done to you?'

'She *is* the one,' said Ed, dribbling a little. 'Well, *was*, anyway. Tara was my plus-one, my one-plus-one, which still equalled one, indivisible, wholly and eternally one – '

'Ed,' said Alan, kindly but firmly. 'You need to stop talking now.'

'Sorry,' said Ed, pulling himself together. 'It's just that – '

'I know,' said Alan, desperately hoping along with the rest of us that Ed wasn't going to start crying. 'We all know,' he continued, soothingly. 'But if you go around thinking like that you'll never get anywhere. Look at me: I'm sure I could have been happy with someone other than Jess. She happens to be my one but, if the worst came to the worst, someone else could make me happy as well.'

Please let something happen to her, I thought. *Nothing too bad. Just something.*

'You're so strong, Alan,' said Ed, looking at him adoringly.

'You're so gay, Ed,' said Matt.

'You're all such tossers,' I said, a little worked up at the direction the conversation had been taking without my input. 'Of course there's no such thing as the one. What are you, Ed? A twelve-year-old girl? This is my entire point. Bring back arranged marriages, I say. Convert to Islam and get your parents to sort it out for you. Become a Jane Austen character. Marry your friends, for all I care. Choose someone from the phone book.

Anyone can rub along just fine with anyone else, as long as you approach the arrangement with the correct degree of cynicism.'

'Would you like to marry me, Sam?' asked Matt.

'Sure. If I get to thirty-five and I'm single and start going bald like Ed, I'm all yours.'

'And you're all mine,' said Matt, doing something with his beer bottle which I would blush to describe in full.

'Rank!' protested Ed. 'Anyway, Sam, aren't you promised to Claire at thirty-five?'

'Yes, but it looks like she's about to be made redundant, so a fat lot of use she'll be to me then.'

'Sam only makes that sort of joke when he really likes someone,' said Alan.

'Shut up.'

'Claire's perfect for you, Sam,' persisted Alan. 'Why does it all have to come back to money with you?'

'Because we don't have any. Because we're in the middle of the worst recession for decades. That's why. Don't get me wrong. I don't *like* money. Not one little bit. Numbers. Figures. Equations. Spreadsheets. It's boring. People who work with money are boring. You, my friend, are boring. Money itself is boring.' I fumbled around in my pocket in an attempt to make my point. All I could find was a two-pence coin. It was symbolic, in a way. 'I mean, look at this. It's a grubby piece of shit, isn't it? Think how many hands it's been through. No, for me, it comes down to what one can do with money. And that's the problem with this country. All the wrong people have the money. What do bankers and lawyers and footballers do with theirs? They buy disgusting houses and two-bit whores, that's what. I would spend it properly. Money would liberate me to do what I want to do.'

'Which is what?' asked Ed.

'Oh, I don't know. Act. Relax. Keep seeing you guys. Appreciate the good things. Live simply but well. Do a bit for charity.' Ed feigned a yawn. I turned on him. 'Have you ever worked in an office, Ed?' He shook his head; Ed had only ever been a teacher. 'Let me tell you what working in an office is like, then. It is wank. You have to get up when you don't want to, you have to iron collared shirts you'd never normally wear, you have to be polite to people you'd have bullied at school and you have to sit at a desk that is the wrong height, underneath lights that are too bright, near a radiator that is too hot, doing tasks that are boring and pointless. Your superiors are less intelligent than you, your inferiors are more ambitious than you and the only attractive girl in the office is already married and having an affair with the boss. So believe me when I say it's wank. Wank is what it undoubtedly is. Wank, wankity wank wank.' Ed still looked unmoved by the Ciceronian force of my rhetoric. I continued: 'So that is why money is important. Because I don't want to spend the rest of my life chained to an office chair earning a pittance in order to support my ungrateful children and a wife who's knocking off one of the neighbours. I don't want to be a breadwinner, whatever that means. I don't want to win bread. I want to win Oscars.' Ed wasn't the only one to guffaw at this point. 'So let's go out there and marry these rich, ambitious women. Let's hang out where the rich hang out. Let's go to City bars and art auctions and ski resorts. Let's help ourselves to these rich pickings. Let's snare these walking wallets. Let's marry money. Let's, in the immortal words of Al Green, stay together. Let's stay close together. And then we can live long and happily and well instead of short and miserably and emasculated-ly.'

My peroration was greeted with a quizzical eyebrow by Alan, a frown by Ed and a small cheer and a raised beer by Matt. Frankly, I think it deserved a little better. It was a good peroration.

We sat in contented silence for a while and then Matt suddenly got down on the floor and started tearing bits of paper out of one of Alan's notepads and scribbling excitedly on them. 'I have an idea,' he explained. 'I have a much better way of narrowing down the decision-making process. It's based on something I said earlier, about Jess's cooking abilities, intelligence and the attractiveness of her mother.'

'Categories?' said Alan, perking up from his drunken slumber at the mention of his forceful fiancée's name.

'Exactly,' said Matt. 'Now, let's say that the score for the perfect girl adds up to a hundred.'

'What's wrong with twenty-one?' I said.

'Or forty-three and a half,' sneered Ed. He'd lost interest in this game.

'A hundred,' said Matt, firmly. 'It's simpler. But how do we get to that hundred? Of what components is that one hundred formed? Categories, that's what. Attractiveness. Likeability of her siblings. Likeability of her friends. Intelligence. Kindness. Fun quotient. Ability to fit in with existing friendship group. Ability to make friends jealous. Suitability as a mother – '

'I really like this,' interrupted Alan. 'It's a quantifiable formalisation of the subconscious process by which all of us rate girls in any case.'

Not you, I thought. *You've never cared how much Jess fits into your existing friendship group.*

'Oh, whatever,' said Ed. 'You guys are so immature.'

'And all the categories have sub-categories, of course,' continued Matt. 'Attractiveness can be divided into beauty and sex appeal. In fact, sexual abilities should probably have a category of their own – '

'Tara was very good at sex,' said Ed.

'It's not an uninteresting scheme,' I said. 'But the really interesting thing is what weight you give to each of the categories. What does the balance look like?'

'Exactly,' said Matt. 'So let me kick the discussion off by suggesting a maximum of forty points for looks, ten for abilities in bed, ten for how her mother has turned out, twenty for intelligence and twenty for personality. Based on these scores, the perfect girl would add up to a hundred.'

'Why is it so important what her mother looks like?' asked Alan.

'Because all girls turn into their mothers,' I said. 'Fortunately for you, Alan, few boys do.'

'Doesn't personality include intelligence?' asked Matt.

'What's the point of them scoring forty for looks now, if they get zero for how they're going to look in twenty years' time when they turn into their mothers?' asked Alan. 'On that basis, a short-term fittie scores much better than a long-term beauty.'

'Then you keep on choosing short-term fitties,' I said.

'Do they get minus points if they're too intelligent?'

'What's the point of going out with someone who scores ninety out of ninety, but is absolutely dreadful in bed?'

'Under this system, a delightful minger would score sixty, but a boring supermodel only forty.'

'Well, I'd rather marry a delightful minger than a boring supermodel.'

'What about compatibility, then?'

'That's too subjective.'

'Surely any relationship is subjective.'

'Then what's the point of scoring them objectively?'

'What about how old they are?'

'You know you're getting old when you think someone's attractive just because they're younger than you.'

'Half your age plus seven, isn't it?'

'Yes, Sam, but that's a bare minimum not a target.'

'What about how easy-going and kind they are? Or how prone to moods? There's no point going out with someone who's up and down like a yoyo.'

'I very much like girls who are up and down like yoyos.'

'Ayeee.'

And so the discussion continued late into the night until at some ridiculous point someone – I can't remember who now – suggested making up little cards of the girls we knew by taking their pictures off Facebook and playing a version of Top

Trumps using the categories we'd finally decided upon. Claire's personality and Lisa's looks – that appeared to be the perfect, winning combination. Even Ed, who had always had a soft spot for Claire, perked up at that thought. It was just a pity that fit Lisa was mildly annoying and fun Claire slightly plain.

At half past midnight little Alan, who had always been the most lightweight of the group, started to pontificate about what women would say if they walked in on us and promptly fell off the sofa and passed out. Matt ventured that he had overheard female doctors gossiping about men and they were far worse, before going off to be sick in the bath. Just before 1am Ed tried to call Tara so we stole his phone and flushed the battery down the toilet. He went home in a sulk, climbing over a prostrate Alan on his way to the front door and leaving only a newly sober Matt and me vaguely *compos mentis*.

'You really mean to do this, mate?' asked Matt.

'Yes,' I said, trying to still the swaying room by concentrating very intently on a point in the middle of his dimpled chin. 'I know it's all a bit of a joke, but it will be a lot of fun, even if it doesn't work out.'

'Category one: money?'

'Category one: money.'

'With a pleasant sprinkling of other attributes mixed in.'

'Indeed.'

I didn't say the real reason I wanted to take up the challenge: namely that the last month had made me as terrified of ending up on the shelf as the desperate thirtysomething girls I'd just been mocking. I, too, was entering my fourth decade: too old to be a professional footballer, a pop star or, these days, even a politician. I thought back to my cynical bravado at the wedding; the bluff in front of my friends just now; the bet. The truth was I had been protesting too much. Lisa's wedding, my trip to Edinburgh, Claire's teasing, Jess's proposal to Alan... It had all shaken me to the core. Mr Geoffrey Parker was right: I had to give up the Peter Pan act at some point. I would need somewhere to live, someone to live with and someone to support me while I threw myself one last time into acting, the only thing I had ever wanted to do with my life.

Matt and I shook solemnly on the bet and then suggested kicking off by going through our mobile address books and finding the richest-sounding girl possible.

'Here,' he said. 'Let's swap phones. It will be more fun.'

A few seconds later, just as I was about to send an erotic text to one of Matt's gay friends from his phone, mine beeped in his hands.

'It's Mary,' he said, waving it in my face.

'The Christian from the wedding?'

'I think so.' He studied it more closely. 'Did you know that her surname was Money-Barings?'

'Mother of God, give me that blessed phone,' I said.

Chapter Seven

There are many horrible words in the English language that I teach, but few are more unpleasant than 'dumped'. Dumping is something you do to unwanted rubbish. It is a one-way process, an assertive, violent act by a subject to an object, a non-reflexive, unequivocal, irretrievable imposition of the will of one person on an unwilling victim.

Our break-up was not 'mutual'. We did not 'talk it over and come to an understanding'. We did not 'drift' or 'grow apart'. We did not decide that 'we loved one another, but were not *in* love with one another'. We did not agree that 'we had become friends instead of lovers'. She did not shake her head sadly and lie that it was more her than me. We did not agree to stay in touch. We did not resolve to remain friends. We did not assure one another that we looked forward to things being the same as they had been before we'd started going out.

Tara dumped me. I was dumped by Tara. I have been dumped. I am dumped.

I know what Sam would say. He would tell me that it is harder to be the dumper than the dumpee. In Sam's opinion, it is difficult to be the one who ends a relationship as you have all the pain of the loss in addition to the guilt of the act. You miss them; you doubt yourself. You hate the pain you've caused and you hate yourself for putting them through that pain. Sam should know: he has had plenty of experience of being the dumper. And yet, with all undue respect, Sam knows fuck-all.

Right now, would I rather be me, pouring out this adolescent angst, or Tara, happily ensconced in her new lover's £4m penthouse? I would wager that Tara is feeling a lot of emotions right now – greed, smugness, orgasmic joy – and none of them is guilt. Dumpers move on quickly (she has moved on spectacularly quickly). It is the rest of us who are left crying in their wake.

Maybe I should have seen it coming. Maybe I should have presented a stronger face to the world and hidden how I felt. But Tara has always known how I've felt. She knew it the first time I asked her out, five years ago. And she knew it eight hours ago when I fell on our bedroom floor in shock and begged her not to leave me.

I know what you're thinking: it's not very manly, is it, all this begging and complaining? The girl upgraded. Good luck to her. Why would anyone want to go out with someone who ran off abroad to teach English and now works in a rough inner-city school? Who would want to go out with that loser when they could have a rich, older lawyer?

I don't want anyone to feel sorry for me. I've got myself to do that. But let me, at least, attempt to explain what it feels like to be dumped. I could, of course, say that my heart feels ripped out and chopped into a million pieces, that I no longer care if I wake up alive tomorrow morning, that nothing means anything any more, that I'd sooner she'd killed me than broken up with me, but you would only laugh or call me a 'twelve-year-old girl', like Sam did. So let me eschew emotions altogether and attempt to explain it in terms of hard facts: I've known Tara for more than five years. I've spoken to her every single day. I know the first CD she bought and the name of her brother's second pet rabbit. Her grandmother sends me birthday cards. I've seen her practising writing her first name and my surname together. Her friends joked about us getting married. Even her father joked about us getting married. We own a flat together.

These facts are incontrovertible, yet she has taken the entire narrative of my life, our life, twisted it, crumpled it and ruined it for ever. Nothing is sacred now. That holiday we enjoyed in Ireland in the spring? She was probably already thinking how to end it. The flat we bought and decorated together? No doubt she was only wondering which room she would like to screw her new boyfriend in first. The plans we made for the future? They were only sweet nothings and meaningless promises until she could find a convenient moment to break them.

Of course I'm angry. Of course that anger has made me irrational. But, you see, we had *plans* for the future. Or at least, I had plans. I know it's only girls who are meant to do soppy things like envisaging themselves as grandparents or imagining their perfect wedding day or thinking up names they might give to their children. Well, slap me in my soppy face and call me the loser that I undoubtedly am, but I did all those things. I planned for the future. I planned for our future. And now that future is a foreign country I can never visit.

I suppose I could give up on Tara altogether. I could pretend that she never meant anything to me anyway. I could move on, or at least pretend to move on, and have a string of meaningless, semi-enjoyable encounters until I have slept her out of my system. Who knows? It might even make her jealous. She might realise she's made a dreadful mistake and ask for me back. If not, at least I will have had some fun in the meantime.

But who am I trying to kid? As far as Tara is concerned, she hasn't made a mistake at all, let alone a dreadful one. In her eyes, she's just made the best decision of her life. She's twenty-eight now, younger than me, in her prime. Five years ago, she was more beautiful but less confident. Five years from now, she'll have begun to lose her looks. Right now she has the perfect balance to snare the sort of man she appears to want to snare. Older, richer men leave their wives for younger, attractive girls all the time. What everyone forgets in that cliché is that those younger, more attractive girls are often leaving somebody as well. In this case, that somebody – that nobody – just happens to be me.

I'd like to be magnanimous. I'd like to be happy for Tara. I'd like to congratulate her on using her small window of opportunity to upgrade to a better long-term prospect. I'd really like to be able to move on myself. But I can't. I just can't. I can't join in Sam's and Matt's silly bet. I can't adopt their cynicism about romance and marriage. I can't really judge women by categories because there's only one category that counts for me: Tara. I can't do any of this, in truth, because I loved Tara, I still love Tara, and I can't imagine ever loving anyone else.

So what am I supposed to do now? Tell me that, Tara, you fucking cow. Tell me how I'm meant to pick my life up and go back to school in a couple of weeks' time. Tell me where I'm supposed to live. Tell me where and how and when a twenty-nine-year-old English teacher is ever meant to meet someone new. Give me one good reason why I shouldn't shut down my laptop and jump out of the window right now.

Well, there is perhaps one reason, one very good reason, and it is this: I'm going to stay alive until I can win Tara back. So watch this space. Listen to this drunken vow: that fat old lawyer is going down. And if I don't succeed? Well, then Tara will soon discover that hell hath no fury like a man scorned.

Chapter Eight

Mary Money-Barings turned out to be something of a prolific sender of text messages. The first, sent at 1am on the Friday morning that Alan passed out and Ed returned home single and phoneless, said how much she had enjoyed meeting me at Lisa's wedding and wondered if I'd like to go for a drink some time. It was signed with one kiss. The second, sent at 1.01am, apologised for texting so late; she had meant to send it earlier, but must have saved it in her draft folder and rolled onto her phone by mistake during the night. A third, sent at 1.06am, stated that she had got the wrong number and I was to ignore the previous two missives. It contained no kisses.

Ten minutes later, a fourth text arrived, a gem of its genre: 'Hello again. Actually, it is me, Mary, after all. We met in Lisa's parents' bed at her wedding. Do you remember? Please ignore the second and third texts. They weren't true. I'm a bit drunk, I was thinking of you and thought it might be fun to catch up again x.'

Matt and I sat in growing amazement as my phone continued to beep excitedly.

'Jesus!' he exclaimed, appropriately, when a fifth text arrived at 1.30am apologising for the bluntness of the fourth. 'What did you do to this poor girl?'

'Do you really want to know what I did to her, Matt?'

'No.'

'You're sure you don't want to hear how very, *very* inventive Christian virgins can be in bed?'

'No.'

Mary, bless her, had undeniably done something for me, though. I actually found her stream of consciousness rather

73

endearing. Girls think guys are put off by this sort of mad behaviour. The truth is that if we want to go to bed with them – or have some other strange agenda, such as a marriage of financial convenience – nothing puts us off at all. Desperation? I'm all for it. Wild horses cannot stop a man on heat. And, in any case, Mary had rather cleverly kept me interested by not actually allowing me to shag her at the wedding.

I waited a few days to let Mary stew and then called her – somehow, I didn't think text messaging was our medium – on Sunday evening. Generally it is an excellent time to call as most people are feeling depressed and will therefore say yes to anything.

'Hello,' said an excitable voice. Maybe Mary didn't get Sunday night blues. 'Who's this?'

'It's Sam,' I said.

'Oh! Hello!' she gushed. I could hear the sound of singing in the background. 'Sorry, I didn't recognise your number. I deleted it in embarrassment after Thursday night.'

'Don't worry,' I said. 'I've done much worse things on Thursday nights, believe me.'

She laughed. 'I do believe you.'

'And I've thought about much worse things on Sunday evenings, too.'

'Like what?'

'You. Me. Champagne. No clothes.'

Mary giggled. 'Sam, you are very bad.'

'So are you,' I said. 'And yet, simultaneously, very good.'

'Stop it. I've just stepped out of church.'

'Well, go back inside then and say you're sorry.'

'I already have, for that weekend at Lisa's wedding.'

'If you say sorry, aren't you supposed to regret it?'

'I do regret it.'

'Did you remember to say sorry three times then?'

'Sam! You know that's not true.'

'I'm sorry.'

But I wasn't really. We continued our good-natured conversation, ending it by agreeing to meet up on Wednesday. 'There's a really good friend of mine I'd like you to meet,' said Mary. 'You don't mind, do you?'

She wanted to add in a friend as well? Just how sinful was this girl?

I checked my busy schedule of trying to get a temping job, making coffee, hanging out with Matt and failing to get recalls for auditions, and agreed that I could definitely make time for Mary and her friend on Wednesday.

*

The next three days dragged a little bit, to be honest, especially after the excitement of Lisa's wedding and Edinburgh, not to mention the multifarious events of Thursday night, which had combined to give me a three-day hangover. Not for the first time I had failed to reconcile the thirst of a teenager with the liver of a twenty-nine-year-old actor. Alan vanished from view from Friday morning onwards, leaving for work long before we woke up and not returning for days. Maybe his nasty boss Amanda was punishing him for saying yes to Jess in public, or maybe Jess was punishing him for not saying yes quickly enough, or perhaps his father was giving him grief for not asking her first, or his Mum, who had never liked Jess much, was telling him to find someone else, or maybe Alan was punishing himself for all of the above. None of us really knew, although it was almost certain, ventured Matt, that he was being punished for something.

In Alan's absence, Matt took it upon himself to move into his room and dress in Alan's remaining accountant-weekend-wear which Ed hadn't already taken home with him for his new hermit-like existence. Matt called Ed repeatedly, increasingly worried by the lack of response, until we finally remembered that Ed's mobile battery was making its slow journey through the London sewage system back to our taps as drinking water. So on Sunday evening, after I'd finished speaking to Mary, Matt and I went round to Ed's miniscule flat in Hackney and found him sitting in his pyjamas amid a mountain of Tara's discarded clothes and watching *Sex and the City*.

'I'm planning an elaborate revenge,' he declared, idly pinging a bra across the lounge. 'Hell hath no fury like a man scorned.'

'Do you want some company?' I asked.

'No,' he said, pausing *Sex and the City* to scribble down a few notes on a pad resting on the arm of the sofa. 'I am researching how women think so I can plan my elaborate revenge.'

We left him in peace, if peace was what you'd call it, and returned to Alan's, where Matt installed himself in his 'war room', the name he'd given the small cupboard in the corridor containing a computer which Alan, in turn, liked to refer to as his 'home office'. This, explained Matt, would be the base from where he would conduct his campaign to snare a rich wife.

Ever the conscientious armchair general, he was already in place on Monday morning as I was leaving for a temping job that had become available through the agency last thing on Friday evening.

'You know what the most embarrassing thing about your house-husband scheme is, Sam?' said Matt, swivelling on Alan's expensive leather chair to face me.

'The fact that it's so embarrassingly simple that Ed and Alan will hate us for not having done it themselves?'

'No. What's really embarrassing is the fact that you've thought of it but I'm going to be so much better at it than you.'

'What do you mean, failed medic boy?'

'What I mean is, "most gifted actor of his generation currently heading out to a minimum-wage filing job"... ' Matt lowered the fingers he had raised like bunny ears, then lifted them again to continue, '"Heading out, that is, in one of his flatmate's borrowed shirts over which he's already spilled his coffee."' I looked down at Alan's stripy, stained shirt. Matt was right, the bastard. He continued: 'What I mean, Sam, is that you have to haul yourself into the twenty-first century. What are your tactics? How are you going about this? You're attempting to hook up with a born-again trustafarian on the basis of her rich-sounding surname. It's not a very scientific approach, is it?'

'I don't like science,' I said. 'Anyway, seduction is an art.'

'Not this sort of seduction. This is definitely a science.' Matt swivelled back to face his screen and tapped ferociously on the keyboard. 'Your problem, Sam, is that you're limiting yourself by sticking to people you've actually met in the flesh. How many is that over a lifetime? A few thousand at most? And how many of those are going to be even vaguely suitable? A hundred, if you're lucky? Less, if you apply the rigorous criteria you've chosen.' He jiggled the mouse around and clicked a few times. 'You wouldn't choose a job on the same basis, would you? Or somewhere to live? So what I'm doing is opening up the search to the entire world. Or the entire worldwide web, to be precise.'

'Has anyone ever told you that you're a complete gimp?' I said.

'Often,' replied Matt. 'But a gimp who's about to beat you.' He tapped a few more keys, pressed 'return' with a flourish and pointed at the screen. 'Here, look at this.'

I looked. On the screen was a picture of Matt, looking effortlessly tanned and handsome on holiday the previous summer. Below was a short biography which mentioned the word 'doctor' at least three times and the more truthful word 'unemployed' not once. The website was called something like www.obnoxiouslytinyworlddating.com or www. weonlyshagotherrichpeople.net. Clicking through the other profiles, Matt treated me to a cascade of square-jawed private equity directors and glossy-maned blondes who all seemed to have 'boutique fashion' businesses and first names ending in 'a'. The advertising was expertly tailored for Amelia, Olivia, Antonia, Alexandra and their friends. Chat forums included such pressing topics as the best new luxury car dealers in Knightsbridge, the tastiest caterers for weddings in Wiltshire and the most trustworthy heli-skiing guides in Courchevel. The recession clearly hadn't hit this part of the web yet. There were more Russians and Arabs than you could shake a mouse at.

'Fling your options wide open and then narrow them down again according to your own criteria,' explained Matt with a grin. 'A rich, grateful patient of mine got me onto the site. It's invitation-only. If you can't beat them, join them, eh?'

'I've always preferred, "If you can't join them, beat them".'

'Well, good luck with that, mate. And have fun at work today. I'm sure the glamorous city sharks will be falling over themselves to sleep with and marry the guy doing their photocopying.'

With what I hoped was a suitably supercilious snort, I left Matt to his sad online games and ventured into the Square Mile to do an honest day's work. *Pah*, I thought, as I crammed in with the rest of the commuters on the Tube. *If that's the way he wanted to do it, then good for him.* I knew my strengths and weaknesses. Both lay in the real world.

After thirty minutes of inhaling eau d'underground, I was in a slightly less upbeat mood. I didn't like the real world much, I concluded, as I trudged wearily up the long escalator at Bank station. It looked as though my fantasy restoration of the way things used to be would be short-lived. Alan had disappeared to an unknown location, Ed had vanished into himself and his memories, and Matt had swapped the normal world for a shadowy online existence where the only thing that mattered was the size of your trust fund. So much for us all seeing more of each other.

Still, in times like these I had Claire, my reserve bloke. Her permanent office was very close to my temporary one so I rang and arranged to meet for as early a lunch as possible. She was looking well – suspiciously well. In my experience girls only look that happy when they're having a great deal of sex with someone they actually like. It's a cruel trick of nature that women should look the most appealing when they're the least desirous of your attentions. Why can't they look their best when they're sad and lonely and haven't slept with anyone for six months?

'You're looking well, too,' lied Claire after I'd complimented her. I looked distinctly green, having just spent ninety per cent of my morning wage, before tax, on a sandwich. 'What are you up to?'

I explained that I had taken the advice she had given me in Edinburgh to heart and was attempting to find a suitable lifelong partner before gravity took its toll, no one fancied me any more and I was too poor and infertile to have any children.

'Oh, Sam,' she laughed. 'I was only joking.'

'I'm not.'

'So how are you going about doing it?' she asked.

I explained my scheme, but it only made her laugh more and more uncontrollably until our lunch resembled the restaurant scene in *When Harry Met Sally*. Other customers stopped and stared at us, wondering perhaps who this comic genius could be. Claire, however, was most definitely laughing *at* me.

'Sam, you are without doubt the most ridiculous person I know.'

'Thank you,' I said, graciously. If the only compliments you receive are unintentional, I don't see any reason why you shouldn't still take them.

'And if you ever need a helping hand, you know where I am.'

'How kind. But why would I want help from you? I have it all sewn up already.'

*

Wednesday arrived, as Wednesdays do, and I met Mary after work as arranged. Work for her turned out to be a part-time job, which curiously she had never mentioned before, in the bookshop of an evangelical church in a posh, leafy part of Clapham. Perhaps I should have smelt a rat when she texted during the afternoon to ask if I could meet her there.

'So,' she enthused, greeting me with an enthusiastic kiss on both cheeks. Mary was always enthusing about something. 'Are you ready to come and meet my friend?'

I looked in the direction in which she was nodding. *Jesus*. She was nodding towards the church. *Did she want me to come and meet Jesus?*

She did.

'I know it might seem bizarre,' she guessed, accurately, noting the look of sheer blasphemous horror on my face. 'But you and I got off to such a strange start and I need to be honest with you. This is part of me, a really important part of me. And it is important to me that you understand that. Do you understand?'

'No' would have been the simple, honest answer. But she was such a sweet, enthusiastic, pretty, filthy, confusing girl that I really did want to understand her. Wouldn't anyone be intrigued by an otherwise rational person wanting someone they'd met at a wedding to meet their dead, Middle Eastern friend? Plus, there was the money. Or the Money-Barings, to be precise. That's what I really wanted to understand. Had the Money come first or the Barings? Had Mr Money met Miss Barings and declared it a match made in financial heaven? Had Barings married into money? Or were the Barings simply sitting around one day thinking, *Fuck me, our name doesn't sound nearly posh enough as it is, let's add 'Money' in front of it so that no one is in any doubt just how rich we are.*

Maybe I would get a chance to ask her during the evening, just after a sermon about the rich man and the camel trying to get through the eye of a needle.

We linked chaste hands and ventured inside.

The church was old and echoing, with vast pillars stretching up to a high wooden ceiling. The evening light slanted through a giant stained glass window above the altar, catching an antique silver crucifix. Yet an effort had clearly been made to make everything feel as modern as possible. The chairs were arranged in small groups, facing inwards towards a stage. Plasma screens were attached to the pillars. There was a hum of anticipation among a well-dressed, mainly young, congregation of about two hundred. U2 blared out from the hi-tech sound system.

Mary introduced me to a small group, most of whom had the beatific smiles and put-upon demeanours of long-term Christians and therefore had to be kind. Everyone took an intense, apologetic interest in me, explaining how they met every Wednesday evening ('a bonus bit of worship') as well as on Sundays. I joined in as well as I could, listening politely as the guy on my left – a confusing mixture of wide-boy City trader and wide-eyed evangelist – explained how he liked to 'say a little prayer' at work before embarking on each multi-million-pound deal. I wondered, silently, how such a little prayer might go: 'Dear Lord, who was born in a stable and worked as a carpenter, who befriended fishermen and threw money lenders out of the temple Dear, dear saviour, please give me the courage to screw over this small company in this deal I'm about to make, for your compassionate name's sake, amen.'

'It's a pithy description of the Trinity, isn't it?' I said instead, aloud.

'What?'

I gestured at the speakers. 'Bono's lyrics: "You're one, but you're not the same".'

Stock Market Christian laughed. 'Yeah, that's good. Mary told us you were funny.'

'Mary told you about me?'

I could see Mary waving her arms frantically and mouthing 'no' behind us, but Stock Market Christian ploughed on regardless. 'Yes, we had a little prayer session last week in which the leader suggested we shared the burden of sin weighing on our consciences.'

'The leader?'

'Yes, the prayer leader. And Mary had some thought-provoking experiences at a wedd – '

'What are you guys talking about?' Mary had given up on her semaphore and bounded over to intervene.

'The burden of sin,' I said. 'It's fascinating. Although, personally, I must admit that I've never found it much of a burden.'

Stock Market Christian clapped me rather too hard on the back and patted Mary rather too gently on the knee. 'Oh, Mary,' he said, 'I don't know how you find them.'

'Find what?' I was beginning to take an intense, borderline violent, dislike to Stock Market Christian.

'I'm sorry, Sam,' said Mary, hastily taking one of my hands in hers. 'Nothing gets people more excited here than the prospect of a reformed sinner.'

'Who says I'm reforming?'

They all laughed again, a little sadly this time, giving me a chance to take a proper look at Mary. She was attractive, certainly – not as stunning as Lisa, but striking, nonetheless. She had a good figure, full, red lips and the kind of glossy blonde mane that posh girls with too much time on their hands are good at cultivating. She was diplomatic, too, if the last few exchanges had been anything to go by. So why hadn't I called her myself after the wedding? Did I only like her because she had got in touch with me? Could this really work? Wouldn't her brassy self-assurance drive me mad? *Was it just the surname*?

'What made you become a Christian?' I asked my apparent rival. If I was going to make a go of this with Mary, I would have to make some sort of effort with her friends.

'It's a long story, Sam,' said Stock Market Christian. 'But basically, I had a fifteenth-century house in the country, a

Porsche 911 on the drive and a penthouse flat in the Docklands, but still, something was missing.'

Yeah, I thought. *Your testicles.*

'So I came to this church,' he continued, 'and just felt this really real connection when the Holy Spirit entered me.'

'And what happened when the Holy Spirit entered you?' I asked, conscious in a vague, agnostic way that a giggle at this juncture would surely mean eternal damnation.

'I felt really warm and fell to the floor, twitching,' he said, smiling at the memory. 'When I stood up again, I found myself singing out, subconsciously but not against my will, *Ti amo,* which is the Italian for "I love you". I had no idea why I was doing this. But later that evening, I met Mary, who was also there for the first time. I discovered that Mary had studied Italian at GCSE... '

Stock Market Christian left the sentence unfinished as if only a simpleton could fail to grasp the depth of its meaning and declare that he, too, had seen the light thanks to Mary's secondary-education choices.

'I don't get it,' I said. Maybe I *was* a simpleton.

'Don't you see? This was God's way of showing Mary and me that we were less alone in the room.'

It was God's way of showing Stock Market Christian that he was a prick, I thought.

'And also,' he continued, 'there's the fact I sang in Italian. That's quite remarkable, don't you think? I don't even speak Italian.'

I was saved from telling him what I really thought – which was that my grandmother's neutered dog didn't speak Italian either, but even it could probably guess that *ti amo* meant 'I love you' – by the sound of applause which signalled the beginning of the service.

'You've come at a good moment,' whispered Stock Market Christian in my ear. 'We're doing the Holy Spirit this week.'

Before I'd had a chance to ask him what this enigmatic

phrase meant, a man in a T-shirt approached the microphone on the stage, greeted the regulars and welcomed any newcomers.

'I'm afraid I'm your worst nightmare,' he quipped. 'A Christian with a guitar.'

He closed his eyes and proved he had been telling the truth by launching into a modern hymn I had never heard before. Two hundred people stood and sang heartily, some of them nodding vigorously, others raising their hands in orgasmic prayer: *You're altogether lovely / altogether worthy / altogether wonderful to me.* I looked across at Mary, who smiled back. But she wasn't singing about me. I wasn't altogether lovely or worthy. I wasn't wonderful. I was trying to get laid in church.

There were a few more excruciating verses, an almost amusingly trite sermon, and then it was time to 'do the Holy Spirit'. A posh young vicar called Rupert appeared on the stage and showed us a series of images of weeping children to get us in the mood, overlaid with a soundtrack of 'Fix You' by Coldplay. Did Chris Martin know, I wondered? Wasn't the song written for his wife?

The wailing Chris and the crying children worked their magic. Half the adults started crying, too. Thus warmed up, we began to pray together.

'Come, Spirit, come,' said Rupert, his voice shaking into the microphone.

Nothing happened.

'Now we have to wait on God for a bit,' said Rupert, as if God might be on hold on another call.

'*Hooooo, naaaaaaa, widddiiii.*'

God had clearly answered, for a white-haired woman in the front row was singing in tongues. It sounded surprisingly beautiful. Someone next to her broke down, weeping wildly. Others joined in. A few rows back, a man began to shake.

'*Hooooo, naaaaaaa, widddiiii.*'

Two women walked around handing out Kleenex for those

overcome by the Spirit. Then Stock Market Christian came to the front and said that the Spirit had told him over breakfast that 'someone here called Iva – or maybe Eva, the Spirit wasn't that clear – had a sister who forgave her.'

So *that* was that how Stock Market Christian did so well on the trading floor. Still, no one came forward.

'*Hooooo, naaaaaaa, widddiiii.*'

Stock Market Christian returned triumphantly to our little group where I was sitting quietly, trying to avoid Mary's eye. 'Hey, man,' he whispered. 'Can I pray for you?'

'*Hooooo, naaaaaaa, widddiiii.*'

I finally turned to Mary for support, to explain, or at least to ask for an explanation, but she had lain on her back on the floor and was making small snow-angel patterns with her arms and legs while mumbling something at the ceiling. 'Mary,' I said, in my own native English tongue. Still she mumbled on. 'Mary, I'm sorry, I have to go.'

'*Hooooo, naaaaaaa, widddiiii.*'

I got up and ran down the central aisle, not caring who saw me, not caring what they thought. I only stopped to breathe when I was outside in the crisp late-summer air, underneath a huge banner that asked, 'Is there anything more to life than this?'

Yes, I thought, as I took a deep breath and walked more calmly towards the nearest Tube station. *There is a hell of a lot more to life than this.* And with that life-affirming thought, I took out my mobile and called my married ex-girlfriend, Lisa.

Chapter Nine

'You just can't compete with Jesus. Surely you understand that.'

'Why not?'

'Because he's bigger than you, older than you, cleverer than you and a whole lot more like the Son of God than you. Plus, his dad would definitely have your dad in a fight.'

'But Jesus is *dead*.'

'Not to Mary, he's not. And not to a lot of other people, either.'

I never really had Matt down as a Christian. But, as Matt put it, there are Christians and then there are 'Christians'. Matt was a Christian, in the way people used to describe themselves as non-thinking, vaguely agnostic, Church of England Christians in a Christian country, and he didn't care much for some 'Christians'.

'I went to a church like that once,' he said. 'It seriously freaked me out.'

'Me, too. And I wasn't really trying to compete with Jesus. I just thought we might all be able to get along together – on our own, admittedly unequal, terms.'

Matt laughed. 'So you're not going to go out with a born-again, drunk-texting maniac for a frustrating year of sexual abstinence and guilt-laden encounters before settling down to a lifelong marriage of twice-weekly church attendance, grace before breakfast and the missionary position?'

I thought for a moment.

'No.'

Matt sighed with visible relief. 'Phew. I thought I might lose you there. I've seen it happen before and it's not pretty.'

It was still Wednesday evening and Matt had taken a break

from his War Room to greet my return from church. Mary might not have chosen the ideal first date, we concluded, but at least I had found out earlier rather than later that she was a complete nut-job. Often you have to wait until the third month of a relationship before discovering this, or at least until you first go on holiday together. Perhaps, we debated, all potential couples should be thrown into an uncomfortable situation early on – an airline disaster, perhaps, or dinner with all of each other's close friends and extended family – to see if you sink or swim. It would save a lot of time, heartache and money.

'And what about the money?' asked Matt.

'The money?'

'The Money-Barings. Is she not worth the Money-Barings?'

'Now here's the funny thing,' I explained. 'I called Lisa on my way home – '

'You called Lisa?' shouted Matt. 'As in your married ex-girlfriend?'

'Yes. And – '

'God, how many more mobiles am I going to have to confiscate this week?'

Matt lunged for my pocket, but I saw him coming and jumped on the sofa, holding my phone, dangling, above his head so he couldn't flush it down the toilet. I couldn't afford another one. 'Just listen for a moment, will you? I didn't call Lisa because I missed her, or because I was having some sort of existential crisis thanks to twenty minutes in church. I called her about Mary. Her friend.'

'Oh.' Matt sat down again, barely hiding his disappointment at being denied his mobile-confiscating responsibilities. I recognised the face he'd once pulled as a six-year-old when Alan's mum had relieved him of his milk-monitor duties. 'So what did she say?'

'Well, it's quite a funny story, actually. I thought Mary was just a friend of Lisa's younger sister from university. But actually, Lisa and Mary also met on the same course the vicar forced Lisa and Timothy to go on. According to Lisa, everyone in their group seemed to have some sort of ulterior motive for being there. Lisa and Timothy, of course, just wanted to get married in a church. There were two other couples in the same boat. Stock Market Christian was there, too. Lisa remembered him with as little fondness as I will. And then there was young Money-Barings, who had been sent by her ridiculously wealthy father – '

'Sent there by her father?' Matt looked as confused as I had been.

'Yes. You see, after Mary's father retired, he appeared to have had a crisis of conscience about how much money he'd made, joined an evangelical church and gave half of his fortune away to charity. He then told his three children that they could only have access to the rest of it if they followed his example. Mary had been a real wild child. This was his way of saving her.'

Matt smiled. 'So that would explain the apparent contradiction between her behaviour at Lisa's wedding and tonight.'

'Exactly. God knows how much she actually believes it all – '

'Yes, I suspect He does.'

'The point,' I continued, 'is that her choice appears to be between being poor, independent and damned, or rich, shackled and saved. However much she's faking it, it's still a no-brainer.'

'I'm sure God will be delighted that she's going to church for all the right reasons,' said Matt.

'Given that he doesn't exist, I doubt he gives a toss,' I said. 'Although even I don't remember the parable of the daughter of a rich man who found God in order to inherit riches on earth.'

'The irony, though, Sam, is that you and Mary are potentially in a very similar boat.'

'What do you mean?'

'I mean, you might both end up faking it in order to get your hands on the money.'

I sat in dumb silence for a moment while Matt waited patiently for the penny to drop. I used to be as sharp as Matt. Is this what happened when you didn't use your brain at all?

'No!' Finally, I'd got it. 'Do you really think so?'

'It's the logical next step.'

'I thought you said you'd seen people convert to born-again Christianity and it wasn't pretty.'

'I didn't say I'd seen people *pretend* to convert. If you could convince her, and convince her father, then… '

I didn't say anything. So much for being a Christian: Matt was actually far more depraved than I was. It was just like him to egg me on with subtly outrageous suggestions. He wasn't the performing monkey who would have to carry them out. He knew as well as I did that I could never resist a challenge.

'Enough about me,' I said. 'How is your online campaign going?'

'Not so great at first.' He sighed, running his hand over his newly acquired stubble. It suited him. Bloody Matt could spend three days inside by himself and still look better than the rest of us. 'It turned out that all the Russians were men and most of the Arabs were women.'

'Not the best way round.'

'No. But I have been chatting to a nice Spanish girl. Come into the War Room and have a look at her profile.'

*

The following day was uneventful, which is how I like my Thursdays, especially if they follow an eventful Wednesday and precede a ridiculously eventful Friday. One can deal with an uneventful sandwich of a week. It's only when one's life becomes all events, or all non-events, that it is time to take stock.

Eventful Friday, as I shall call it, started with a text message at breakfast time from Lisa: 'Hi Sam. It really was good to speak the other night. Please don't go out with Mary. It would make me jealous. Hope you're well. I'd love to see you soon. Lisa x.'

Make *her* jealous? How did she think I'd felt when she'd got *married* within a couple of years of breaking up with me? Of course I didn't want to marry her myself – just as she didn't want to go back out with me. Our break-up had been genuinely mutual. We'd fallen rapidly in, and then slowly out of, love. We were better afterwards as friends than we had been as unhappy boyfriend and girlfriend. Still, none of this seemed to stop our relationship remaining complicated. I read the text a second time then deleted it, which somehow made it easier. Out of inbox, out of mind.

More to cheer myself up than anything else, I got dressed in one of the good suits my father had given me ten years previously, once his middle-aged paunch had finally defeated him. The last time I'd had a chance to wear it, I reflected ruefully while tying one of my better ties, was while playing the young barrister in *A Voyage Round My Father*, which had started at the Edinburgh Fringe and transferred to London. My father never came to see it, but I still have the *Guardian* review which described me as 'thrillingly promising'. That was five years ago.

Still, I felt good, for some perverse reason, as I walked from the station to work that morning. Sometimes, I thought, as I joined the mirthless throng of workers, you have to embrace being right at the bottom of your luck curve before it starts to turn. Adversity was good. If I couldn't make a living out of my art, I could, at least, turn my life itself into an art of sorts. There was nothing wrong with living as if in a soap opera. Nothing wrong with trying everything and seeing where it led you. Nothing wrong with being confused and whimsical and different. Today, I resolved, as I took the office escalator two steps at a time, was going to be a good day. I would be thrillingly promising at temping. And very well dressed.

A little too well dressed...

At the top of the escalator I was met with the beaming smile and bone-crushing handshake of a genial giant.

'It burns,' said the giant. He had a light German accent. Or maybe Dutch.

'I'm sorry. What burns?'

He laughed. 'No, no. *Esbern*. It's Danish. And you must be Max Anderson-Bickley.' The genial Dane looked me up and down appraisingly. 'It's good to meet finally.'

If I'd been sensible, I might have mentioned that I had absolutely no idea why it was good to meet this guy finally, given that there had been no preamble to this encounter. I would certainly have pointed out that I wasn't called Max. Sensible Sam would have explained that he was merely an out-of-work actor-cum-intern who had turned up overdressed on a dress-down Friday he didn't know about in order to feel better about not having a proper job.

But I wasn't feeling sensible, so I simply said: 'Yes, it is great to meet you too, *finally*,' which seemed to be enough to satisfy Esbern because he led me towards a large meeting room on the top floor which even I knew from my week's worth of temping was reserved for this venture capital consultancy's more important clients.

'It's very good of you to come here to meet us,' said Esbern as we walked. 'It certainly beats corresponding by email.'

I nodded and murmured and generally made the non-committal sort of noises I imagined important clients of the firm might go in for. I talked about my weekend in the country, my plans for my next city break and the nightmare traffic around Battersea. I think I might even have passed favourable comment on a hideous and expensive piece of modern art hanging in the corridor.

Whatever it was I said, it was enough to satisfy the Dane. 'Of course, we normally go to our clients' premises ourselves,' he continued, as we got into the lift. 'It's good to see the office, kick, how do you say, some tyres...' He laughed as if this was a joke. I decided to laugh, too. 'But when it comes to a start-up like yours, and a start-up with such potential, then, well, it's really the intellectual property that excites us.'

I laughed again and Esbern looked at me strangely as the lift's doors opened. I'd misjudged it this time. The intellectual property reference hadn't been a joke. It was very difficult to judge with this man.

I turned the laughter into a cough – a trick taught by a teacher at drama school that had often been useful to prevent corpsing in various third-rate plays since. 'Yes,' I spluttered, as I was finally ushered into a spacious room I'd only entered previously in order to collect half-finished plates of biscuits. 'Exciting intellectual property, indeed.'

Many people don't believe in the concept of love at first sight. Lust, yes. Love, no. Love takes time to develop, time to mature. Love is familiarity, respect, understanding. Love is not the desire to get jiggy every second of the day. And as someone who has often enjoyed the latter in a distinctly loveless form, I always used to agree with them. But the moment my Danish venture capital friend opened the door to that sacred room, that holy of holies, and introduced me to Rosie, whose business card confirmed her position as a junior analyst and whose smile established her as the most beautiful girl I had ever met, I changed my mind. You can laugh at me – and God knows, I'm laughing about it now – but I didn't just want to sleep with Rosie. I didn't want to shag her or date her or shack up with her money. I wanted to love her. And I wanted her to love me.

Rosie was not perfect, even at first sight. Five years previously, I would have said that her brown hair was a little too long and her legs a little too short. I might not have taken to the freckles on her nose or the small spot on the left of her chin. I would certainly not have approved of the slightly frilly shirt she was wearing. But I was a man now, or almost a man, and I didn't care about such trivialities. When she smiled, it was as if she was sharing an intimate secret. When she talked, I hung on her every word. When I spoke, she made me feel endlessly and irresistibly fascinating. And all the time there danced behind those laughing green eyes an intelligence, an irony, an understanding that life was one big joke which she wanted to share with you. To me, Rosie was perfect. In those ten seconds, I found love. I found it at first sight.

As the meeting progressed, however, I was reminded that Rosie's principal motivation in being in Meeting Room 12 was not love. She seemed to like me well enough, but more importantly, she liked 'Max' and his business idea.

'It's a wonderful idea,' said Rosie.

'The best we've seen for a long time,' agreed Esbern.

'Is it really?' I asked, as bashfully as I could. It's not easy pretending to be someone who is pretending to be modest.

'Of course it is,' said Rosie. 'It's genius.'

'What is your favourite bit about it?' I asked, fumbling desperately.

'Oh, we like *all* of it,' said the Dane, giving nothing away under pressure.

'Definitely,' enthused Rosie. 'But it's not really about us, Max. This is your idea. So, what's *your* favourite bit about *your* new business?'

'I just like how, er, new... ' I started to say before checking myself. My brain was planning on telling my tongue to say, 'I just like how, er, new-y and business-y it is.' That would not do. I took a deep breath and decided to take a gamble. These people were deferring to me. There must be a reason. I looked at them both authoritatively, imagined I was Michael Douglas in *Wall Street* and said: 'I like it because it's a fucking good idea which is going to make us all very rich. Now, I believe I'm paying you clever, expensive people for your clever, expensive time so I suggest we get on with it.'

I'd made the right call. They both laughed and agreed it was time 'to get on with it'. I sat back expansively in my leather armchair while Rosie dimmed the lights and fired up a PowerPoint presentation. Of course! I should have guessed that was what 'it' would involve. I had listened to Alan discuss his job enough times to know that nothing counted as work in the world of finance unless it involved a PowerPoint presentation.

The first slide showed an artfully framed bicycle. Rosie pressed a button on the remote and it dissolved prettily to be replaced by the second slide: a man in a suit riding a bicycle. Rosie smiled at me and I smiled back for far too long, before remembering to smile at the Dane as well, who smiled across at Rosie. *What the hell was all this about?*

Eventually, by slide 10, I had got the gist of my business idea. It involved providing a garage system for commuting cyclists in central London. The logic, according to Max, as re-packaged and summarised by Rosie, was that cycling had expanded exponentially in the capital over the last few years, but cyclists were worried about the security of their increasingly expensive bicycles. They were also worried about smelling like stale cheddar at their desks. So the 'Max House' – I'm afraid I'm not making this up – would provide them with a secure haven for their bike during the working day and a shower room to use in the morning. Slides 11 to 19 dealt with the results of the surveys carried out by Rosie and the Dane's firm (and, I suppose, mine, too) into whether or not people would use it. Slides 20 to 37 were more irrelevant pictures of people cycling – strangely none of them was pictured in offensive lycra, running red lights or under the wheels of a bendy bus – while slides 38 to 60 dealt with financial projections and marketing techniques. The last dozen showed the ways in which their firm, Taylor Williams, could help.

Just as I was dropping off, Rosie flicked to the final slide, number 73 – a handsome businessman on a tandem with his photogenic daughter. Then Esbern turned on the lights and asked what I thought.

'It's excellent,' I answered, truthfully. Their presentation had indeed been excellent. They had successfully polished the turd that was Max's idea. Even a rank amateur could see that it was not a goer. People cycle to save time and money. They don't want to pay over the odds in the middle of a recession to share a shower in the morning with people they don't know in a location nowhere near their office.

I examined the eager faces of Rosie and the Dane. Surely now was the time to back out. Perhaps if I owned up to Rosie that this was a case of mistaken identity, she'd like me on my own terms. She might admire me for having had the balls to see it through. She might come and watch my next play, whenever that might be. We'd fall in love. We'd get married. In years to come, we would look back and laugh at this meeting. 'Oh, the Max House,' we would chortle to our cute and clever grandchildren. 'The dreadful idea that brought us together. Now, has Granny ever told you – '

'On a personal note… ' My reverie was broken by the Dane building up to another heroically dull monologue. I tuned back in as he continued: 'I'd just like to say how much we admire you as a person. It is a brave thing to quit somewhere as secure as Goldman's on the remuneration you were on in an economic climate such as this and break out… '

I tuned out again, thinking ferociously this time. *They thought I was a former Goldman Sachs banker?* No wonder they wanted to indulge me. They didn't want my idea. They'd give up on it if it ever went beyond an initial feasibility study. They wanted my stupid money. Max could afford the consultancy fees Taylor Williams had started charging recently in addition to taking equity in a start-up. Max could afford to come up with an idea this bad and not go bankrupt. So that meant… Well, that meant that Rosie thought I was very rich. And beautiful, charming girls, even those with freckly noses, hair that is slightly too long and legs that are marginally too short, like very rich men.

'I would love to join you both for a celebratory lunch,'

continued Esbern. 'But I'm afraid I have another meeting. In any case, I would only be a burden on you two young things.'

He laughed, and we both laughed, too. We had correctly identified a joke this time.

'Lunch is on me,' I gambled wildly; all thoughts of contrition and honesty suddenly vanished.

'Nonsense,' said Rosie, holding open the door. 'It is on me.'

'Well, it's on Taylor Williams,' said the Dane. Rosie and I laughed again, and Esbern blushed at having made two successfully identifiable jokes in a row.

I shook his hand goodbye and escorted Rosie triumphantly downstairs. We walked out into the street and straight into an unsightly commotion, at the centre of which flailed a fat, balding, red-headed, ill-shaven drunk. Rosie and I looked at each other and smiled. 'Difficult economic times,' I quipped, Max-like. 'He's probably just been made redundant.' She pretended to laugh and we turned in the direction of our restaurant. Then something made me stop and look again. I dropped my bag and plunged into the middle of the crowd.

'Ed,' I yelled, pulling the fat, balding, red-headed, ill-shaven drunk to his feet. 'What the hell are you doing?'

'My revenge plan didn't go so well,' he said, smiling ruefully, and collapsed into my arms.

Chapter Ten

There is nothing wrong with strong women. Strong women close business deals, bring up children, fight wars, grow crops, fly planes and generally keep the world turning. It is only weak men who cannot deal with them. But overexposure to unnaturally determined females in the weeks following Jess's proposal left me longing for the more fluffy, demure variety of womankind.

It all continued to go wrong as soon as I woke up with a raging headache on the Friday morning and had to clamber over a prostrate Sam and Matt en route to the office. It was all very well for them, sleeping off their hangovers until it was time for a fry-up, daytime TV and a spot of rich-wife-hunting. Some of us had work to do.

Work itself was predictably unpleasant. No sooner had I approached my pod than Amanda announced to the rest of the team: 'Well, screw me sideways if it's not Mr Jessica Gallagher in search of a dowry.'

The rest of our team sniggered, the pathetic little sycophants that they are. I might have been senior to them, but Amanda outranked all of us put together and had clearly briefed them in advance. No one does office politics quite like Amanda.

'Well, shag me diagonally and shut the hell up,' I retorted, uncharacteristically. My head was pounding from my drinking session and I really wasn't in the mood for this. Maybe some of my wilder friends' lack of inhibitions had worn off on me.

'Oooh,' cooed Amanda, mockingly. 'It's good to see you stand up to one woman in your life.'

'And it would be good to see you sufficiently happy with your lot not to drag everyone down to your own miserable level. At least someone's actually asked me to marry them. And meant it.'

I knew straight away that it was a stupid thing to have said. The shocked looks mixed with carefully concealed mirth on the juniors' faces informed me, if I didn't know already, that I would pay for this hollow victory, sooner or later. You can't buck the office hierarchy.

'Right,' said Amanda briskly, a small twitch in her right eye betraying the true extent of her anger. 'Shall we get down to work?'

Of course I didn't know then that this early morning encounter with Boadicean brawn was only a taster of what was to follow, a mere hors d'oeuvre for an à la carte evening of recriminations and unnecessary arguments with the other two most important women in my life: my mum and my self-appointed fiancée.

It was my mum's turn to make life more difficult first. On leaving the office I rang home to tell my parents that they were not going to be losing a son but gaining a daughter-in-law. My dad was delighted, mainly because I didn't tell him that it was Jess who had proposed (thank God she hadn't completed my emasculation by asking him for permission), but also, I think, because he has a small, secret crush on her. It's not difficult for girls to win over their prospective fathers-in-law. All they have to do is listen attentively, flirt gently and give off a quiet impression of being fertile, honest, intelligent and unlikely to embarrass the extended family by giving the grandchildren ridiculous names or ending up in jail, divorced or on reality television. It is much the same in reverse for men and their prospective mothers-in-law.

Convincing the in-law of the same sex, however, is a much thornier task.

'Your father tells me you're engaged,' said my mum after he had congratulated me warmly and handed over the phone. 'Is it Jess?'

'No, Mum, it's someone I met on the street this morning. Of course it's Jess.'

'Then commiserations,' she said. 'I think you'll be very unhappy.'

My mum seems to think I'm still at the primary school where she used to teach, my ability to make sensible autonomous decisions stalled for ever at the age of ten and three-quarters.

'I've told you before, Alan,' she droned on, 'she's bad news, that girl. You could do much better. What about Lisa? You always got on very well with her.'

'She's married, Mum. I went to her wedding, remember?'

'Or Hayley? Your father and I always liked Hayley.'

'She's a lesbian.'

'Or Claire? We liked her when Sam brought her round last Christmas. What's wrong with her?'

'Nothing at all is wrong with Claire, Mum. She's a good friend. But I just don't fancy her.'

'Well, I didn't fancy your father when I first met him. But we soon – '

For the first time in my life I hung up on my mum. It wasn't just that I had no intention of listening to the technicalities which had led to my birth – like most children with two siblings, I like to cling to the notion that my parents have only made love on three occasions, at least two of them on Valentine's Day – I was also genuinely offended that my mum still hadn't come round to Jess after all this time.

I'd feared it from the start, of course. I didn't introduce Jess to my parents for ages – partly because Jess can be a bit of an unintentional snob and I stupidly thought she would dump me if she saw where I had grown up, but mainly because I knew that my mum, the world's least successful class warrior, just wouldn't take to her. The first time they met, three years after we'd started going out, at an awkward Sunday lunch in London, my mum excelled herself by disparaging Jess's job before we'd even finished our starter – 'You can only be a barrister if you've been to private school, can't you?' The atmosphere didn't improve when she asked during the main course whether Jess's mum cooked her own roast or had a servant to do it for her. The parting promise that 'we shouldn't leave it so long until next time' was happily broken on all sides.

Maybe it's not a class thing at all. Maybe my mum only likes my female friends who don't constitute a threat. Maybe she doesn't think anyone is good enough for me. Or perhaps it's simply third-and-final-child syndrome. Whatever it was, she had never made any effort to be anything more than coolly civil towards Jess and it really, *really* annoyed me. There were flaws in my mum's relationship with my dad, but I didn't point them out. So what business of hers was it who I ended up with? I was the one who had to live, sleep, procreate, holiday, grow old and die with the person I married, not her. She could just see them at Christmas, and funerals.

It was not, therefore, in the best of moods that I turned my phone off for the evening and went round to Jess's flat after work. I was always going to Jess's flat after work, partly because she lived nearby, on the South Bank, but mainly because she disliked north London almost as much as she appeared to dislike Sam.

I arrived before Jess had got home and bumped into her flatmate, Olivia, lugging a large suitcase down the stairs.

'Congratulations,' said Olivia, putting down her case and surprising me with a hug. She worked in the same chambers as Jess and I hadn't known her very long. 'Can I see the ring?'

'No,' I said, a little too abruptly. I'd managed to bury that painful incident at the back of my mind and didn't welcome it resurfacing. 'It's at home.'

'Well, then, you better bring it along to your new home,' said Olivia with a smile sweeter than I deserved. 'Or I think we both know you'll be in a lot of trouble.'

'You're moving out?' I asked, dumbly gesticulating at the suitcase.

'Of course,' said Olivia. 'And more importantly, *you* are moving in.'

'It's the first I've heard of any of this.'

Olivia shrugged. 'Really? Well, welcome to the rest of your life with Jess.'

After I'd helped Olivia to load the rest of her stuff into her brand new Mini – most of Jess's friends were far too flash for my liking – I let myself into 'our' flat with Olivia's key and sat, fuming, in the empty bedroom to await the return of my fiancée. This would probably become our study, I thought bitterly. She would paint it 'fuchsia pink'. If I was lucky, I'd be allowed a small corner for my music collection, a desk and a laptop which she'd monitor ruthlessly for any signs of suspicious online activity. The bedroom would be lightly fragranced with a hint of pine. Socks would have to be stored in my third of the cupboard, and not on the floor. The radio alarm would be set permanently to Magic FM. We'd have to make the bed together in the mornings. The bathroom… No, don't get me started on the bathroom.

'YOU'RE GOING TO MAKE ME USE SCENTED BUBBLE BATH, AREN'T YOU?'

It was a strange accusation with which to greet Jess when she finally arrived home an hour after me. But I was so worked up that I felt an uncharacteristic desire to be entirely irrational about everything. The result was a full-blown, no-holds-barred argument during which we danced around each other like prizefighters, landing painful blows in all the weakest spots. There's no point spending years getting to know someone really well unless you can use that knowledge to your advantage in a fight.

So I accused her of being manipulative and she countered by calling me lazy and vacillating, to which I retorted that she was controlling, which prompted her to tell me that I never listened to her, which I didn't hear because I wasn't listening, which made her even more angry, which made me angry as I had run out of insults to hurl at her, so I just shouted something nonsensical and she shouted something nonsensical back and called me stupid so I called her fat and then she threw a shoe at me, which I caught because it wasn't a very good throw, so she started laughing, and then I laughed, too, and we had furious make-up sex and everything was okay again.

It wasn't an unfamiliar pattern.

As we lay together afterwards in our new bed, which wasn't really 'new' at all, of course, because I had slept there a thousand times before, Jess asked me what was really wrong and I told her the truth because we were in a grown-up relationship. So I said that I was concerned about losing my independence, that I was also a little worried about missing my friends, who seemed to be having a whole lot more fun than me (I didn't mention the specifics; she'd disapprove). I told her that the whole engagement thing had left me feeling doubly shaken because it had come out of the blue for me, and that I felt as though I was no longer in control of anything and I didn't like it when she made decisions without me.

I rambled on, sometimes coherently, often not, while Jess listened and soothed and explained and skilfully made everything seem all right again without actually giving an inch on one issue of importance. Did I want to get married? Then what did it matter if she had asked me? Did I want to live together? Then what difference did it make if we lived at hers or mine? I could never throw Sam out of my uncle's flat. Matt could take my place and keep him company. Neither of them could survive in London, in any case, without mates' rates.

We barely left that bed until Monday morning, ordering in food and DVDs, making love and discussing our future – honestly and openly – until I was in no doubt that this was the girl I loved, and wanted to love until the day I died.

We spent the rest of that week in post-engagement bliss, too, rushing home from work simply to spend time together. And then, on Friday afternoon, just as I was about to leave work early in order to pick up the more traditional engagement ring I'd had commissioned, Amanda stuck her head round her office door and beckoned for me to join her inside.

'I really do have to leave soon, Amanda,' I said, determinedly. She had been very quiet since the recent outburst. Perhaps my tactic of standing up to her had worked after all.

'That's okay, Alan,' she said with a small smile. 'It won't take long.' She closed the door behind me, took a chair and smoothed down her expensive charcoal business suit. Amanda never really did dress-down Fridays. She gave another fake half-smile. 'Now, I don't really feel I've congratulated you properly on your engagement. So, congratulations. Being engaged suits you. You look happy. More confident. And so you should. It's an exciting time for a young man, of course. You'll be thinking of getting a bigger place together, probably. Maybe even starting a family. Your career will be taking off as well, I hope.' She frowned, every conniving muscle in her taut, attractive face playing its part, and pushed a stray strand of blonde hair back behind her ear. 'It would certainly be a very bad time for your job to go wrong. Just imagine how awful the timing would be if you got a poor review now. Just imagine if you were passed over for promotion. Or even sacked. Would Jess still marry you? She's in love with a hotshot young accountant, right? Not a loser washout.' Amanda edged her chair a little closer to mine, her blue eyes boring directly into mine. 'So what's it to be, Alan?'

I looked at my boss evenly. 'I'm afraid I have no idea what you're talking about.'

Amanda leant forwards, put a hand on my knee and whispered in a voice of mad, piercing authority: 'Fuck me, Alan. Fuck me before you get married to that fat barrister tart of yours or I'll destroy your career.'

Chapter Eleven

If ever there were a case of Beauty and the Beast, it was the moment Ed collapsed drunkenly into my arms while Rosie, the divine junior analyst, looked on in confusion. One moment we were en route to an expensive lunch to celebrate Max's dreadful new business idea. The next I was cradling a foul-smelling pugilist who kept on mumbling the name 'Sam'.

But it wasn't as if I had much choice. Ed needed help, and no one else appeared willing to step in. Tempting as it was to waltz off in the other direction to continue the courtship of my rich wife-to-be, I wasn't about to leave a mate in trouble.

As the crowd slowly regrouped around the two of us, there stepped forward a short, almost square man with the neck and the vowels of an East End boxer.

'Mate of yours, is 'e?'

I nodded. I didn't want to speak unless absolutely necessary. Speaking would have meant breathing in afterwards and smelling Ed.

'Fiery little fucker, isn't 'e?'

Ed stirred a little, vomited over my shoe and then passed out completely. 'What happened?' I asked the square man.

'Fucked if I know, mate. I'm jus' standin' on the door at that law firm over there and he runs at the barrier shoutin' some bird's name. Tara or summink. Pissed as a fart. An' before lunch an' all. Well violent, 'e was, when I frew 'im out.'

I nodded again.

'What's your name, son?' asked the square man.

'Max,' I said, hoping Ed wouldn't wake up.

'Well, Max. You're getting your mate's dribble all over your nice threads.'

I looked down at my father's expensive suit, my only suit, and eased my comatose friend into a more comfortable position. 'He's had a rough time,' I explained, sticking out a hand to hail a cab. 'I better get him home.'

'A bloody men'al home, more like,' said the security guard, heading back into Tara's cavernous glass law office, which appeared to be the signal for the rubbernecking crowd to disperse and leave us to it.

The first three taxis didn't stop. The fourth slowed down to take a closer look at Ed and then quickly switched off its light and sped away. Finally, Rosie, whom I had barely dared look at since the whole episode had started, walked into the middle of the road, put out an arm and forced the next cab to come to a squealing standstill.

'I'd like you to take these two people to wherever it is they would like to go,' she told the driver, handing him one £20 note and me another. 'You can charge them double if they make any mess.'

Rosie helped me ease Ed into the back while the driver, a young man with a Bluetooth headset attached to his ear as if he was expecting to take an emergency call from Jack Bauer at any moment, looked on sullenly, almost willing Ed to be unwell again so he could claim his extra fare.

'This is far too kind of you,' I said to Rosie as I straightened up to say goodbye. 'I feel bad for bailing on lunch but, you see, Ed's a very old friend and his girlfriend dumped him recently... ' I tailed off and gestured at his nodding, limp head. 'Well, he didn't take it too well.'

'Not at all,' said Rosie. 'You're a good man, Max.'

'No, I'm not,' I said, truthfully. I was not good, nor was I Max.

She extended a hand, which I held for just a little bit too long. There was an awkward silence. I didn't want to leave. I liked being Max and Rosie. But what were the chances that I wouldn't get found out? In all likelihood, there would be a message from the real Max apologising for missing the meeting the moment she walked back into the office. And me? Well, I would have ruined my temping as well as my acting career, not to mention my chances with this perfect girl with the slightly too long hair and the slightly too short legs.

Still, in for a penny… I took out a Biro and told Rosie I had just set up a new email address: 'max@maxhouse.co.uk'.

'Didn't like the dot-com address, then?' she said, taking the proffered bit of paper with a smile.

'No. Thought I'd keep it local. UK-based, you know.'

'I know.'

Phew. She knew.

'Bye, then.'

'Bye.'

I climbed into the cab and closed the door. There was a knock on the window. I wound it down.

'And Max. Shall we do that lunch another time?'

'Definitely,' I said, smiling to myself as the cab pulled away. I loved this new breed of young, confident women. I loved Rosie.

In the seat next to me, Ed stirred, fixing me with briefly comprehending eyes. 'Max?' he slurred. 'Why did she call you Max?'

'It's all a game, mate. It's all one big stupid game.'

I took Ed 'home', by which I mean my home, which was actually Alan's, or Alan's uncle's, or at least had been Alan's/Alan's uncle's before Matt moved in and became a squatter. Definitions had become a little blurred of late.

We arrived noisily, prompting Matt to burst out of his War Room. If he was surprised to see me in the middle of the day, accompanied by Ed in that state, he didn't show it. He quickly helped me take Ed's clothes off, gave him a shower and, after a brief argument, put him in Alan's, i.e. Matt's, bed to sleep whatever it was off.

'It's just like the good old days back in A&E,' said Matt,

scrubbing his forearms — a little unnecessarily, I felt — with antiseptic soap afterwards. 'Now, how on earth did you bump into him?'

I explained how my bizarre morning had seen me attend my own business meeting, get promoted from temp to chief executive, fall in love with Rosie and then cancel a business lunch in order to rescue one of our drunken friends from a square man. Matt listened increasingly open-mouthed, occasionally prompting and laughing. He was an excellent listener, Matt.

'My word,' he said, when I'd finally finished. 'It makes my own adventures today look quite lame.'

'What adventures?'

Matt took me back into the War Room and closed the door so that Ed's snores grew fainter.

'Remember that Spanish girl I showed you on here earlier this week?' He pulled up her profile on the laptop. 'Bonita. Beautiful name. Beautiful girl, no? Looks fairly normal, right?'

'Right.'

He flipped down the lid. 'Wrong. She's a student at LSE, a very rich student judging by her online chat, so I asked if she fancied meeting up for a coffee this morning. She said she fancied it very much, which was a good start, as I fancied her very much, too. But then she suggested meeting at the Imperial War Museum, which I thought was, well, a little odd. But no matter; there's nothing wrong with being quirky, and at least we'd have something to talk about. Anyway, I turned up early so that my beautiful Spanish date wouldn't have to hang around waiting for me. Eleven o'clock came and went. Nothing. Half past eleven — still nothing. And all the while this strange dumpy creature sat on a bench nearby. I ignored her. In desperation, I actually approached three other passers-by, in full view of this girl, and asked them if they were Bonita. And can you guess who the real Bonita turned out to be? This strange dumpling, of course.'

'That's embarrassing,' I said.

'It wasn't the best start to the date. Still, I wouldn't have minded all that much if she'd turned out to be as friendly as she was online. You win some, you lose some, right? Looks aren't everything. We might have passed a pleasant hour together. But her first question was, "Do you want to go downstairs and look at genocide or shall we start on the first floor with the Holocaust?" After ten minutes, I bowed out, feigning an important work call, and returned here.'

Matt slumped down in his chair, apparently shocked to the core that people might twist the truth to present a better image of themselves online.

'You need to get out more,' I said, gesturing at the low ceiling and limited light in the War Room. 'This is not healthy.'

'And what you're doing is?' he retorted.

'At least I'm keeping my acting skills honed.'

'I'm sure your next casting director will be delighted to hear all about your latest production.'

'Science versus art. I think we're quickly learning which seduction technique is more successful.'

Matt stared vacantly at his laptop and didn't say anything.

'Having said that,' I continued, 'there is one vaguely scientific thing this artist could use a little help on.' I scribbled down an email address on a scrap of paper. 'Can you make it so that any messages sent to this address are forwarded to my Hotmail?'

'max@maxhouse.co.uk? You actually are depraved, Sam. You can't really be serious about taking this further?'

'I've never been more serious about anything in my life,' I said.

'Even though you realise it will end in tears when she inevitably finds out?'

'Tears of happiness, mate. I spoke to Claire on the way home in the cab – '

'When are you just going to marry *her*?'

'I spoke to Claire on the way home in the cab because I hadn't seen her for a while and thought she would be amused by what had just taken place. Well, she was, as it happened. All the more so because she'd heard people talk about this Max character before. Until fairly recently, he used to go out with one of her colleagues who remembers him mentioning his business idea. Max Anderson-Bickley, chief executive of the Max House... Well, you don't forget a name or a company like that. Claire made a few enquiries and rang back to tell me that Max left the country recently at short notice – partly because he's under investigation for tax evasion, partly because he's just got a job advising a Russian oligarch in Abu Dhabi. So on that account, at least, it looks like I might be off scot-free.'

'And what about his business, which you now appear to be running?'

'I'll quietly tell Rosie that I've reconsidered the idea and have decided it's the sack of shit which she already knows it to be. Then I'll pretend to go back to my old banking firm, feign redundancy within a couple of months and tell Rosie I've decided to become the actor I've actually been all along. By that point it won't matter because she will have already fallen deeply and irretrievably in love with me.'

'Genius,' said Matt. 'Why don't you just tell her the truth now?'

'Because, my slow-witted friend, it's both too late and too early: too late to own up because I've already gone too far down the Max route; too early to tell her I'm becoming the actor I already am because she hasn't yet fallen in love with me. We've started on a lie. I just need to work her slowly back towards the truth.'

'And what makes you think she'll fall in love with you?'

'We have a connection. Plus, she's after my "money".'

'And you're after hers. What a delightful couple.'

'She's well-bred, charming, ambitious, intelligent and beautiful. She's clearly going to make as much money as she will no doubt inherit. What's not to like?'

'And by the time you end up penniless, or rather admit to her that you're penniless, you think she won't mind because she'll never be able to leave you?'

'Exactly.'

'Sam, you're the most arrogant man I've ever met.'

'Not arrogant, Matt. Just desperate. And I like a challenge.'

Matt smiled and swivelled back to face his monitor. 'Okay, last thing I do in my War Room before I go and join the real world again.'

'You're giving up on this bet?'

'I didn't say that,' he replied, enigmatically.

After a couple of minutes of what Matt assured me was relatively simple computer wizardry, I had a new email address. 'Let's check it out, shall we?' he said, sending an email from his own account to max@maxhouse.co.uk. 'Now, log on to your Hotmail.'

I logged on and duly found the empty test email from Matt with the subject line: 'Cock'. We went for a celebratory pint. An hour later we returned and found a new email above the 'Cock' one, from rosie.morris@taylorwilliams.com, with the rather more sober subject line: 'Invoice'. Matt's technical wizardry had come just in time.

'Dear Max,' read the sober email. 'It was great to meet you finally this morning. Esbern has also asked me to pass on his best wishes. I hope you don't mind my sending an invoice so quickly, but our accounts department is very rigorous about this sort of thing at the moment. We're very much looking forward to continuing our working relationship with all relevant stakeholders going forward. Best wishes, Rosie.'

'Fucksticks!' I buried my head in my hands. '*An invoice! A working relationship! Best wishes!* Fuckity fucksticks!'

'Well, don't pay it,' said Matt, failing to hide his smugness that Rosie clearly didn't fancy me. 'You don't owe them anything. Get out while you can.'

I nodded. But just as I was about to log off I noticed that the genial Dane had been cc'd into this formal email. Above it had popped up another one, also from Rosie, but with the rather more interesting subject line: 'Lunch II'.

'Max, hello!' it started, which seemed to me an excellent way of formulating a greeting. 'So good to meet you earlier. Esbern has just told me to send you a boring email about the invoice, but I wanted to drop you a quick personal line as well. Very sorry about our lunch. I'm holding you to a repeat. Hope your friend is okay. Rosie x.'

'Matt,' I said quietly. 'Let's open that invoice and see how much it comes to.'

'No,' he said, attempting to delete it.

I pushed him out of the way and opened it. 'Five thousand! For that poxy little presentation! Who has five thousand pounds?'

'Max probably does.'

'Bully for Max. I certainly don't.'

I had no money at all, in fact, I thought, slumping down in the spare chair. No money, no prospects, no career. Just a lot of debt. But I did have Rosie – or at least it looked as if I might be able to have Rosie. What if Rosie was my saviour? And if her price was five thousand, so be it. It was a small price to pay for salvation.

'A small price, if it works,' said Matt. 'For the record, I repeat that I really do think this will end in tears.'

'Tears of happiness and liquid gold. You have to spend money to make money.'

'And how do you know that?'

'From my former high-flying career at Goldman Sachs.'

'And where exactly are you going to get the money from?'

'Now that is an excellent question.'

It was indeed an excellent question – and a weighty one, too, with which I bored Matt and myself rigid for the rest of the afternoon. If Ed hadn't still been passed out, I would probably have bored him as well, until he passed out all over again. Could

I just delay payment and let the interest rack up while hoping for a miracle? Or maybe I should get on to my useless agent and get her to land me another well-paid advert? Then again, she hadn't got me so much as an audition for months. So perhaps I should sack her and get a new one? Or set up Max's business myself? Or a better one?

'For the love of God, please just give up on the invoice,' snapped Matt at last. 'Or go back to Christian Mary.'

'Christian Mary is not Perfect Rosie.'

We were just thinking of heading back out to the pub when my mobile rang.

'Hello, Alan,' I said, answering it. 'Do you have five thousand pounds you'd like to lend me?'

'No, Sam, I don't. But I do have one hell of a problem at work.'

Chapter Twelve

'So are you going to fuck Amanda backwards or is she going to screw you sideways?'

'That's really not funny, Sam,' said Alan.

But it *was* funny. It was one of the funniest stories I had ever heard. Of all the people to be sexually harassed in the workplace, Alan was by far the least likely candidate. Why couldn't I have a job with an attractive fortysomething boss preying on me? Life was unfair.

'I reckon you report her to an employment tribunal,' said Ed, who was sitting on the sofa, dressed in Alan's pyjamas and clutching a bottle of headache pills.

'I reckon you call her bluff and do nothing,' suggested Matt.

'And I reckon you screw her.'

'Sam! This is serious.'

Alan was right, of course. This was serious – certainly serious enough to warrant cancelling our Friday night plans and holding a four-way summit in the living room. But what was the poor guy supposed to do? Sleep with Amanda and ruin his relationship with Jess? Or turn down Amanda and ruin his career? Personally, I thought a great deal more of Alan's career than I did of his relationship with Jess. If I were in his situation, it would be a no-brainer. But you can't really say that to a best mate – especially when he's been with his girlfriend for eight years and has just got engaged. There is a small window of opportunity in the first three months of a friend's new relationship in which you can give your truthful, negative opinion. And they either thank you for helping them see the light and move on, or they ignore you, stay together and your own friendship is never quite the same again. Either way, I had missed that window.

'More to the point,' said Alan, calling the meeting to order again, 'why on earth does Amanda want to sleep with me?'

'Now, that,' I said, 'is the unspoken question on all our lips, and one to which I believe we have no answer. What the hell have you done to the poor woman? Is your office so starved of male eye candy that you actually constitute a catch? Are you Messrs January, February *and* March in the accountants' pin-up calendar?'

'Maybe Amanda is one of those sex addicts you read about in magazines.'

'What kind of magazines do you read, Ed?'

'Ones that help me to understand the incomprehensible, rapacious creatures that women are.'

'Amanda is simply a bitter and disturbed misanthrope,' explained Matt, the unemployed doctor turned amateur psychologist. 'She would rather see other people miserable than be happy herself.'

Alan nodded vigorously. This seemed to fit his experience of Amanda. 'You're right, Matt: she's probably jealous of my stable relationship, given that hers have always been so screwed-up.' A brief smile flickered across his face at the thought of his boring, happy, stable relationship. The smile quickly turned to a frown: 'On the other hand, maybe she just wants me to sleep with her because I'm one of the few people left in the office who haven't.'

'Really?' said Ed. 'She's even more of a player than Sam.'

'Then again,' continued Alan, a worried frown now permanently fixed on his face, 'it might just be her way of getting back at me because I stood up to her the other day. I was really quite rude.'

'Oooh,' said Matt. 'Stand up to her, did you? I bet that turned her on.'

The others droned on with their teasing and their theories, but there was a missing dimension that no one else knew about, and that I didn't mention because I was too ashamed. It came to me in a sudden shock of recollection during Matt's amateur diagnosis of Amanda's mental health problems. *Could this be it, then? Was this Amanda's revenge?*

Earlier that year, I had been a plus-one at Alan's firm's summer party, which Jess had been unable to attend, and I'd met Amanda for the first time. She'd struck me as a fairly fun person to spend an evening with: borderline psychotic, admittedly, even on a first meeting, but otherwise attractive, flirty and unbelievably direct. I'd never slept with an older woman before so thought I'd give it a whirl when she suggested it. Unfortunately, she forgot to tell me that her boyfriend was also there that evening. Taking an untimely break from the party downstairs, he had caught us *in flagrante* on her desk, whereupon he'd screamed blue murder, picked up a knife (one that was meant for opening letters, fortunately, not arteries) and chased me, my trousers flapping helplessly around my ankles, the length and breadth of the office. I'd eventually holed up behind a photocopier in Human Resources while Amanda went to call security, leaving her soon-to-be-ex boyfriend hurling a torrent of expletives in my general direction.

I'd finally got out of the party with everything except my dignity intact and thought that was the end of it. However, I'd stupidly given Amanda my number earlier in the evening and was bombarded with text messages over the next few days, each one more extraordinary than the last. Her boyfriend had dumped her, which was understandable, and she blamed me for it, which was not. I'd felt bad for the guy, of course, but it was hardly my fault, was it? Amanda hadn't even mentioned his existence, let alone the fact he was at the same party. How was I meant to know that some coked-up, cuckolded banker was going to appear with a letter-knife mid-coitus and force me to hide behind a photocopier?

I'd rung Amanda to apologise, in any case, which was another mistake because she told me I could make up for it by taking her out for dinner. I recognised an arch manipulator when I saw one and offered lunch instead, if only to placate her. It was not a success. After paying the bill, she said that if I didn't go to a hotel room with her right then, she'd get back at me by making Alan's life hell. I assumed she was joking and politely declined. We'd parted fairly amicably.

And that, I thought, was finally that. She'd find someone else to push around. I'd go back to playing with people my own age. I'd kept the whole thing a secret for so long that I'd almost forgotten about it myself. And now, several months later, as these drunken and half-forgotten scenes swam hazily into focus, it appeared that she wasn't joking after all. She really did mean to get back at me by punishing Alan. *The sins of the actor would be visited upon his flatmate.* If so, Matt's psychological appraisal had been far too generous: she wasn't a misanthrope; she was a bloody nutcase.

Of course, I should have owned up straight away. I should have told Alan that this was probably all my fault and had little to do with Amanda's jealousy of his stable relationship with Jess, or her apparent desire to complete a full house by copulating with the entire office. Alan would have been understanding, in the quietly forgiving way he always is. But by the time I had weakly joined the others in recommending prevarication and prudence – print out all her emails, said Ed; carry a recording device next time she asks you into her office, suggested Matt – it was far too late to come clean. The only consolation was that I appeared to have at least a few months to make everything all right again. Amanda's deadline for the fulfilment of her indecent proposal was Alan's wedding day itself.

'And when exactly is the happy day?' asked Matt,

'I'm not sure. Next summer, maybe. You'll have to ask Jess,' said Alan, entirely seriously.

'Wow, you really are under her thumb,' said Ed.

'Yep, under her thumb and wrapped around her little finger.' Alan laughed. Perhaps he didn't mind being trapped under one of her podgy digits. 'There's something else, too; another reason why I came round tonight. Jess appears to have decided that we're going to live together. In her flat.'

I jumped.

'But it's not all bad,' continued Alan, hastily. 'I think I'm going to be allowed a small corner of the spare room for my PlayStation.'

'You fight that good fight, mate,' said Matt.

'So *that's* where you've been,' I said. 'You've moved in with your fiancée without telling us.'

'She's not my fiancée yet. Until *I* propose to *her*, she's just my flatmate.'

'I'd like to see you say that to her face,' said Ed.

'She is not your bloody flatmate,' I said, surprised at my own anger. 'I'm your flatmate. We are your mates. And don't you forget it.'

'I'm not forgetting it,' said Alan, gently.

'Yes, you bloody are,' I said, not so gently. 'This is the beginning of the end, I tell you. First you move in with her, then you get married, then you knock her up and then we never see you again.'

'We'll get you round for dinner,' said Alan.

'I don't want to come round for fucking dinner, Alan. I don't want Classic FM and seating plans. I don't want to "bring a bottle" and "something for pudding". I don't want to ask how the kids are getting on or fantasise about swapping wives over coffee and After Eights. I want to go out and get drunk with you, like the good old days.'

'And when were those good old days, Sam?' Alan's voice was reasoned, measured, as if talking to a recalcitrant toddler. 'When did we last go out together on a whim in London and get drunk? Three years ago? Four? They're old days, mate. And how good were they, anyway? Time's moved on. We've moved on.'

'I don't want to move on. I want things to stay the way they are.'

Ed and Alan exchanged looks across the room — looks which, roughly translated, said: *Why is Sam being such a dickhead?*

'Why are you being so weird about this?' said Alan, at last.

'I'm not being weird about it,' I shouted, knowing full well I was. The guilt of my Amanda secret was making me aggressive, but it was the news that Alan was definitely and finally moving out that had really got me. Here it was, at last, in all its stark reality. I'd feared it long enough, of course, but always refused to prepare for it. A small part of me had even convinced myself that this day would never come. I didn't want to grow up. For all my talk of settling down, there was no way that I was ready, no way that I was sufficiently mature. Alan, Matt, Ed, well... They were like my family. I didn't want a divorce.

At least that's what I should have said. Again, Alan would probably have understood. He might even have felt similarly himself. But instead, like the fool that I am and the dick than I can be, I started to insinuate that Jess was to blame for taking our friend away from us. Alan, by nature averse to any unnecessary confrontation, became increasingly irritable. Eventually he snapped.

'Why don't you just come out and say it?'

'Say what?'

'Say that you don't like Jess.'

'I don't like Jess.'

'Fine.'

'Fine.'

'She doesn't like you much either.'

'I've never liked her. And I wish I'd said that eight years ago.'

'Fuck you, Sam.'

'Fuck you, too.'

'Just go and fuck yourself.'

'You fucking go and fuck yourself.'

Alan sprang to his feet and moved towards me, his fists raised. I was a head taller, but he was a great deal angrier. The others got up, too. For a moment I thought we were going to have a full-on fight. But who was fighting whom? I was the one who deserved to get hit by all the others.

Alan, though, had already decided which side he was on. 'Actually, fuck all of you,' he said, dropping his fists and heading towards the door. 'I came round because I thought you might listen, because I thought you might care about the situation I've got myself into at work, because you're my oldest mates. I came round to say that I was moving into Jess's, but also to say that I've spoken to my uncle and he's happy for you, Sam, and you, Matt, to stay here. I thought that might make you happy. I thought you might even be happy for me and Jess…' He shrugged and tailed off. 'And instead it ends up like this. Well, I tell you, I don't want *this* any more. I've got Jess. I don't need you guys. You know what I think? I think you're just jealous. That's what your sad little bet is really about.' He pointed at me and Matt. 'A couple of losers who can't even keep a girl beyond a couple of months. A couple of losers trying to get what I already have. Well, good luck with it. And good luck with finding somewhere else to live, guys. You've got a month to move out.'

And with that Alan turned his back on his friends and returned south of the river to his new flatmate, or his fiancée, or whatever else he wanted to call the woman he loved and I had so clumsily criticised, the Thames a stinking metaphor for the chasm that now separated us.

*

During the recriminations that inevitably followed, the general consensus – with which I found it difficult to disagree – was that I had acted fairly appallingly.

'Basically, you're a complete tosser,' summarised Ed. 'Surely you realise that you missed the window of opportunity to criticise Jess years ago.'

'I know,' I said, apologetically. If only I had listened better to my own internal monologue when I was policing my earlier thoughts about Amanda.

'You're worse than Alan's mum,' continued Ed. 'Sure, none of us is mad about Jess, but that doesn't mean that we know better than Alan what's good for him.'

I said nothing. I really did think I knew better than Alan what was good for him. Alan's mum and I had always got on very well in that respect. I was her favourite pupil.

'So where are we supposed to live now?' I moaned.

'We?' questioned Matt.

'Well, obviously not Ed — he's already got a shoebox with negative equity he can call his own until Tara decides to sell it. But you and me, Matt. You're not leaving London, are you? We're in this together, right?'

I looked at Matt pleadingly while he stared at his shoes. 'I don't know, mate,' he said, eventually. 'I just don't know. I mean, it hasn't exactly been a resounding success so far, has it? You were on the verge of committing a cardinal sin with an evangelical Christian while simultaneously convincing another impressionable young woman — whom incidentally you owe £5,000, if you ever want to see again — that you are the CEO of a promising start-up. And me? Well, I've had a blind date with a Spanish fascist.' He shook his head ruefully. 'Alan's right, you know. We *are* losers. This *is* a silly scheme. I'm up to my eyeballs in debt. I've got a degree in medicine, a further three years of pointless specialist training behind me, and I'm squatting here in my engaged mate's uncle's flat in the vain hope of trying to get married to someone rich. I should be moving around the country, trying to get locum work. Or moving to Australia. Moving anywhere, in fact, that isn't here.' He thumped the sofa and finally looked me in the eye. 'I'm sorry, Sam. But you're on your own now.'

But I didn't want to be on my own. I've never wanted to be on my own. 'Come on,' I pleaded. 'Just one more month. Just see me through that and then I'll give up, I promise.'

'Really?'

'Promise. One more month to find myself the money for Rosie. And one more month to find you a rich wife as well. Then I'll apologise to Alan and we can all go on with our lives as before.'

'Who says I need your help, anyway?' said Matt, trying and failing to conceal his wounded pride that the bet wasn't going too well for him.

'I have a particularly cunning plan which is foolproof, even for a fool like you. It's the art of seduction meets the science of seduction. And it involves Claire.'

'Claire?'

'You'll see.' I turned to Ed. 'Now, are you with us or are you against us?'

'Neither,' said Ed.

'What do you mean? You're not planning another drunken attack on the security guard at Tara's office, are you?'

'No. This is a much more sober and subtle plan.' Ed rustled around in his man-bag. 'Do you remember me telling you that I was going to become a masculinist – that I was going to stand up for men's rights?' He handed me a few sheaves of paper. 'Well, I wasn't joking. In fact, I turn your question back on you: are you with us or against us?'

'Ed, what the hell is this?'

'It's a blog I've written. The *Guardian* has picked it up and it's going to appear in the paper tomorrow.'

The Male Eunuch
by Ed O'Brien

I'm not saying we now live in an entirely feminised society any more than anyone has ever lived in an entirely masculinised society. Cleopatra seduced and used

Antony. Helen of Troy launched a thousand ships. Queen Elizabeth I sank a few dozen.

We men in modern, feminised Britain are not tyrannised by women, as men themselves have tyrannised women for much of history. There have been no castrations. No male rape. No prostitution and slavery.

But, at some point in the early twenty-first century, Western man started to lose the battle of the sexes.

It didn't happen overnight. Most people haven't even noticed it's happened. There have been no running battles in the street: bra-burning women clashing with Y-front-burning men. Germaine Greer has not challenged the editors of men's magazines to unarmed combat in Trafalgar Square. The Gherkin in London has not been torn down and replaced by a giant, symbolic vagina. Calendar months have not been re-synchronised to a twenty-eight-day menstrual cycle. History has not been renamed her-story. The revolution is quiet, subtle, deadly. It's a femme fatale of a revolution.

The few men who have noticed don't even appear to care that much. We still have our jobs – for now, at least. We can still vote. We're not throwing ourselves under horses at the Derby.

But look a modern man in the eyes, *really* look him in the eyes, and ask him what is he *for?* Is he a hunter? A gatherer? A warrior? A hero? 'There is an electric fire in human nature,' wrote John Keats, 'so that there is continually some birth of new heroism.' But where is our fire today? Sanitised, domesticated, tamed and curled up in front of a modern electric fire watching costume dramas with our girlfriends. All men want to be heroes – it is one of the many aspects of boyhood we never relinquish – but modern life offers precious few opportunities for heroism. It is difficult to be a hero in Tesco.

So what are we left with? What are we meant to do now that all our other traditional roles are on the verge of being eroded? Women dominate, or soon will, the workplace – rightly so, in my opinion, for they are better team players, better communicators and better manipulators than men. They're better at the dating game than us. They certainly hold all the cards when it comes to granting and denying sex. Ogden Nash put it well: 'I have an idea that the phrase "weaker sex" was coined by some woman to disarm the man she was preparing to overwhelm.'

Historically and biologically, men have just two distinct advantages over women. One is that, with the exception of a few hockey goalkeepers, men are bigger and stronger. But what use is this to the modern, civilised man? I am not going to convince a girl to come to bed with me by beating her in an arm wrestle. An employer would not be more inclined to give me a pay rise just because she'd defer to me in a fist fight. I cannot – and would not – sit on a female traffic warden in the hope that she would withdraw my parking ticket. We men are lumbering, impotent beasts of burden in this brave new world of emotions and mascara.

Our only remaining edge, then, is that it is the woman who gives birth. To date, at least, this requires a man – to inseminate, if not to provide afterwards. But every day we read about diminishing sperm counts, the rate no doubt accelerated by the expensive phones we carry around in our pockets so that our girlfriends can summon us back home to take out the rubbish. And even if we are fully functioning, we still have to find a partner. The latest statistics suggest that there are one million fewer single women than men in Britain.

Then there is the unspoken Armageddon scenario: what if women suddenly decide en masse that they no longer want to be inseminated by men they know? What if they want designer babies to go along with their designer clothes? What if your girlfriend pops into a sperm bank, orders a blue-eyed, Oxford-educated six-footer with an IQ of 150 and a decent tennis backhand and, nine months later, asks you to be his godfather?

Then, my brothers, we are truly fucked.

I have seen the future: the future is pink. So now is the time to daub the present in great swathes of blue. Now is the time for men to be men again. Now is the time for us to reassert our masculinity before it vanishes for ever. Then women can have their cake and eat it. We can eat ours. And we shall all grow old and fat and jolly together.

'What do you think?' asked Ed when I'd finally got to the end, barely able to read any more through tears of mirth.

'What do I think?' I handed it back to him at arm's length. 'I think you should ring the editor of the *Guardian* immediately and beg, bribe or blackmail him not to publish this drivel.'

Chapter Thirteen

Psychologists like to talk about the grief cycle of denial, anger, bargaining, depression and acceptance, which can apply as much to the end of a relationship as to death itself. I went through most of these stages in the first few weeks after Tara wrecked my life – all of them, in fact, apart from acceptance.

Most of all I felt depressed – depressed and drunk. For the first two days I didn't get dressed, or didn't get undressed – whichever way you wanted to look at it – and simply sat on the sofa in the pyjamas Tara had given me the previous Christmas, swigging from a bottle of cheap vodka and alternating between re-watching old box sets we'd bought together and listening to wrist-slitting music on the iPod she'd left behind. 'Dry Your Eyes' by The Streets. That was the soundtrack to the early days. It didn't work.

Sometimes I would convince myself that Tara would walk in the door at any moment. In my more lucid moments, I would kick the wall repeatedly in a torrent of impotent anger until I fell on the floor, exhausted and weeping among the empty bottles.

Whoever said that alcohol numbs the pain has never tried drinking to get over a failed relationship. It does not numb anything; it fuels everything: the pain, the anger, the loneliness, the vivid images of Tara – how she used to be, and worst of all, how she was now, spending time with her old lawyer, laughing with her old lawyer, sleeping with her old lawyer…

The anger became uncontrollable. So did the drinking. And with the alcohol came the bargaining. Sam may have thought he'd achieved something by flushing my mobile phone battery down the toilet, but all it did was make me think he was more of a prick than usual. What did Sam understand about this kind of thing, anyway? Tara's number was seared across my heart; her email address lodged irreversibly in my head; her Facebook page re-checked on an hourly basis for incriminating updates. These days, there are many ways to get hold of someone who's destroyed your life. Too many ways.

Traditionally, it is women who make the most convincing mad-ex stereotypes. To judge by the newspapers, they are very good at pouring paint over sports cars, cutting up expensive suits and forming internet groups to discuss how tiny your penis is. Sam, who barely has any possessions to ruin, and whose demeanour suggests he is perfectly well endowed, had one ex who took her revenge by turning up to all his plays and heckling his character whenever he spoke. What she didn't seem to realise was that the last laugh lay with Sam in making her sit through his plays.

My point is that jilted men don't really do revenge – not calculated, cunning revenge – the way women do. Traditionally, a tiny minority of men are better at the psycho, criminal end of the revenge spectrum. The rest of us just get over it and get on with it.

But I didn't want to get over it, so I created a mad-ex male prototype all of my own. When I called Tara repeatedly from my landline, she was initially quite understanding. She was in the wrong, even though it felt right; she had done a bad thing, even though it felt good. So she felt duty bound to listen sympathetically while I ranted insanely at her. But then, inevitably, she grew tired of my demands that she justify herself and stopped taking my calls. So I started withholding my number. When that no longer worked, I would call her office switchboard and ask to be put through to her even when she was in meetings – *especially* when she was in meetings. On one glorious occasion I pretended to be a client I'd once heard her mention and succeeding in joining a conference call. I got as far as ascertaining that her new guy was also in the room before announcing, on speakerphone, that I had enjoyed our threesome with a male escort in Soho the previous weekend.

No blow was too low or too pathetic when it came to poor Tara. Until she deleted me from her friends list on Facebook, I wrote regular messages on her wall. Then I wrote messages on her friends' walls. Finally, I updated my status – the one thing they couldn't touch – so that the few remaining mutual friends who hadn't severed all contact could see 'what was on Ed's mind' regarding Tara. Ed, it is fair to say, wasn't thinking very nice things about Tara.

I begged, bullied and berated her to come back to me. I rang her parents and asked them to help make her come back to me. I fabricated a letter from our mortgage company saying that she wasn't allowed to leave as we had taken out a specific couple-only mortgage. Tara wrote back, tersely and firmly, saying that this had to stop. There was a vague hint that if it didn't, she might have recourse to some of her legal knowledge. The letter came on headed notepaper which included her 'partner's' name at the top.

Well, I knew a threat when I saw one. I knew that none of this was helping. I knew that I was acting like a dick. But I just couldn't help myself. Tara is – was – my life. Without her, there was nothing, just an awful absence, an absence of Tara. At least if I spent my time riling her, we still had some sort of contact.

This is what formed the basis of my thinking – if you can call it that – the day I got in a fight outside her office and was taken home by Sam. I know it sounds ridiculous, but I was actually going to see Tara because I wanted to share the strange history of my article that was appearing in that weekend's *Guardian*. I'd first written down a few rushed, loosely connected thoughts in a blog for the bit of the newspaper's website that anyone can write for and no one reads. A university friend, who worked occasional shifts there, saw it, stopped it being posted and suggested I sex it up a bit for the paper instead. I spent an entire week proudly rewriting and editing it (it was my summer holidays; teachers have to fill the time somehow), and thought it only fair to give Tara some advance warning of its contents. The only problem was that I still hadn't quite got my daytime drinking under control and ended up trying to hurdle the security barriers.

Writing the article had actually brought something of a revelation in itself. I no longer felt angry with the older lawyer; I felt sorry for him. Both of us had been manipulated by Tara. And if she could do that to us... Well, what had started out as a directionless rant crystallised into something much stronger. The specific became generic. I was no longer writing about me, Ed O'Brien, and my pitiful life post-Tara, I was writing about all men, all of us in the same situation, whether we knew it yet or not: Alan forced to kowtow to the unholy trinity of Jess, Amanda and his mother; Matt losing out to girls for every job he went for; Sam driven to lies and subterfuge to find a mate.

Then the article appeared. What could have been a fairly forgettable blog had become a monster, trailed on the front page of the print edition with the strapline: "'Soon, my brothers, we will be truly fucked": the future of gender politics by Ed O'Brien'.

It wasn't the only line that came back to haunt me. *A femme fatale of a revolution... It is difficult to be a hero in Tesco... We men are lumbering, impotent beasts of burden in this brave new world of emotions and mascara...* Had I been drunk when I'd written this?

The readers certainly seemed to think so, judging by the comments they left online.

'Is this writer high?' wrote big_guy29. 'How exactly could a building look like a "giant, symbolic vagina" in any case?'

'I am an expat in Riyadh, Saudi Arabia, where I don't think it is accurate to say that women hold all the cards when it comes to granting and denying sex,' wrote Bob.

Others were downright offensive.

'I'm a female traffic warden and I'd definitely have Ed in a fist fight.'

'Well, I'd like to castrate Ed for one. Or at least cut off his fingers so he can't write again. Look at his ugly ginger byline photo. No wonder he can't get a woman.'

'Sack of shit,' summarised one, succinctly.

'Gay,' opined another, even more succinctly.

Others were, at least, vaguely witty.

'I'd like to use this forum to challenge the editor of *Nuts* to unarmed combat in Trafalgar Square,' wrote 'Germaine Greer', who was almost certainly not Germaine Greer.

'This is drivel,' wrote 'Sam Hunt', who almost certainly was Sam Hunt. 'What Ed needs to do is to have a good night out with his friends and get laid.'

Of all the hundreds of comments, I found just one that actually tackled the issues I had raised or which could be construed as positive in any way.

'Saynotospermbanks.com,' it demanded, enigmatically. I looked up the site and was disappointed to find nothing there.

'Don't be disheartened,' said the journalist friend who had stitched me up in the first place, when I rang up to moan.

'Don't be bloody disheartened?' I shouted. 'The caption under my picture says "Is this the future leader of the new suffragits?"'

'I'm sorry,' he lied, laughing. 'We meant to write suffragists, but typos happen. Anyway, the readers always savage new writers online. I bet you get a much more positive response via your email.'

Naturally, bile poured into my inbox as well. Tara wrote a markedly un-positive email, her anger and embarrassment only tempered by the concern she evidently felt: 'Ed, are you okay? I had no idea it was *this* bad. Do you want to meet up to talk? Somewhere public… ?'

But my treacherous journalist friend turned out to be at least partially right, as I was also bombarded with a torrent of man-love from emasculated men all over the world. 'I would never admit this openly,' wrote Tom from Washington DC, 'but you are completely right. Thank God someone has come out and said this at last. I'm not saying I don't like the way the Western world is going, but I do think we should debate it.'

'Spot on, Ed,' wrote Pete from Liverpool. 'Everyone always discusses women's post-feminism role. What about men's? What are we *for* any longer?'

Others just used the article as an excuse to sound off about their girlfriends. *How come they were allowed to be moody once every twenty-eight days? Why did guys always find themselves apologising? Why did girls always talk about 'training' their boyfriends? Why did all the sacrifices come on our part? What exactly did girls give up for marriage compared to blokes?*

I didn't agree with most of these comments. The main reason I was so upset was because I had enjoyed making sacrifices for Tara and now they all seemed pointless. But there was one final email, at the end of the following week, just as they were beginning to die out, which made me think.

'Fair shout, mate,' it said, 'but if you really believe all this, what are you going to do about it?'

And I thought, yes, that is a fair shout, Al from Earls Court, Australia. If these were my convictions, did I have the courage to see them through? And where would they logically lead?

I was just contemplating this when another email popped into my inbox, from Sam's friend, Claire.

'Hello, suffra-git,' it said. 'Do you fancy a drink some time soon?'

Chapter Fourteen

'So basically, Sam, you have a month,' summarised Claire.

It was the day after Alan had stormed out to go and live south of the river with Jess. Matt and I had joined Claire for a coffee in Covent Garden.

'Yep,' I confirmed. 'A month in which to find some money for Rosie, make her fall in love with me and move in with her before Alan evicts me. Otherwise, I'll be spending this Christmas on the street.'

'You could just apologise to Alan now and hope he lets you stay there.'

'I don't know about that,' said Matt. 'I spoke to Alan again this morning and he's still fairly livid. Sam's basically insulted his entire life. By criticising Jess, you criticise him. That's the way he sees it, anyway.'

'I just can't believe you left it so long after the window of opportun – ' said Claire.

'Look, I know about the bloody window of opportunity, okay? Anyway, Matt, it's not as if you're entirely blameless in this whole thing. You moved into our flat without even asking Alan. And you didn't exactly stand up for Jess when I put my foot in it.'

Matt glared at me and sensibly decided to change the subject. 'Claire,' he said, 'Sam was telling me yesterday that the two of you had a cunning, foolproof plan to find some rich women.'

Claire laughed, sat back in the comfortable Starbucks armchair and started to describe the shambolic discussion we'd had on the phone only a few hours earlier. This was a great girl, I thought, as I watched her speak. Not that pretty, admittedly.

Not that cool, either. But pretty damn cool, nonetheless. How many other girls would decide to take a holiday from work to help out two old friends on a silly plan like this? How many other girls would find this amusing instead of infantile? At what age was it we'd jokingly arranged to marry each other if we couldn't find anyone else? Thirty-three? Thirty-five? Why couldn't it be sooner? And why didn't I bloody fancy her?

'So what do you think?' Claire asked Matt when she had finished.

'I think it's an excellent idea. We should have done it from the start.'

Matt was right: we definitely should have thought of this earlier. The plan was fairly simple: namely that to snare rich women we had to go to where rich women hung out: premieres, art openings, auctions, etc. We couldn't rely on our friends, or our friends' friends, or strange, unvetted people we met online. We had to cast the net wide. We had to go out into the community – a very exclusive community, admittedly, but a community nonetheless. Our task would be made a whole lot easier if we weren't just two predatory blokes working alone, but two cousins accompanied by their sister / cousin. Claire was nobly volunteering to join our very dysfunctional family.

'I can't wait,' she said. 'I haven't acted for a very long time.'

'You never really did,' I said, laughing.

'You must act well enough at your job to pretend you don't find it irredeemably boring,' said Matt.

'And you must have acted a little with that new boyfriend of yours to pretend he wasn't physically and morally repulsive.'

'He's not my boyfriend any more, Sam.'

'I'm sorry.'

'No, you're not. And neither am I. Anyway, don't think I'm just doing this for you guys. I want to find another entertaining man of my own. Preferably a rich one.'

'Because you want to spend another five years having fun with alpha males before marrying a safe beta?' I quoted.

'Exactly.'

'Well, this is going to be fun,' said an unconvinced Matt, who had no idea what we were talking about.

*

Yet fun it undoubtedly was. Matt and Claire might have pointed out that there was no real need for me to join them, given that my chief concern was finding money for my primary target, Rosie. But I didn't have any money for Rosie. And what was my alternative: hanging round with Ed while he publicly sabotaged his chances of ever meeting another woman again? I have always been very bad at saying no to anything, in any case. Lisa used to describe this as my greatest failing, which I think says a lot about why we eventually broke up. I have always modestly thought it my greatest attribute.

As much as possible, Claire tried to limit our activities to freebies, of which there were an enormous number in London, if you knew the right people, or knew how to blag. Claire, it turned out, was equally good at both, partly thanks to her sister who worked for a PR company and provided her with a long list of daily events. You would never have known we were supposed to be in the middle of a recession. Champagne, or at least fizzy white wine, still flowed at book launches, film launches, art gallery launches, fragrance launches... Anything that could be launched was launched, trumpeted with expensive and entirely unnecessary fanfare. Not that we were complaining. Chaperoned by Claire, we crawled from party to party, living strange nocturnal lives of half-remembered conversations, vol-au-vents and elaborate deceit. In the course of one evening I was a literary agent to the stars, an extra in *EastEnders*, a composer of advertising jingles and a reclusive avant-garde poet who spent most of the year in a cave in Wales. This last idea came from Claire, who took great delight in testing me with surprise introductions and then leaving me to sink or swim.

'And how do you pass the time in your cave?' asked the attractive publishing intern Claire had introduced me to, floundering around rather sweetly for a topic of conversation.

I mimed at the confused intern, and then at Claire, until the latter finally took the hint.

'I'm afraid my cousin Samuel took a vow of silence three years ago,' she explained. 'He feels that to speak would ruin his art.'

'Samuel?' I remonstrated, once I'd dragged a giggling Claire away to the vol-au-vents on the other side of the room. 'Cave-dwelling, poetic hermit? Just you wait...'

Later that evening, at a party to celebrate the first album by a new band no one would ever hear of again, I interrupted Claire's conversation with a drummer who was exactly her type and asked if she wanted to be paid now or later and whether the agency's price included the 'full girlfriend experience'.

'Bastard,' she mouthed as the drummer looked around for an escape route.

'One-all,' I mouthed back, smiling.

Matt seemed to enjoy himself as well over those few weeks – in his element simply being himself, the charming unemployed doctor. Everyone loves doctors, especially the pneumatic actress at a premiere who thought he was a plastic surgeon and might be able to provide a free nip here and a complimentary tuck there in return for her own favours. Matt, however, was far too honest – far too foolish, in my opinion – to allow her to continue in her misapprehension.

In the cab home after the music industry party – a cab paid for on expenses by Claire's unknowingly generous firm – Matt complained of another problem with being a doctor, employed or otherwise. Every profession has its 'Room 101' question. For barristers, it's how they can justify defending someone who is probably guilty. For teachers, it's how they spend their overly long summer holidays (no one should *ever* ask Ed how he spent his summer). For me, and many other actors, it's what production I've been in last. And for doctors it was any question that started with 'Would you mind having a look at...' in the middle of a social engagement.

'Someone actually came up to me tonight and took their sock off to show me their in-growing toenail,' said Matt. 'And then one of the band's groupies asked if Chlamydia was still contagious if they had sex with another girl and the band just watched. I mean, come on, what am I? A walking, unemployed Google?' He swivelled round in the front seat to face us. 'Guys, I'm very grateful and everything, but I'm not sure this is really working. Sure, I'm having a good time, but I'm not convinced these parties are the best places to meet rich women. As far as I can tell, there is a tiny bunch of rich blokes at the top of all these fun media industries, while everyone else is paid a pittance, but pretends not to mind because at least they're doing something interesting for a living, their colleagues are entertaining, the parties are free and the drugs are subsidised.'

'He's got a point,' I said to Claire.

'Speak for yourselves, boys. That room was swarming with eligible people.' She flicked a couple of business cards at us playfully. 'I can't do everything for you.'

'But Claire, we *need* you to do everything for us,' pleaded Matt.

'Okay.' She laughed. 'Well, I've got another plan for tomorrow, but it does involve spending money.'

'I haven't got any money,' I said.

'It's not your auction brainwave again, is it?' Matt asked Claire.

Claire giggled. Earlier that week, she had had the genius idea of taking us to a modern art auction at Sotheby's on the grounds that it might be swarming with rich, bored women. Instead, it had been swarming with rich, bored sheikhs. The afternoon had almost ended in disaster when, after a long liquid lunch, Matt thought it would be amusing to raise my arm during the bidding for a Rothko. The guy with the hammer spotted me and, for a horrible, long minute, it looked as if I might be the proud owner of a few square metres of colourful stripes and £36m worth of extra debt. Fortunately, someone speaking frantically into a mobile at the back of the room eventually raised their hand and I was saved.

'I'm sorry, my friend,' said the owner of the rival hand afterwards. 'You looked as if you really wanted it.'

'No, not really,' I said truthfully, patting the young sheikh gratefully on the back.

'Oh, I love your charming British modesty. I could give it to you, if you really wanted.'

'Give it to me?' I had sudden visions of wealth beyond my wildest dreams. I would hang it in Alan's flat. No, I'd sell it and buy my own flat, my own house, set up a theatre company of my own, spend my life with whomever I wanted, travel, do good works...

The Arab laughed. 'Well, not exactly *give* it to you. But I'm happy to sell it to you for a fraction more than I bought it for. It was only really a business investment, in any case. For my father. I mean, look at it.' I looked at it. 'How do you say, "It's a horrible piece of shit"?'

I agreed that that was exactly how you said it and we parted on friendly terms.

Back in the taxi, Claire laughed at the memory. 'The look on your face, Sam, when you thought you'd found an Arab sugar-daddy... '

'The look on yours when you tried to flirt with his brother and spilled tea over his white robe.'

'Anyway.' Claire hastily changed the subject. 'My plan for tomorrow is nothing like the auction. There's a one-off performance of *Tosca* at the Albert Hall.'

'*Tosca*, eh?' said Matt, perking up. Matt liked opera, for some strange reason.

'It's expensive, though,' warned Claire.

'No problem,' said Matt. 'You sometimes have to spend

money to meet money, right?' It had become something of a slogan over the last few weeks.

'Right. And goodness, will we meet money tomorrow night.'

'Will we?' I asked. 'What does it look like?'

'Shut up, Sam. Tomorrow night is a huge charity bash on behalf of the Prince's Trust. Everyone who's anyone is going to be there. And tomorrow, we can be a someone, too. My sister has some clients who can't make it.'

'In the same way as prostitutes have clients?'

'Sam! It will be fun. Why are you being so stubborn suddenly?'

'Because I don't have any money, Claire. Because I'm tired. Because I haven't acted for months. Because all I really want to do is see Rosie again and I'm nowhere closer to sorting out any of my life.'

Claire took one of my hands in hers. 'Well, I'll lend you the hundred pounds for the ticket. It's all for a good cause, right?'

'Right.'

'For charity and for Matt.'

'I'm not sure I see the difference.'

'Thanks, Sam.'

*

I'd worn white-tie once before – when playing the butler in a drama school production. The people at the Albert Hall that charity evening looked as if they had been born in white-tie, as if they got dressed in it in the morning and walked the streets during the day in full regalia as if it were the most normal thing in the world.

'Just look how the other half lives,' whistled Matt as we were ushered into an auditorium of plunging golds and reds, the silk rustle of floor-length dresses, the tinkle of glasses and animated conversation.

'Just look how we're *going* to live,' I replied.

'What *is* it with posh women?' asked Matt, wide-eyed. 'Is it the breeding? The genes? The expensive grooming? The clothes? Those worldly voices that make them sound so damn shaggable? I tell you, mate, they put a lot of the girls we grew up with to shame.'

'From my limited experience,' I replied, 'their main attraction lies in the fact that they've spent the best years of their lives in single-sex boarding schools, with only contraband long-handled hairbrushes for company, and are therefore desperate to make up for lost time.'

'Are you two going to gawp all evening or are you going to get busy?' demanded Claire, giving us both a little shove. 'Come on, boys: divide and conquer. Go forth and multiply.'

There was an hour-long drinks reception before the opera started which I determined, on behalf of the charity, to make the most of. I loathe opera and I challenge anyone who professes to like it to prove that they are anything other than a snob. The fact that it is mainly attended by twats does not make it a superior art form. The extortionate ticket price does not guarantee interpretative genius. I have spent £9 and seen more artistic integrity from someone eating his own penis while playing the ukulele at the Edinburgh Fringe. I like opera's sense of occasion – I enjoy dressing up as much as the next thesp – but the performance itself is always three hours of your life you will never get back. *Fat bint sings to ugly man, then dies.* It's a complete waste of time. Opera music – now that's a different thing altogether. I love singing along in the bath to the thumping extracts on Classic FM. But fifteen of these in a row with a loosely woven plot that no one can be bothered to translate from the Italian 'because it spoils it' (it's not the Qur'an, for Allah's sake; have you heard how facile some of the lyrics are?), when the only thing really spoiled is the sense of smug superiority felt by those in the audience who studied Latin at school? Well, no. Opera music has its place: in short clips on *The X Factor* and ice cream commercials. And the bath. Nowhere else.

Not that I shared any of these philistine thoughts as Matt, Claire and I mingled with the rest of the audience, champagne flutes in hand. It wasn't that sort of evening. There was a gentle, pleasant buzz of acceptance and belonging. Outside, anything could be happening for all we knew, for all we cared. Inside this womb we were safe, in body, mind and spirit, content that our generous charitable pounds were going towards nourishing our cultured souls, as well as helping those considerably less fortunate than ourselves. Money, wealth, exclusivity. Was this not what I had wanted all along? Role play on a grand scale, an entire theatre of possibilities, a comic cast of hundreds, a thousand potential plot twists, grand entrances and flamboyant exits.

It was an atmosphere that seemed to suit Matt as well. *Here, at last, I am in my element,* his elegantly tailored body seemed to cry as he glided effortlessly around the room, a quiet word here, a suitable nod there. Within a few minutes he was locked in deep conversation with a wealthy-looking older woman and her attractive daughter. Claire, meanwhile, had fallen in with her sister's crowd. They laughed uproariously as Claire related some amusing vignette. Her sister's dashing boss held her gaze for a little too long.

I was just warming up by talking to a nice waitress studying at my old drama school when I saw two alarming and highly unexpected sights approaching from opposite ends of the room. One was Christian Mary, accompanied by what could only be her parents; the other was Rosie, accompanied by what could only be a boyfriend.

I gawped at Rosie. I think everyone in the room gawped at Rosie. She was wearing an off-the-shoulder red dress that seemed to caress the ground as she walked. A diamond glistened at her throat. Her eyes danced with intelligence, her smile was a beam of celestial light, beatifying anyone it touched, her brown hair was piled high in the silky crown of the anointed one. No one that night would have said that her legs were a little bit too short or her hair a little bit too long. Tonight, she was perfect.

The short, ugly bloke accompanying her knew that, too. He steered her towards the canapés with all the confidence of someone who knows that every other caveman wants to club him and ravish his woman. This is why some men go for trophy wives, I thought, as I looked on enviously. It's better than having a nice house or an expensive car. It says something about you that nothing else can quite articulate. *Well, well,* we think, *if* she *sees something in him, then maybe...* We might all have wanted to kill Rosie's companion but, were we to be introduced, we would probably show him a great deal more respect than we would have if he had come to the party alone.

Not that there seemed to be any chance of getting the short ugly man away from Rosie. He stuck to her side, bristling like a suspicious bull terrier whenever a potential rival spoke to her. She might have given him confidence, but he clearly wasn't confident enough to leave her alone for very long. I felt a tiny glimmer of hope. I just had to see Rosie again. Just had to see her alone. *I had to get that bloody money to pay the invoice.*

It was, I think, at that moment that I began to scrape the very bottom of my moral barrel. Much of what preceded that evening was unintentional, unscripted, unplanned. But as I looked again at the incomparable Rosie caught up on one side of the room, still unaware that I was there, and saw Mary approaching me, now *sans* parents, from the other, her eyes bright with recognition and forgiveness, I suddenly had a very clear plan. *These two girls didn't know each other...* Returning my glass to the waitress and advising her that her current profession was a much better bet than the one she was training for, I turned and embraced Mary wholeheartedly.

'Sam!' she exclaimed, flinging her arms around me. 'I was worried about you.'

'I was worried about me, too,' I said. 'That church... '

'I'm sorry. I just felt so bad when you ran out.'

'*You* felt bad?' I took a deep breath. 'You can't have been feeling as bad as me. The weight of sin bearing down on me. The realisation of what a bad person I've been, how bad we all are, fundamentally.'

Mary nodded understandingly.

'But I also felt this great love,' I continued. 'I felt that I was loved and cherished, understood and nurtured, no matter how bad I'd been. So I prayed. *Man*, did I pray. *God*, did I pray. That's why I haven't been in touch for ages. I've been praying non-stop. I've barely left my room for prayer. And I think I've seen the light. I really do. I think I now know the direction my life is going to take. And then you appear here tonight… Well, it must be a sign. It's like a prayer answered.'

'Oh, Sam!' Mary looked up at me through tears of delight. 'Would you like to come and meet my parents?'

'Oh, Mary! I would like that very much indeed.'

Mary took me by the hand as if I were the prodigal son and led me off to meet Mr and Mrs Money-Barings. I was suddenly glad it was a white-tie function because if one of Mary's creators had not been wearing a tailcoat and the other a dress, I could easily have got them mixed up. They were equally tall, square and masculine. Poor Mary. If I had been her, I would have hidden her mother away in Dorian Gray's attic so as not to warn potential suitors of what she was going to turn into.

Having worked out which Money-Barings was which, the next problem was trying to follow what they were saying. I'd studied Received Pronunciation, of course, at drama school – I had been using it the whole evening – but the dialect spoken by the Money-Baringses was something else altogether. At first I thought they were speaking in tongues. Then I wondered if they were both trying to clear something from the backs of their throats or had, perhaps, brought an ageing labrador with them that evening and were attempting to call it to heel. Finally, I managed to tune my ear into their wavelength and we had something approaching a conversation.

'Like opera, do you?' barked Mr Money-Barings. The trick to understanding him, I soon realised, was never to expect a full sentence.

'Yes, sir,' I lied.

'Rubbish,' shouted Mr Money-Barings. 'Full of ponces.'

I laughed, despite myself. 'Actually... ' I said, in a voice I barely recognised. I think I may even have pronounced it 'Ashley'. 'Ashley, I hate opera. But you know, all for a good cause. Rugger. That's my poison.'

Mr Money-Barings looked as if he wanted to hug me. 'Mary,' he cried. 'Good egg you've got here. Meet recently, did you?'

'At a wed – '

'At church, Daddy,' interrupted Mary with a firm smile.

'Church, eh? Excellent.' He turned to me. 'And what do you do, young man, when you're not in church? City? Insurance? Stockbroking?'

'Sam's an actor,' said Mary.

'Yes, I'm afraid so,' I said. 'But I'm also starting a small business in the City.'

''Fraid so? Nonsense. Fine living. Very fine. As long as you're not one of these opera ponces.'

As if on cue, a bell rang to announce that the opera ponces would start their poncy singing in ten minutes. Mr Money-Barings clapped me warmly on the back, 'For whom the bell tolls, eh? Ponce alert. Great to meet you, Sam. Come and visit us in the country some time, if you're passing.'

When have I ever passed the country, I thought ruefully as the Money-Baringses rummaged for their tickets. Still, I was confident of eliciting a proper invitation. 'It was lovely to see you again,' I said to Mary, kissing her dangerously close to her lips in front of her parents. 'Will you be in church next Sunday, if I come back?'

'Oh, Sam!' said Mary, which I took to mean yes.

Another warning bell sounded. Mary rushed off to join her barking, homophobic father and mute, masculine mother, and

I rummaged around in my pocket for my own ticket. Just as I'd started climbing the stairs to the gods, searching in vain for Rosie, I heard a familiar voice behind me.

'Max,' it whispered urgently.

I didn't turn round at first. Who was Max?

'Max,' it whispered again, louder this time.

Oh, fuck. I was Max.

I turned to see Rosie, a vision in resplendent red, all alone on the stairs, her face flushed with champagne.

'I thought I saw you across the room,' said the vision.

'Hello,' I said, for I was tongue-tied and the only other thing I could think of to say was, *Please come home with me now.* In the circumstances, 'hello' seemed safer.

'How is your friend?' asked Rosie.

'Oh, that's just someone I met at – ' I started to say before blushing and realising she was talking about Ed. I grinned, sheepishly. 'Oh, he's fine. Slept it off. Now he's writing drivel for the newspapers as a means of public therapy.'

Rosie laughed. 'Yep, I read that. But it took me a while to recognise the photo from the tramp you'd introduced me to.'

'And how is your, er, friend?' I grimaced, involuntarily.

'Oh, Kevin? He's trying to grease up the Prince of Wales in the foyer. He's our office accountant.' She flashed a charmingly sheepish grin of her own. 'Anyway, I only agreed to come with him because I've got a crush on Prince Harry.'

I laughed.

'Anyway,' she continued, 'Kevin doesn't really like opera. He only came for the networking opportunities.'

'Philistine.'

'Philistine.'

'Do you like opera?'

'No. I hate it. You?'

'No.'

'Philistine.'

'Shall we go somewhere else?'

'Yes.'

And with that, I took Rosie's hand and we hurtled down the stairs together, past a startled-looking Matt, who was now sitting with the mother/daughter combination he'd met earlier, past Claire, who was no longer flirting with her sister's boss but perched grumpily in the corner with her BlackBerry, past the waitress I had befriended and out into the glorious autumn evening.

'I feel like I can breathe at last,' said Rosie, laughing. We linked arms and began to stroll aimlessly away from the Albert Hall.

'Me, too.'

Rosie stopped, took both of my hands in hers and moved very close. 'But look at us now, Max. All dressed up with nowhere to go.'

But we did have places to go. With the remaining £300 on my fifth credit card, we spent the best evening of my life, the evening to end all evenings, in which the only drink we drank was champagne, the only music we heard became our own, and the only person I cared about in the world was the girl on my arm. It ended, inevitably, in her bed, breathless, delirious, and with Rosie shouting out, at the top of her voice, the name of a man neither of us had ever met.

Chapter Fifteen

'Love lasts a long time, but burning desire – two to three weeks,' said Carla Bruni, who looks as if she knows a few things about both. Until Rosie, that had always been my experience, too. Even Lisa and I, who went out for eight months, only lasted so long because neither of us had the courage to finish it. But Rosie? Well, she was different – very different. After a month, there was even more burning desire and passion than there had been at two to three weeks. After two months, there was respect as well as affection. After three, I found it difficult to imagine life without her. And after four... Well, whisper it quietly, but I think I was actually in love with her. Not head-over-heels, over-in-a-month, get-bored-later infatuation, but proper, lasting, in-depth love. So *this* was what songwriters and poets had been banging on about for all these centuries.

Not that those four months after the Albert Hall were without their complications. For starters, I had to grow used to being Max, even as I tried to kill him off. The first step was to announce after a few weeks that I was shelving his business plan. 'I just don't think it will work in the current economic climate,' I said one morning over breakfast in Rosie's house in Parsons Green. 'I think I'll go back to banking.'

'No worries,' said Rosie, laughing. She was always saying 'no worries'. 'Although I'm afraid you'll still owe Taylor Williams for the consultancy fee. My boss is getting a little concerned about it.'

If truth be told, I had been getting more than a little concerned about it myself. It wouldn't be long before interest would start kicking in on the invoice, and I already had more than enough debts accruing interest without worrying about another one. That £5,000 would be the release fee: the point at which I no longer had to worry about the strange way in which we had met.

But however hard I tried, I realised how difficult it would be to kill off Max altogether. One night, when we were lying in bed, Rosie randomly said: 'Lunch.'

'What?'

'Lunch. We never had that lunch you promised.'

'Isn't this more fun, though?'

Rosie giggled and pressed herself up close. 'Yes, Max, it is.'

'You know, Rosie, I've been thinking,' I said, seizing the moment. If she was being post-coitally whimsical, this was as good a time as any. 'I've been thinking about my name. Max. It's a bit of stupid name, isn't it? *Max. Pepsi Max. Maxed out. To the Max.* Ridiculous. I thought I might change it to something more sensible. Sam, maybe. That's my middle name.'

Rosie looked at me strangely. 'Why would you want to do that? No one changes their name in their twenties. Especially to something as stupid as Sam. Anyway, your name is one of the things I like most about you. It's so… it's so manly. Now come here, Max… Oh, Max, Max, MAX.'

For the first couple of weeks, I pretty much lived at Rosie's, pretending I'd taken some old, accrued holiday from the banking job they'd kept open for me. But as time progressed, the deceptions inevitably became more and more complex. Any weekday evening spent at hers I had to remember to turn up in a suit and leave sufficiently early, and in the right direction, for Blackfriars in the morning. On one nerve-wracking occasion, she insisted on accompanying me right up to the door of Goldman Sachs – I cursed myself for not pretending I'd moved to a bank with offices in Canary Wharf, miles away from hers – before kissing me goodbye. Fortunately, her phone rang, and while she was distracted I bolted round the corner and back to Islington, spared the ignominy of Rosie watching me pretend that my swipe card for the bank's doors had broken.

There were other pretences to keep up, too. Most painful was maintaining the illusion of living a banker's lifestyle. Not only did I have debts up to my eyeballs, I also had very little income. The people at the temping agency that had got me the job at Taylor Williams were livid that I had apparently absconded from the placement and were unwilling to find me a job anywhere else. 'Either you go back and work there and mend our relationship,' they told me, 'or we don't find you another job ever again.' I said it would have to be the latter; life was stressful enough without working in the same office as Rosie under a different name and a very different job title. Divine junior analyst Rosie had not fallen in love with Sam the temp.

Sam the temp, on the other hand, was in love with Rosie exactly as she was. None of her evident wealth or ambition mattered any more. It was her that I wanted, and damn the consequences. Over the next four months I fell so deeply for her that none of the obvious complications seemed to matter much either. Something would turn up. I would make everything okay again in the end. The deception itself became intoxicating. All my senses were heightened by the possibility of being found out and the determination not to become so.

Yet still the black cloud of money hung over me. I managed to get another couple of credit cards, but the limits became tighter and the demands for the existing ones more aggressive. I worked as many shifts as possible in the same old coffee bar in Camden during the day, but it only made tiny inroads into a debt that spiralled faster than I could pay off even the interest.

So I turned, in desperation, to my friends. But the truth was that I hadn't been a very good friend of late. In fact, I had been spending most of my time with Rosie's friends instead, surprising myself by how much I actually liked them. Normally, girlfriends' friends are a nightmare. The girls are a lose-lose: either they're attractive and you fancy them, or they're ugly, jealous types who resent you for taking their friend away. The guys, on the other hand, simply can't be trusted, for obvious reasons. Rosie, however, had a nice little group from university which I quickly became part of. Most of the time, I didn't even care what we did, as long as we did it together.

After I'd started spending all my time at Rosie's, Ed had apparently decided to return to the shoebox in Hackney that he and Tara still hadn't sold. Apart from writing a slightly disparaging online comment at the end of his *Guardian* article, I hadn't had any contact with him for ages. Alan seemed to have allowed Matt to stay on at his flat for a while, but Matt wasn't around all that much, either. On the few occasions Rosie had come round to 'mine', I had asked him to go and stay somewhere else so I could put up a broken but presentable plasma television screen from the local tip and pretend that this two-bedroom flat was a banker's bachelor pad and not a squalid bedsit shared by two unemployed people. Matt had readily agreed, not least because things seemed to be working out very well with the girl – Debbie – he had met at the opera.

Debbie was a north London Jewish princess who ran a successful kitchen business, selling over-priced interior decorations to other rich, successful north London women. Her only flaw was that she appeared to have fallen twice for men who were 'not the family type' and was bringing up two children under the age of five by herself. Matt, it seemed, exactly fitted the profile of the man she was looking for: a stay-at-home father-figure with excellent first-aid skills. Debbie's widowed mother, who lived next door, had also taken quite a shine to him.

'A doctor as a potential son-in-law?' I prodded when we met up for lunch one day in the new year. 'She must be very excited. It's just a shame you're not employed. Or Jewish.'

'Who said I told her I wasn't Jewish?'

'Shit, Matt, you're worse than me.'

'Well, I didn't exactly lie to her,' he continued, grinning sheepishly. 'Not at first. I just didn't correct her when she started talking about Jewish things. And well, by then, it was too late. One day she told me she had some Jewish cousins in Norway, so I told her that my granddad was Norwegian, which is true, even though he isn't Jewish, which I didn't mention, and so any doubts she might have had about why my hair is so blond were probably cleared up. Also, in case you were wondering, I don't have a, well, you know, *thingy*... Anyway, before I knew it, one thing led to another and I was swapping stories with her younger brother about our bar mitzvahs.'

'And how was your bar mitzvah?'

'Emotional. So emotional, in fact, that I barely remember anything about it.'

We both laughed at ourselves. 'Just look at us now,' I said, pointing at the Gap Kids carrier bag he was holding, full of clothes for Debbie's children, and smoothing down my father's suit, which I had put on at Rosie's house that morning. 'We've almost made it, haven't we? Almost fulfilled what we set out to do.'

Matt smiled. 'Yep, almost. We don't have to work at all.'

'Well, you don't.'

'We're in the pub in the middle of the day.'

'Yep, until you have to go and pick up Debbie's eldest from nursery school.'

'We're not losing touch with our friends.'

'Well, not all of them.'

'All we have to do now is get these two to marry us.'

'And move them a bit closer together. The same street, ideally.'

Matt clapped me on the back. 'Thanks, mate, for persuading me to keep going a bit longer. It was all worth it to meet Debbie.'

'No worries. I'd love to meet her properly. I'd love you to meet Rosie, too, as long as you can remember to call me Max all night.'

He laughed again. Maybe this was the right moment.

'Matt?'

'Yes.'

'Do you have five thousand pounds?'

'No.'

And that was that. No hard feelings. Just a simple, direct 'no'. He didn't have the money. And why should he ask Debbie to help? He had won her on his own merits, by being himself, or at least a non-Gentile version of himself. I was the one who'd dug myself into an awkward, deceitful hole.

No one else seemed that willing to lend me a shovel, either. Ed had less money than the average sixth-former he taught, and although I'd written Alan a letter of apology which, frankly, grovelled well beyond the call of duty, I thought it probably wasn't wise to ask him for a loan. We were back on speaking terms, but it would take a while to patch up some of those stupid things I'd said. Our friendship meant too much for me to risk blowing it again.

Most disappointing of all was Claire's reaction. She'd been uncharacteristically blunt and unfriendly when I'd called after the opera.

'Well, that was great fun, thank you,' I'd said. 'What are we three musketeers going to get up to next?'

'Nothing,' she'd said.

'What?'

'I have to go back to work and stop spending all this money. Anyway, haven't you two got what you wanted?'

And that was that. Claire went back to work in a grump and I didn't see her again for months. A scheme that had begun with the intention of spending more time with each other had ended up driving most of us apart.

Still, there was Rosie — she was my life now. I had actually learned to do everything right in this relationship. I listened, even when she was being boring. I bought her thoughtful presents. I didn't fart in bed. Maybe that's what all the other failed relationships in my twenties had been about — practice for the one that actually counted. If I could just keep this going, everything else would somehow work itself out. The game of relationship musical chairs I had banged on about at Lisa's wedding appeared to have stopped and I was perfectly happy with where I was sitting. I'd grown bored of the dating game, now that I'd found someone I really liked. I had grown up, despite myself. Frankly, I'd become a little bit like Alan.

I don't say all this to excuse what happened next – there are no excuses for what happened next. There was, however, a very good reason: I had exhausted all other options over those four months to pay that bloody £5,000 invoice. The interest was still mounting and I couldn't stall Rosie and her firm indefinitely. Mary, then, was the only person left who could 'kill' Max. Thanks to the duplicitous hole into which I'd dug myself, Mary and Rosie had become inextricably entwined.

*

Since the opera Mary and I had stayed in fairly regular contact, often going for a coffee during the day – whenever my busy schedule of making coffee for other people or pretending to be a banker allowed – or meeting up at church, if I felt able to convince Rosie I had to work late. My apparent conversion had spread like wildfire among the Clapham Christians, much to my embarrassment. The closest I came to pulling the plug on the entire charade was the evening the vicar asked me to come to the front and 'testify' in front of the congregation about my amazing Damascene moment. I'd conducted a serious search of my conscience, but to my mild alarm found it to be almost entirely clear. Anyway, I knew enough about the Bible by then to know that God wasn't that bothered about different grades of sin. Human beings are inherently sinful. This was no worse than the things most people got up to in an average day. The important thing was saying sorry afterwards. And meaning it. In any case, I've always thought God had something of a sense of humour. Ultimately, I convinced myself with weasel logic, this was all for a good cause. God was love, wasn't he? And anyway, Mr Money-Barings wasn't exactly a textbook example of selfless, tolerant Christianity in action.

So I put in one of the finest performances of my life at the front of that church. The vicar cried; I cried; the congregation cried. Jesus wept. And when the man with the guitar appeared on stage, I sang along with the best of them, often in my own key. *You're altogether lovely / altogether worthy / altogether wonderful to me.* I did the Holy Spirit. *Hooooo, naaaaaaa, widddiiii.* I made snow angels on the floor alongside Mary. I listened attentively while Stock Market Christian told us about his latest multi-million-pound deal. And through it all, I out-Christianed the Christians. If someone made a joke of which I felt Jesus would disapprove, I censured them. Whenever Mary attempted to renew any level of sexual contact beyond kissing, I would point her to the relevant Bible verse. 'Not before marriage, dear,' I would say. 'Not again before marriage, at least.'

It made me feel marginally better about Rosie that I wasn't being sexually unfaithful, even if the levels of emotional infidelity and deception were far worse. Mary, meanwhile, grew increasingly frustrated the more fervently religious I became. 'What's happened to you, Sam?' she demanded one evening. 'I've never seen the Spirit take someone like this before. Being a Christian doesn't mean you have to be completely boring, you know.' But we were the golden couple of the church, much to Stock Market Christian's annoyance. The beautiful trust-fund girl and her lost-actor convert: it was a happy ending Mary appeared unable, or unwilling, to resist.

As for me, I was so into the part that there were some days when I questioned whether I actually had gone native. There was a peace in that church, a purpose, a sense of community, role-play or no role-play, which I wasn't sure I had ever found elsewhere. There were also a lot of good people – kind, generous, loving people who thought hard about life's questions and believed they had found an answer. Who was I to say they were wrong? Could this be my way out, too? My absolution? Could I become Sam again? Write off my sin along with my debt?

But Rosie was my sin and my debt, the girl I was unable to resist, and still unable to be entirely truthful with. So when Mary finally invited me down to Gloucestershire to spend a Sunday in late January with her parents, I accepted and told Rosie I would be away for business, which was a fairly accurate description of how I saw the excursion.

The Money-Baringses lived in a small, pompous village near Stroud in Gloucestershire, where we attended a church service led by a small, pompous vicar.

'Be nice to the ponce,' said Mr Money-Barings with an attempt at a wink as we left. 'Might be back here soon yourself, eh?'

The old homophobe quickly warmed to me again, just like the night at *Tosca*. Alan has always had a problem with Jess's parents and vice versa. Ed used to turn into a nervous wreck around Tara's father. Personally, with the exception of Mrs Geoffrey Parker, Lisa's mother, who took an instant dislike to me, I have never found any difficulty with the parents of girls I've been interested in. Their daughters, yes. The parents, no. All you have to do is flirt gently with the mother and convince the father you're a solid sort by discussing manly things neither of you understand, such as quantitative easing or the Middle East peace process.

Mrs Money-Barings was also on fine form on our second meeting. 'I'm sorry I was so quiet, Sam, that night at the Albert Hall,' she said as we sat down to a Sunday roast in their cavernous dining room. 'I'm afraid London's just not my scene. Is it your scene?'

I wasn't sure if I had a scene, but I said it was, as that appeared to be the answer she was looking for. Tucking into my lunch, however, I could see what she meant. Gloucestershire was very definitely *her* scene: several dogs wandered languidly around the hall; a fire was roaring next door in the drawing room; Mrs Money-Barings had already changed out of her church clothes into a threadbare old jumper and corduroys. It was a very pleasant setting, to be honest, and for a while I let myself be carried away by an enjoyable fantasy of Rosie and me one day living somewhere like that. I would play the piano in the evenings. Our friends would come round for weekend house parties. We'd walk the dogs. Maybe I could build a theatre in the garden.

'And what are you up to at the moment, Sam?' asked Mr Money-Barings over coffee. 'Any plays in the offing?'

I looked around the table at his wife and daughter. I'd half expected them to withdraw after dessert – sorry, *pudding* – to allow Mr Money-Barings and me to crack open the port and chew a *Romeo y Julieta* while discussing whether or not we should return to the Gold Standard. Maybe I'd been watching the wrong era of films as research.

'Well,' I said, taking a gulp of coffee, '*Ash*ley, I've got a bit bored of waiting around to be cast in something while keeping my business ticking over, so I've decided to put on my own production.'

'That's great, Sam,' enthused Mary. 'Isn't that great, Daddy?'

'Not opera, is it?' barked Mr Money-Barings. 'No pon – ?'

'Darling,' interrupted Mrs Money-Barings. 'Please.'

For a man who professed to have found God late, I felt Mr Money-Barings had a rather unhealthy obsession with homosexuality. Had he only read the Old Testament?

'No,' I reassured him. 'Not opera. Actually, I think you'll rather like it. It's going to be a musical about the Prodigal Son. Looking at it in a modern light, and so on.'

'That *is* great,' said Mr Money-Barings. 'Expensive business, I imagine.'

'Well, yes, the production won't be cheap. But I thought I'd finance it through a loan from the company I run.'

Mr Money-Barings rose to his feet, went next door to the drawing room and returned with a cheque book.

'I think we can do better than that,' he said, producing a fountain pen from his jacket pocket.

'No. I couldn't possibly.'

'Nonsense, boy. You're as good as family.'

Mary winced, opposite.

'No, seriously, I couldn't. It's an expensive production.'

'How much?'

'Well, it's going to cost five thousand, all-in.' Then I remembered Claire's opera ticket. 'Sorry, five thousand one hundred, if we include the lighting guy.'

'There,' barked Mr Money-Barings, sliding over my get-out-of-jail-free card. 'Now, who's for a walk?'

Chapter Sixteen

I'd argued with Sam before, of course, at various junctures over the last twenty-five years. When we were seven, we fancied the same girl and used to shove each other outside the classroom so we could sit next to her in Geography (Sam always won, incidentally). Then, aged twelve, Sam went through an annoying phase of setting alarm clocks for different times in the middle of the night and hiding them all over my bedroom, which I didn't find very amusing. It was the one occasion my mum got really angry with him. Inevitably, there was also the odd spat over the years while sharing a flat in London. Most of the time, I put up with his many foibles, but occasionally I'd flip and we'd have an argument to clear the air. It's difficult to be angry with Sam for very long.

The row over Jess, however, cut very deep. I know you shouldn't care what your friends think about your girlfriend. I know that no one else can really understand a relationship from the outside, because a relationship is between two people, not an entire group, and that often the couples who are most outwardly gregarious and happy in company are miserable alone. But it was impossible not to care – my friends were important to me. Although I didn't *need* their blessing – Jess was not a trophy for which I demanded applause or recognition – it would be nice to think they didn't loathe her.

Sam's outburst also made it difficult for me not to question my entire relationship with Jess. First my mother; then my friends… Was I the only person who actually saw anything good in her? Was it more likely that all of them were wrong and I was right, or the other way round? They couldn't all just be jealous, surely? Was I simply too lazy to find anyone else? And why had it taken so long for me to ask her to marry me? For the first time in my life I began to have doubts.

And yet I think I'm as aware of Jess's faults as anyone. The blinkers don't stay on after more than eight years. She can be difficult, awkward, manipulative, snobby and self-obsessed. But she's also loving, kind, funny, intelligent and wonderful in bed (or at least, I think she's wonderful in bed; I haven't really slept with that many other girls). I could make long lists all day with Jess's negative points in one column and the positives in the other. Both lists would be of roughly equal length. But what would be the point? The only real point is that I love her. And that, I thought, was what I had to make everyone who disapproved realise. Frankly, our relationship was none of their business, but still, I wanted the wedding to be a celebration, not a funeral.

Not that we had even got close to setting a date. Jess wanted a winter wedding so we could go skiing for our honeymoon. For what it was worth (this was another argument I probably wouldn't win), I preferred the idea of getting married the following summer – partly, I think, because it would allow me to postpone confronting the issue of Amanda's ultimatum.

All these myriad problems – some voiced, others kept bottled up – combined, I think, to put an unbearable amount of pressure on our relationship. Maybe I should just have told Jess about Amanda's indecent proposal. Perhaps I should have explained that I had argued with my friends about her. But I didn't. Whether through a misplaced desire to protect her or simple cowardice, I kept everything to myself and the relationship suffered as a result. Christmas approached and the engagement ring I'd had commissioned still lay uncollected at the jeweller's. Every day I meant to pick it up and every day I made an excuse to myself. It was symbolic of a malaise that seemed to have taken root the moment we'd started co-habiting. Other friends who have moved in with their girlfriends – fiancées, even – and become their 'flatmates' have told me it was the best decision they had ever made. Whereas before they had had to trek across London to have quiet sex without their flatmates overhearing, check diaries to see when they were free and endure constant arguments about not seeing enough of each other, moving in together solved all these problems in one fell swoop. Ironically, a move you would expect to be trapping was actually liberating. Girls know they've 'got you', my co-habiting friends told me, so they give you much more freedom to do as you wish. Their nesting instinct satisfied, you are free to stay out until 3am on a Saturday with your mates, as they'll always know if you haven't come home eventually. It's difficult to lie to your 'flatmate', or indeed your flatmates. I knew far more about Sam's life when I was living with him than any girl who thought she'd got close to him ever did.

I, on the other hand, didn't seem to have any friends left to go out with until three in the morning. Ed, I was alarmed to read in the *Guardian*, appeared to have embarked on some kind of kamikaze mission to ensure no woman would ever speak to him again. Matt, who rang occasionally to keep me updated, appeared to have quickly shacked up as a house-husband to a Jewish princess. And Sam? Well, we didn't speak for a while, leaving me trapped with Jess, Jess's friends and Jess's bubble bath, which I had surprised myself by taking quite a shine to.

Throughout the weeks that followed my moving in with Jess, it upset me more than I could really articulate not being in contact with Sam. We had shared everything since we were children and I really wanted him to share my happiness – if that was the right word for it – now. I would certainly be a whole lot happier if he was part of it. I also wanted to know how his little scheme with Matt was going. Sam was fun to live vicariously through. It was like watching a movie featuring a slow car crash from which everyone eventually emerged, shaken but unscathed. But Matt didn't give me many details. Maybe he thought I would be shocked.

So when I saw a letter arrive through the post one Saturday

morning in December – a proper letter, no less; not a misspelled text message or a dashed-off email – bearing Sam's handwriting, I pounced on it eagerly. Long, amusing and heartfelt, it contained everything I hoped for. Sam explained why he felt weird about my moving out, how he had never had any stability in his life, and how our flat and our friendship was one of the few constants he enjoyed. He admitted that he was prone to looking back nostalgically at the 'good old days' when he should be looking forward to the rest of his life. And to that end, my moving out was really a good thing because it had persuaded him to take some proactive steps to squire a young junior analyst at Taylor Williams called Rosie Morris by assuming the identity of a banker called Max Anderson-Bickley... And so it continued, for several pages, to detail his recent adventures. I felt a small pang of jealousy that he was having all the fun, along with a modicum of disapproval. Most of all, I felt relieved to be back in contact with my friend.

There was a short passage on Amanda, in which he asked if there had been any progress. He also apologised for being insensitive in recommending I screwed her sideways and repeated his recommendation to keep a record of anything she did.

There was no glowing praise of Jess – maybe that was asking too much – but he did apologise for being rude. 'I didn't really mean what I said,' he wrote in the concluding paragraph. 'I didn't really want you to go and fuck yourself. I wanted you to go and fuck your nice fiancée, Jess. And most of all, I just want you to be happy.'

Well, I don't mind admitting that I almost cried as I put the letter down in the small corner of the fuchsia-pink study I was allowed to call my own. Sam had called Jess 'nice'. Not 'beautiful' or 'lovely' or 'just right for you', but still, it was a start. Soon we'd be having him over for dinner parties, Classic FM and After Eights.

That weekend I bought a new fountain pen and started to

compose my reply. We were grown-ups now and it felt right to be communicating in a grown-up way. In any case, there was something I wanted to ask Sam that I thought would come across best in a letter: I wanted him to be my best man, whenever Jess decided our wedding was going to be. I was ready to forgive him.

I also wrote about Amanda and about how I had begun to feel more confident when dealing with her at work. She wasn't stupid, after all. Alcoholic, manipulative and amoral, yes. But not stupid. You didn't get to her position by being stupid. All I had to do was keep my nose clean and she would have nothing on me. Others in my team would vouch for me, if she decided to give a bad report. She had, however, been suspiciously quiet and pleasant of late. Amanda was only quiet when she was scheming.

My letter went on to mention plans for our engagement party, my hopes that my mum would get on with Jess, my concerns about Ed, etc.

In the end, none of this was relevant, because the letter was never sent.

The following Monday, I went to work as usual, wearing my Monday socks and Monday shirt, and left my half-finished reply next to Sam's letter on my desk. When I returned home, later than usual because Amanda had made me stay to do some extra menial work, both letters had vanished. I went through to the bedroom, where Jess was standing in the middle of the room, melodramatically ripping them into tiny shreds. How long had she been waiting there to start doing that, I wondered.

'What's wrong, darling?' I asked.

'I think you know what's fucking wrong,' said Jess, who never usually swore. She gave up ripping, screwed the paper into a tight ball instead and hurled it at me. 'You bastard.'

'Sweetheart,' I said, genuinely confused. My conscience was clear. 'I don't know what I've done.'

'You don't know what you've done, *sweetheart*?' She

mimicked. 'You're having an affair with your boss. That what you've fucking done. And your nasty little friend Sam is laughing about it. Take recording equipment, he sniggers. Keep a record. What, so he can whack up in your old flat over it?'

I actually laughed, despite myself. Only Jess could come up with a phrase like 'whack up'. And the misunderstanding about the recording equipment was so ridiculous. That wasn't what Sam had written at all. She was always so quick to misinterpret him, I protested.

Jess, however, wasn't in the mood to see the funny side. And could I blame her, really? I explained the Amanda situation, and I think she was just about willing to believe that I had done nothing wrong, but she was still livid that I hadn't told her about it.

'I didn't tell you about it because I knew you would react like this,' I explained, which, judging by the shoe she aimed at me, was the wrong explanation.

'I just don't understand why Amanda would want you so much,' she said, once I'd finally calmed her down a few notches on the Jess-Richter scale.

'Oh, thanks.'

'I blame Sam,' she continued, giving me another filthy look. 'I don't know why, but I just sense he has something to do with this.'

'Why do you always have to blame him for everything?' I said.

'And why do you always have to excuse him for everything?'

'Because he's my friend.'

'And I'm your fiancée.'

'He's my friend. You're my fiancée. They're not mutually exclusive.'

'They are from now on.'

'What?'

'You have to choose, Alan. Either you drop contact with Sam or you don't marry me.'

'That's unfair.'

'Life's unfair. Anyway, what kind of friend gets up to the ridiculous things he's been doing with this Rosie girl? That silly bet made me really angry, too. Sam *and* Matt, but especially Sam. It makes a mockery of marriage.'

'He's only doing it because he's got no other choice at the moment. Anyway, it's just his bit of fun.'

'Fun? It's immoral. That's what it is. I hate him. I've always hated him.'

'Sam's going to make an effort with you. He said you were nice in his letter.'

'Nice? Fucking *nice*? And that's a compliment, is it, Alan? I'm not going to be very nice if I ever see him again.'

'But he's going to be my best man.'

'Not if you get married to me, he isn't. I'm not having a best man who thinks I'm "nice".'

'So the wedding day is all about you, is it?'

'Yes, Alan. It is.'

And that, it would seem, was that. Perhaps I should have been more forceful. I should, at the very least, have got upset that Jess was reading my private correspondence. I should have pointed out that we couldn't go on like this, that she couldn't expect to call all the shots. I should have pointed out that Sam had tried to make more of an effort with her than she had with him. She had been against him from the start.

These are all things I could have done – should have done – to save more heartache later. But I was already on the back foot for not having told her about Amanda's threat. What's more, bitter experience had taught me that arguments could drag on for days, even weeks, when Jess was in a mood like this. She wasn't such a good barrister for nothing. No, it would be much quicker and easier to admit full culpability and give her whatever she wanted.

So instead of standing up for myself, instead of standing up for my friend, I found myself apologising, for things I had and had not done, for things I might yet do; apologising for the state of the world as a whole, while agreeing, fervently and apologetically, that Jess was right, I was wrong and that the invitations for our engagement party, whenever she decided it might be, would not include Sam.

And then I waited until she was in the shower and rang him anyway.

Chapter Seventeen

After my business trip to Gloucestershire, I felt like the cat who'd got the cream, killed an army of mice and scratched the family dog's eyes out all in the course of one glorious Sunday afternoon. As soon as Mr Money-Barings's cheque had cleared my bank account, I was able to send off my payment to Taylor Williams's accounts department. I also sent Claire a cheque for £100 for the Albert Hall night, with a note thanking her for helping me to become a very happy man.

Over the course of the next few weeks the final stages of the strategy could be implemented: I was made redundant from my non-existent banking job, my fictional flat was repossessed and I officially moved in with Rosie. This would be the acid test – perhaps she only liked me for my perceived money – but any fears were quickly assuaged. Rosie was as much in love with me as I with her. Occasionally she would tease me gently about not having a job or not being the 'rich man with a plan' she'd first met. And I'd simply laugh, and make her laugh, by saying I was going to 'get back on my bike' (she loved that weak joke) and come up with a better plan than the Max House. I felt progressively less guilty, day by day. It was still the real Sam she had grown to know; it was still Sam she had fallen in love with, not Max. She made me want to become a better person. I actually believe I did around her.

Rosie was even enthusiastic when I mentioned that I had done a bit of drama at university and might give it a go again. I finally summoned up the courage to sack my agent and found a better one. Now that my life was no longer one big act, perhaps I would have more luck with my career. I could even try my hand at something else. In the meantime, I had Rosie to support me. I no longer had to maintain the illusion of a being a banker. Max was dead. Long live Sam and Rosie.

'And what about Mary?' asked Matt, when we met up for a midweek daytime game of pitch and putt in late January to swap our news.

'I'm trying to fizzle it out gently,' I said. 'But it's not that easy.'

'She still likes you, does she? Why?'

'God knows.'

I hoped he did, because I was pretty damned confused: the more Mary's barking father took a shine to me, the more she seemed to like me as well. I'd expected an argument about the cheque on the way back from Gloucestershire, but Mary didn't even seem to care that much. He had lots of money, I suppose. 'Anyway,' she'd said, 'the production will make the money back, won't it?'

'Yes,' I lied, knowing full well that there was no production and that, even if I were to stage one, I would almost certainly lose the loan. There's no money in theatre, unless you find the lead actress on reality TV or re-work a pop group's hits into a narrative that would embarrass a three-year-old.

Back in London Mary and I saw less of each other, but I still felt I had to keep her sweet, if only in gratitude for how she had unwittingly helped me out with Rosie. Ultimately, I hoped it would fizzle out completely into a simple friendship, which, I reassured my conscience, was all we'd really had anyway since I'd become manically Christian and decided I no longer wanted to fool around with her in bed.

'Maybe she was just using you all along, mate,' said Matt after we'd finished our golf round and were safely back in the bar.

'Using me?'

'Yes. For your body.'

'It is very possible.'

I sat back in the comfortable armchair at the nineteenth hole and took a deep swig of my gin and tonic. It had been paid for by Matt, who had been lent some money by Debbie, but still, it felt good.

'You know what, Sam?' said Matt. 'You look really happy.'

'You know what, Matt? I am. I'm no longer living a lie.'

'No, mate. You're living the dream.'

'Never say that again,' I laughed. But it was true. It did feel as though I was living the dream. Now that Max was out of the picture, and Mary was well on her way to joining him, I was able to devote all my time to Rosie. We had become inseparable, spending our time reading, eating, drinking, going out with her friends, having sex, talking about going travelling, talking about the future... Ironically, she didn't actually have very much money at all, despite the cut-glass accent, the nice clothes and the worldly confidence. The house was part-owned by her five siblings and her job didn't pay quite as well as I'd imagined. None of this mattered, though. It was Rosie I wanted.

Later that evening, Matt and I joined Debbie and Rosie for our first dinner all together. 'So, it's the two career girls and their workshy other halves,' joked Rosie after we had all sat down.

'Your better halves,' I said. 'You're looking at someone who's just got a part in *Richard II*.'

Matt stared at me. 'Mate, you didn't tell me this earlier.'

'Well, I wanted to tell Rosie first. She was the one who pushed me to go for the audition. Anyway, it's only a fringe venue and I'm just second spear-carrier or something.'

'A very lovely second spear-carrier,' said Rosie, kissing me.

'And how's *my* work-shy better half?' Debbie asked Matt.

'Exhausted,' he replied. 'Took Sarah to your mother's, cleaned the house, picked Sarah up from your mother's, took David to gym club, picked David up from gym club – '

'Okay,' said Debbie, laughing. 'We get the message. And where are the kids now?'

'Scrubbed, washed, handed over to your mother and tucked up in bed.'

'Well done, dear,' said Debbie, picking up the wine list.

Just before pudding, Matt and I arranged to visit the men's together at the same time, prompting ribald jokes from the girls about us going to check our teeth and gossip about them.

'Mate, Rosie is awesome,' gossiped Matt as we washed our hands and checked our teeth for spinach.

I thanked him while quietly thinking how much better I'd done in comparison. This was the first time I'd met Debbie properly and she'd already struck me as manipulative, bossy, and frankly a little bit boring. And how on earth could Matt put up with doing all those menial household chores, even if he did get to escape for an occasional surreptitious round of golf?

Still, I had learned my lesson about commenting on friends' girlfriends.

'And so is Debbie,' I replied as I dried my hands. 'Debbie is absolutely bloody awesome, too.'

Matt clapped me on the back. 'Hasn't this all worked out rather well?'

*

The only sadness in my new, perfect life was that I hadn't yet introduced Rosie to Alan. I thought they'd get on really well. Having someone I really cared about had made me understand him and Jess better. I wanted to tell him that. Most of all, I wanted to show him that the spreadsheet he'd made of my strengths and weaknesses the previous summer was both right and wrong. By 'pretending to be something I wasn't', I had indeed convinced a rich(ish), successful woman that I was an attractive catch. Ultimately, though, I felt I had done it on my own merits.

But there still hadn't been an opportunity for them to meet. Since Alan and I had made up, we'd gone for a clandestine beer on a couple of occasions when Jess was working late, but Rosie had never been free at the same time. Alan, I discovered, was on an even tighter leash than usual: Jess had seen my apology letter and wasn't very happy about any of it. According to her, I was an amoral scoundrel who didn't deserve to be friends with her fiancé. She had therefore given him a choice: me or her. Alan was never going to make that decision, so we'd had to conduct a clandestine friendship of whispered telephone calls, furtive emails and occasional stolen lunches, as if I were his mistress or unrecognised love child.

A kamikaze part of me really wanted to take Rosie along to Alan's engagement party at the end of February. He was my best friend; she was my girlfriend. Why couldn't they meet? But it was just too risky. I didn't know how Jess would react to her. She didn't even want *me* there at the party, let alone a random girlfriend who knew me as Max. My ex, Lisa, was good friends with both Alan and Jess, and would probably be there, too. Then there was Claire. Would she be nice to Rosie? Or would this weird thing of being rude to each other's boyfriends and girlfriends continue? And then what if Amanda turned up? No, she wouldn't be invited, surely. Still, none of it bore thinking about. There would be awkward questions about how Rosie and I had met, and so on. Much easier to introduce her gradually to the others at a less high-pressured occasion.

So I kissed Rosie goodbye that morning and said I would be home late because of a preliminary meet-up with the rest of the cast of *Richard II*.

I've never really thought much of engagement parties. They seem to be just one more excuse to put yourself at the centre of attention and make everyone else feel lonely and inadequate. Engagement parties are weddings-lite, with poor imitation speeches, cheaper wine and worse-dressed people. They last too long to be forgettable and not long enough to be enjoyably forgettable. Worst of all, it is almost impossible to get laid. Everyone is on their best – by which I mean worst – behaviour.

The only mild diversion is scoping out potential targets for the wedding itself.

At least that's what I used to think about engagement parties. But surely this one was going to be different. This one was Alan's. I was going to miss having Rosie on my arm, but otherwise it would be a collection of most of my favourite people, together in the same room.

My misgivings should have first been aroused when the gorilla on the door – it was a swanky bar in Embankment, within a stone's throw of Alan's office – produced the guest list, which had two columns: one for Jess's friends, the other for Alan's. The column that contained my name was a quarter of the length of Jess's. 'Sam Hunt' had been angrily scored out in red ink and, it would appear, equally angrily added in blue ink again at the bottom. I could only guess at what machinations had gone on behind the scenes.

'It looks like someone desperately wants you here and someone doesn't,' said the surprisingly astute gorilla, stamping my hand and admitting me into the cavernous downstairs bar.

As my eyes adapted to the low light, I could only make out people who probably weren't that keen on seeing me. Right at the bottom of the stairs stood Lisa. At first I pretended I hadn't noticed her, stooping to tie my shoelace, checking my phone to see if I had any messages and attempting to make it to the bar, all in one subtle, fluid movement. But she knew me – had known me – far too well to fall for any of these pathetic tricks.

'Sam,' she said. 'Hello.'

I tried to look surprised, but quickly gave up when I saw the pitying look on her face. We shook hands before realising this looked ridiculous and so had a kind of awkward hug instead, which looked even more ridiculous, so she turned the hug into a kiss on one cheek, whereupon I came back for a second cheek, which she hadn't anticipated and so pulled away, leaving me hanging like a mutant goldfish, attempting to nibble the air near her earlobe.

How *are* you meant to greet your exes? You can't exactly shag them hello, can you?

Lisa, however, didn't seem overly concerned with social niceties. 'Why did you never get back in touch with me after my text message last autumn?' she demanded, without further small-talk or air-nibbling.

Well, there were many answers to that question. One, as I have already mentioned, was that I didn't think it was fair for her to be jealous when she had moved on significantly more quickly than me. Another was that I was quite enjoying playing around with her friend at the time, partly to spite her. And the third – and most important – reason was that my life was far too complicated as it was without meeting up with Lisa alone. I had a sneaking suspicion that her marriage to Timothy James wasn't going all that well – he wasn't here with her tonight, for starters – and the last thing I wanted was to deal with the ex-sex that might have followed an encounter *à deux*. Ex-sex always seems like a good idea at the time – it's often the best idea ever at the time: all the excitement of an unexpected one-night stand with all the familiarity of someone who knows what you like – but all it does in the long run is re-open deep and festering wounds.

These were all truthful reasons, but I wasn't sure Lisa really wanted the truth so I simply lied and said that my phone hadn't been working very well. Lisa, it would seem, actually did want the truth, though, because she took my lame lie as an excuse to open deep and festering wounds of our own by revisiting our relationship, most of which was now over three years old, and mentioning every mistake I'd made. How could anyone have such a forensic memory, I wondered, as she pointed out all the bad things I had done and said, and all the nice things I hadn't done and said. This post mortem – made doubly painful by the fact I was still alive – came so out of the blue that I changed the subject by asking her about her marriage, which was also a mistake because it set her off on another tirade about how the whole thing was completely overrated.

'I think I've got bride depression,' she said, eventually.

'And what's that?' I asked wearily, hoping that this, at least, wasn't my fault.

'It's a new condition I've read about which affects newly-wedded women who put too much store on getting married. They plan the wedding itself for so long that they imagine married life to be an endless continuation of champagne, white dresses and dancing. Then reality bites and it's forty years of sharing the housework, fighting over the remote control and hosting joint dinner parties at which you embarrass, bore and infuriate one another in equal measures.'

I laughed, which made Lisa laugh as well. 'I'm sorry, Sam,' she said, touching my arm. 'I bet you're really glad you're not married to me.'

I shrugged. There wasn't really a right answer to that one. 'Yes' was too hurtful. 'No' was too dangerous. Anyway, there was a mountain of evidence – a ring, a wedding, a new name – to suggest we might just have left it too late. Fortunately, Lisa ploughed on before I had to say anything: 'And I'm glad I'm not married to you, either. No, it's Tim for me. Till death do us part. Preferably his.' She laughed again, falsely this time. 'No, I don't mean that. It's just that I still care about you, Sam. You're fun. You're nice, sometimes. And that's why I want you to be happy.'

'But you didn't want me to be happy with Mary?'

'I didn't say that.'

'You warned me off her when I rang to ask you about her. It comes to the same thing.'

'No, it doesn't.'

'Are you jealous?'

'A little.'

Ha, I thought. *I've made her say it out loud.*

She continued: 'But mainly I warned you off because Mary's a bit of a psycho.'

'How do you mean?'

'Well, she uses people. And she's a faker as well. I saw it on that course the vicar made us go on. You see, her father... '

Just as Lisa appeared to be on the verge of actually saying something interesting, I had to stop her. Over her left shoulder I could see Mary herself approaching, arm-in-arm with Stock Market Christian.

Stock Market Christian got to us first. 'Brother!' he exclaimed, embracing me.

'Brother?' I recovered quickly. 'Brother! What on earth are you doing here?'

'I was involved in a litigation case with Jess once and we stayed in touch.'

Jesus, it was a small world of objectionable people in London. Maybe this sort of thing could only happen at engagement parties, where a hundred people's complex lives all cram together into one confined space, living proof of six uncomfortable degrees of separation.

Stock Market Christian continued: 'I haven't seen you at church for a while, Sam. Where have you been?'

'Oh, you know, praying, meditating, fasting. Christ *is* the Church, you know, and not just *in* church. He is everywhere.' I placed my hand on my heart. 'He is here.' I placed it over Mary's breast. 'He is here, too.' Mary smiled sweetly. Stock Market Christian scowled so I placed it over his firm pectoral muscle as well. 'And here, too, of course.'

Lisa stood next to me, open-mouthed. 'Sam, what the fuck are you playing at?' she demanded, when she was finally able to speak. 'And don't even think about putting your hand on my tit.'

I lowered my hand and decided I'd had quite enough of Lisa's questions. All things considered, this was an excellent time to go to the toilet. Having kissed Mary chastely hello, I started to work my way through the crowd, leaving Stock Market Christian to explain to Lisa the biblical significance of the FTSE's downturn: 'We just have to pray extra hard that none of us is denied a bonus, even as Peter denied our Lord before the rooster crowed...'

I let the voice of hypocrisy fade out and focused instead on Alan, who was making his way towards me through the crowded bar, his arms outstretched in preparation for the biggest man-hug of our lives.

'Mate,' I said, because that was all that needed to be said.

He mumbled something back, his voice muffled by my shirt.

'I'm very glad you could make it,' said Alan after we'd held the hug a little too long and started to worry it might look a bit gay (surely, by the time you reach your own engagement party, you shouldn't worry about people thinking you're gay?).

'Wouldn't miss it for the world,' I said.

'And now you're here, I wondered if you might be able to say a few words later,' Alan continued. 'You know how Jess isn't that keen on having you here and so on, but if you were just able to say a few nice things about her at her engagement party, I'm sure it would make everything okay.'

I smiled and accepted readily. The night might have started with a haranguing from an ex-girlfriend, and a vaguely awkward encounter with someone in a category all of her own, but it was finally picking up. Matt and Debbie joined us and enquired about Rosie, whom Alan said he was still dying to meet. Ed arrived late, with Claire, and was met with much good-natured joshing about whether she'd had to unchain him from Downing Street's railings. I also chatted to Alan's mum for a while and told her that she should give her son a break. On the other side of the room, I could see Jess surrounded by a group of friends, smiling and laughing. I would say some very nice things about her, I resolved. I had got fairly good at lying by now.

At half past ten, when the room was well lubricated and the party in full swing, Alan handed me a microphone and I clambered onto the bar so I could see everyone. To my surprise, and slight annoyance, the first thing I noticed was Ed and Claire snogging in the front row. *What was that all about?* I decided to ignore them even though I could feel my face flushing. I had just started to say some pleasant lies about Jess – how we hadn't lost a friend but gained a new one – when I looked up and saw Matt's horrified expression. I knew that what I was saying was untrue, not to mention a little bit naff, but surely it wasn't *that* bad. I stumbled on with my speech and then looked up again. Matt wasn't looking at me. He was looking at the door. I followed his gaze. Rosie had just walked in, closely followed by Alan's boss, Amanda.

'Sam Hunt, you're a lying bastard!' shouted Rosie across the bar. She didn't need a microphone.

'I'm sorry.' I blustered lamely across the loudspeakers. 'We appear to have a heckler. Perhaps security could deal with them. Security. SECURITY.'

But neither security nor wild horses could stop Rosie. Even as fear gripped my stomach, I found myself thinking how magnificent she looked, full of righteous anger and feminine determination. I would never meet a woman like this again, I thought. I never deserved to meet a woman like this again.

'This man seduced me under a false name,' she cried out. 'He pretended to be something he wasn't so he could move in with me. He stole money in order to pay an invoice – '

'An invoice?' called out Mary from the middle of the crowd. 'How much for?'

'Five thousand pounds,' said Rosie.

'You lying shit, Sam Hunt!' shouted Mary. 'I thought you liked me. I thought you liked my family.'

The two girls looked at each other, momentarily unsure whether to fight each other or fight me, the lying shit. The sisterhood won. They started to push their way through the crowd, screaming hysterically, Mary brandishing her champagne flute as a weapon. In other circumstances, I might have been amused to see two girls fight over me. Not this time. This was dreadful. This was Rosie. This was Alan's engagement party.

I put down the microphone with a quick apology and started to make my way through the crowd. I had to get out of there. But the crowd didn't seem inclined to let me leave. They wanted me to get my just deserts. Part of me wanted me to get my just deserts as well. Cathartic punishment. Start from the beginning again. Do it right this time.

Or maybe the crowd just wanted to see a fight. Strong arms reached out to grab me. Someone – I swear it was Stock Market Christian – even threw a surreptitious punch. The fact it was an engagement party seemed to have been forgotten.

In the confusion, someone else had been forgotten, too. Making her way to the bar, Amanda picked up the microphone and tapped on it twice to check it was working. 'Hello and good evening,' she said. The crowd fell silent. Stock Market Christian stopped hitting me. 'I won't take up too much of your time,' Amanda continued. 'It would be nice to see you continue to lynch that man. He came to our office party this summer and behaved very naughtily, so I'm not all that fond of him, either. But if Sam's not up to making a proper speech, at least someone should.'

Everyone looked at me and then back at Amanda. She had clearly been drinking, but her eyes had lost none of their calculating intelligence. I had no more idea than anyone else what was going on.

'Anyway,' she continued, 'I think we're forgetting the real reason we're here, which is the happy couple, of course.' She gestured at Alan, who looked as white as a sheet. 'Now, I know Alan fairly well, having had the pleasure of working with him for the past few years, just over the road here. So I can safely say that Jess is a very lucky woman, not least because – '

'No!' shouted Alan. 'This isn't true. I won't let you get away with this.'

'What isn't true, Alan?' replied Amanda, calmly.

'I *knew* it!' yelled a tearful Jess.

Amanda replaced the microphone on its stand as Alan made his way up to the bar to grab it from her. 'Don't worry, Alan,' whispered Amanda. Her voice was no longer amplified, but those of us near the front could still hear her; the room stood in stunned, embarrassed silence. 'Jess will probably forgive you. After all, she'll have to forgive herself for last night.'

'And what's that supposed to mean?' said Alan, finally arriving next to her.

'Oh, Alan. Did Jess not tell you about Sam?'

Some people have recurring nightmares in which they're naked in the middle of a crowded street, or stuck in an examination room without knowing any of the answers. Mine used to be standing alone on a stage in front of a packed audience and forgetting all my lines. But ever since the night of Alan's engagement party, the only thing that can make me wake up sweaty and screaming in the dead of night is the vivid and horribly real recollection of what happened after Amanda said those words.

I tried to shout back my case, of course. It was one thing to face one's deserved, cathartic comeuppance, quite another to be accused, publicly and falsely, of sleeping with your best friend's fiancée. But it was all to no avail. Why should anyone believe me? I had hardly revealed myself to be a model of propriety that evening. Amanda's accusations were passed around the room in a rapid chain of Chinese whispers that didn't even need embellishing. The party descended again into a cacophony of shouts and chaos. At one point I remember catching sight of Alan's tearful face and realising that even he didn't believe me. All this must have finally made sense to him. *That* was why I had never got on well publicly with Jess, he must have been thinking. We were hiding our secret lust.

As for what anyone else was thinking, I'm really not sure because the rule of the mob had taken over. Drinks rained down liberally on my head. A few people shoved me. One tried to trip me up. 'Slag,' called out someone. Other shouts rhymed with my surname. 'I fucking hate you!' screamed Rosie, looking as though she meant it. 'You've got a tiny cock,' added Lisa for good measure, her face contorted with rage. If they could have buried me in the sand and stoned me to death, I think they would have.

Well, screw this, I thought. *Screw all of this. I'm done. I'm out of here.* And so I flailed and jostled and shoved my way out of that basement hellhole, out into the street above and past the astute gorilla on the door, who smiled apologetically, perhaps for failing so spectacularly to do his job, and asked if the people who desperately didn't want me to be at the party had won.

'Yes,' I said, ruefully. 'They appeared to be in the majority.'

He waved down a cab for me to take home. I climbed into it gratefully, before realising I had neither money nor home. The driver threw me out at the end of the street and I spent the night on a park bench, as remorseful as I was angry, as cold as I was completely and utterly alone.

Chapter Eighteen

I've had some long, dark nights of the soul before, but nothing that compared to that wintry park bench. By 3am I was worried that I might actually die. By 4am I was worried that I might not die. Every time I closed my eyes, I could see Alan's shocked, white face. The distant rumble of traffic became Amanda's low, mocking laugh. And whenever I remembered Rosie's look of righteous betrayal, I wept warm, uncontrollable tears of loss and self-loathing.

By the time dawn broke, cold, grey and forbidding, I had resolved to do whatever was necessary to sort out the mess I had created. This was not about my happiness any more, I realised. I'd tried to make myself happy, and look where that had got me. My happiness could go hang, for all I cared. No, this was about everyone else's. It was about righting wrongs. It was about apologising – to Alan, Jess, Amanda, Rosie, Mary, Lisa, Mr Money-Barings. There were so many apologies. And once I had said sorry – and meant it – to everyone I had ever met, I would give the clothes on my back to charity and go and live in a monastery somewhere for the rest of my days.

But it's all very well having good intentions – I've spent my entire life having good intentions – it's quite another thing to carry them out. I slumped back down into a frozen ball on the bench. Was this where it all ended, then? I had no money, no job, no home and, it seemed, precious few friends. My phone had beeped incessantly throughout the night with messages of foul abuse – much of it warranted – which provided me with a small, unexpected token of comfort. The more everyone chastised me for the way I'd behaved, the more I realised just how indefensible my behaviour had been. I bathed in their loathing and my self-loathing. I heaped their opprobrium on my own head and used it to subject myself to the fiercest of cross-examinations. What *had* I been thinking? Had I really believed such a deceit was sustainable? In what possible way was my behaviour morally justifiable? What had started out as a prank – a bet – had come to a disastrous end, hurting real people with real emotions. I'd once told Ed that it was all one big game; I was wrong. *This isn't a fucking play any more, Sam*, I remonstrated with myself. *This is real fucking life.*

On a selfish note, it hadn't worked out particularly well for me either, had it?

I could deal with the warranted abuse, then. They couldn't match me for that. What I couldn't bear was the torrent of bile for something I hadn't done. It offended me to the core that anyone – least of all my friends – could believe I'd slept with Jess. It offended me because she wasn't very attractive. But most of all, it offended me because I would never do that to Alan. I haven't even slept with any of my mate's exes (even when one of Matt's, who was a definite nine and a half out of ten, asked me to). I have strict rules about this sort of thing. Friends come first.

I got off my bench and started to jog around the park to thaw myself out. *What did Alan think?* That was the important thing. That was the crux of the matter. Did he believe what Amanda had said? *Surely he didn't believe a word of anything she said*, I thought, perking up as my brain started to thaw. She was an inveterate liar and manipulator. And if it wasn't true about his sleeping with Amanda, then he *must* realise that what she'd said about my sleeping with Jess wasn't true either. Surely he would see reason. Yes! I took out my mobile to call Alan. No! The abuse had overloaded the battery and it had given up the ghost. So I jogged for a solid twenty minutes until I managed to find a public phone box. Like the tramp that I was, I reversed the charges to Alan's mobile, the one number I knew by heart.

To my surprise, he accepted the operator's request.

'Sam?' said Alan. 'Where are you calling from?'

'My mobile's dead so I had to go to a phone box.'

Alan grunted.

'Actually, mate, you wouldn't believe how hard it is to find a phone box these days,' I babbled, skirting a little around the main issue. 'Everyone's got mobiles, I suppose. But at least you can still reverse the charges. I didn't know you could still do that, did you? After we've finished chatting, I'm going to try and get some Polish lessons, a part-time job in IT and a sensual massage with a happy ending.'

The line went dead. I tried again, via the same operator, who wearily put me through.

'Listen, Alan,' I said, hurriedly. 'I'm sorry, I've spent the night on a park bench, I'm delirious, I'm hypothermic, I'm nervous, I'm talking shit. But please don't hang up. None of what was said last night is true.'

His voice was flat, expressionless. 'It doesn't matter much if it's true or not, does it, because my life is ruined. Jess thinks I've slept with Amanda. She's left me. Whether she's with you or not, I don't know… '

The operator interrupted: 'Look, this is all very interesting, but this isn't a free call. If you don't accept to pay the cost, I'm going to have you cut you off.'

Alan laughed hollowly. 'Cut him off, then. After all, that's exactly what I intend to do. I'm sorry, Sam, I don't know what to believe any more. However, I have been thinking a lot all night and have come to the one conclusion I can be sure of: namely, you're a complete cunt and I never want to see you again.'

And with that, he hung up, leaving me to smash the receiver back onto its cradle and stomp angrily out of the booth. So *that* was what Alan thought. *What a prick*. Maybe he really had slept with Amanda. Ha! Well, then, this served him right. This served him bloody right. He had tried to have his cake and eat it, and now he was going to end up miserable and alone with no friends…

I stopped myself, suddenly aware of the irony. It was not for me to judge my friends. It was for me to forgive them, to understand them, even. Whatever Alan had or had not done – and I had always trusted him before – it was clear that he was happiest with Jess. It was fairly clear that he made her happy, too, however she chose to show that. The more I thought about it, the more I realised that Alan and Jess were the one constant I'd actually had over the last few years. Ultimately, I liked consistency, however much I tried to struggle against it. Girlfriends came and went. Friends, too. Matt moved in with Jewish princesses. Ed started kissing Claire at engagement parties. Lisa got married and became depressed. But through it all, Alan and Jess loved and endured. My mission of atonement slowly became clear. It was to make amends for ruining their engagement party by making sure they got back – and stayed – together.

*

Not that I had the first idea how I was meant to go about doing this. Until I had proved my innocence – or at least exonerated myself from a few of the more serious charges – no one appeared particularly keen to be seen dead with me. So much for a friend in need. Alan, of course, was out of bounds. Claire had probably joined the feminine chorus of disapproval. Even Matt found his loyalties to two of his best friends torn when I turned up at Debbie's house around lunchtime. 'I'm sorry,' he said, opening the door with a baby in one arm and a bottle of milk in the other. 'But I just don't think it's fair to Alan for me to see you at the moment. Plus, Debbie doesn't seem to think all that much of you, either.'

So it was that I found myself, at 3.30pm the same afternoon, hanging outside the rough secondary school at which Ed taught, feeling like something of a paedophile.

'What are you doing here?' demanded Ed when he finally

emerged from his classroom, looking fraught after a day of confiscating phones containing happy-slapping videos and trying not to get stabbed in the back with a kitchen knife while writing on the whiteboard.

'I'm grooming your pupils.'

He recoiled sharply before realising I was joking. *God, just how bad was my reputation?*

Pretty bad, I discovered, after I'd persuaded Ed to take me back to his shoebox for a shower and a bite to eat. The engagement party had, I learned, come to a fairly abrupt end after I'd departed for my open-air hotel. Amanda had slunk away, her moonlighting completed. A tearful Jess had exited quickly afterwards, pursued by distinctly un-teacherly shouts from Alan's mother. Meanwhile, Rosie had decided to suspend her non-aggression pact with Mary and poured a gin and tonic over her rival's head. Alan stepped in to check Mary was okay, at which point Stock Market Christian had lamped him one, prompting Matt to lamp him one back and a second near-riot had ensued. Apparently, it had been quite difficult to get back into the party mood after that.

Worse revelations were to follow when Ed logged on to Facebook and showed me a new group that had been created that morning called 'Sam Hunt is a cunt'. It was difficult to argue with the sentiment, but did it really have to have 372 members already? The group's description contained a rather inaccurate, badly written account of my recent adventures. Its creator, I noticed, was Alan Muir. Its two 'officers' were Rosie and Mary, united again in anger. As for the rest of the members, I didn't even recognise half of them. There was someone from Nepal on there, for fuck's sake. Was this the global village everyone kept on banging on about? The United Nations of Sam's cuntdom.

'Hang on, Ed,' I said, scrolling down a bit further. 'You're a member of this group as well. So why are you not being horrible to me, like everyone else?'

'Well, you *are* a cunt, Sam. But you're my cunt.' He laughed.
It did sound a bit anatomically ridiculous put like that. 'Plus, you
were good to me when I was in trouble. And I don't believe you
slept with Jess. But most of all, we brothers have to look after
one another when the chips are down, the claws are out and
violent women are attacking us, objectifying us and using us for
our bodies.'

'Hang on. You think that I was being used?'

'Yes.'

'Even though I lied to two women for their money, assumed
a false identity, pretended to be a born-again Christian in order
to get my hands on an elderly man's money and slept with an
older, attached woman I later ignored... *I* was being used?'

'Yes. They were all using you to get what they wanted as well.
Amanda wanted attention. Rosie wanted affection. Mary
wanted to get married so she could have a good shag at last. The
fact that you had to lie to get what you wanted shows exactly
how society uses men. We are expected to fulfil a certain
stereotype – to project a rich, successful, macho image – in
order to attract women.'

'I thought we weren't macho enough, according to your
ridiculous newspaper article.'

'No, *you're* not. You weren't, anyway. But when you became
what all men actually are – the shits that women secretly want
us to be – you were punished for it. And that, my friend, is the
problem with modern gender politics. No one knows how
they're meant to act so you're screwed either way.'

'Ed, I'm really not sure you can portray me as the victim. I'm
the cunt here, remember.'

Before Ed could share more of his illogical wisdom, we were
interrupted by the doorbell. He went to answer it while I waited
in his front room, straining my ears in an attempt to pick up the
faint murmur of hushed, urgent conversation. Eventually it fell
quiet, the door was shut again and I went out into the corridor
to see what was going on. There, only a few feet away, stood

Jess, the real victim in all of this. We both stopped and stared, a no-man's land of recriminations and history between us. And then, with slow steps, as if effecting an exchange of hostages, we walked towards each other until we were within touching distance, and she raised a hand as if to slap me before dissolving into violent, shuddering tears. I held her, awkwardly at first, then tighter, weeping too, apologising over and over again.

'I had no idea it would turn out like this,' I said, after we had cleared Ed out of the way and sat down on the sofa together. 'I'm sorry, I just don't think sometimes… I don't think most of the time… and well, this really was the last thing I wanted.'

'Me, too.' She sniffed and blew her nose again. 'Thank you for saying that. But I came to tell you that I'm sorry as well.'

'*You're* sorry?'

'I'm sorry for trying to take your friend away from you.'

'Don't be ridiculous.'

'I'm not being ridiculous,' Jess snapped. It was good to see her old temper return. 'I *was* trying to take Alan away. I was trying to take him away because I loved him and I worried he wouldn't love me back. I was trying to compete with the rest of you the whole time. And that's what I've now realised was ridiculous.'

I laughed encouragingly, which was a mistake as she rounded on me again. 'Anyway, you guys think you have it so hard, don't you? *There's too much choice to settle down just yet. My girlfriend traps me. I'm going to lose touch with my friends. I'll never be able to sleep with anyone else again.*' She reverted to her normal voice. 'Yes, I know what you talk about among yourselves. But please, don't think it's all that easy for women, either. We fall for someone, and we fall for them hard, but then we spend the whole time scared that they're going to string us along for eight years before running off with someone else once they've found their feet a bit more in the world. Because you can, can't you? Growing older is easy for you. You get better with age while twenty-five-year-old girls just stay the same. And meanwhile we're getting older, too, which means less attractive, as well as more familiar to you and therefore even less attractive in your eyes. No, don't shake your head. That's the fundamental difference between guys and girls, isn't it? The more we like and know you, the more we want to settle with you. The more you like and know us, the more you think, *To hell with this, I've nabbed her now, and if she likes me, I bet lots of other women will, too, so I'll go and get myself an upgrade until I get bored with her as well.'*

I stared at Jess open-mouthed. No woman had insight like this into a man. Was she a hermaphrodite? Had she tortured Alan to give up the inner workings of our psyche?

Jess took advantage of my surprise to continue: 'You know what the real problem is with men, Sam? You think a relationship is like a job interview – a one-off assessment at the beginning, after which you either get the girl or you don't. And once you think you've got us, you relax and don't make an effort any more. A long-term relationship for a woman, on the other hand, is a never-ending, performance-related, 360-degree appraisal. And it's one you often fail.'

Jess heaved a huge sigh, as if trying to shift the weight of the world from her shoulders. It didn't seem to work. She continued: 'Those are some of the stereotypes about men and women, anyway. The truth is that we think a lot like you as well. Has Alan been freaking out about getting engaged? Probably. But I can tell you that I've had a little freak-out of my own. I'm also worried about losing touch with my friends. I'm also worried about never sleeping with anyone else again. One day, if I forgive him for what he's done, and he forgives me for what I haven't done, we'll probably have children together. And how much do you think that will trap me? How much do you think that terrifies me? More to the point, how much do you think it annoys me that I'm going to have to spend most of the rest of my life competing with his bloody mother for his affections?'

'None of us exactly fits the male stereotype, either, do we?' I said, eventually finding my voice. 'Ed the suffragit. Matt the unmarried house-husband. Me... well, me. And in Alan you could not find more of a rock. You will never find anyone who loves you more than him.'

'Alan fits the male stereotype perfectly. He cheated on me with Amanda – a woman who is better-looking, more successful and a great deal thinner than I am.'

'Why are you so sure he cheated on you with Amanda?'

'I read the letter you sent Alan, and it all makes sense, doesn't it? Amanda blackmails Alan with his career and he's too weak to stand up to her. He also gets a final fling into the bargain. You heard what Amanda said at our engagement party.'

'It meant nothing,' I said. 'She's manipulative and a bit of a drunk. She was just winding him up.'

'I saw Alan's face,' said Jess. 'I know that look of guilty terror.'

'And I know that that look is just terror. Nothing more.'

'Nonsense.'

I shook my head vigorously. Jess continued: 'There's something else, too. After reading your letter to Alan, I wrote to Amanda and told her to leave him alone. As you know, I'm not the kind of person to let this sort of thing lie. Well, it was a fairly stupid thing to do, all things considered. After you'd been bundled out of my engagement party, Amanda passed me on her way out and whispered in my ear, "You must be Jess. Never think you can get one over me by writing such slanderous drivel. Oh, and by the way, your fiancé is a dreadful shag."'

'Well, there you go,' I said. 'You wound up Amanda and she decided to take it out on you.'

'She took it out on me because it's true: she's shagged Alan and wants to steal him from me.'

'Rubbish. I trust Alan. I always have done, always will. I know him better than you.'

Jess started to protest, but I continued: 'Anyway, this is more about me than him. Amanda is just a psycho trying to get back at me.'

Jess listened patiently while I told her the full story of what had happened at Alan's office party in the summer. When I got to the end, she gave a half-smile and said, 'So this actually is your fault, then, whichever way you look at it?'

I didn't have it in me to smile back. 'Yes. But I'm trying to make amends. Just tell me what I have to do to put things right and I'll do it.'

'The way I see it,' she said, authoritatively, 'is that the two of us finally have something in common: the fact that everyone hates us right now. But if we can work together to convince Alan we didn't sleep together then he might be persuaded to have the balls to convince me that he didn't sleep with Amanda. Then no one loses face and we all waltz off happily into the sunset.'

We stayed up most of the night on Ed's sofa – discussing how we would go about doing this, as well as talking about normal stuff: jobs, families, friends. It was a conversation we should have had years ago – eight years ago, to be precise. I had never got to know Jess, I had only got to know 'Alan's girlfriend': Alan's girlfriend who had taken him away from his friends; Alan's girlfriend who had kept him under the thumb; Alan's girlfriend who had never made much effort with us. I hadn't liked 'Alan's girlfriend' much. Alan's girlfriend hadn't liked me that much, either. But Jess? Jess, when I finally met her eight long years later, was very likeable indeed. She was a little bit brash for me – a bit brash, a bit fat, a bit posh, very much not my type – but she was funny and bright and so evidently perfect for Alan. Earlier that morning I had resolved to get Alan and Jess back together because I felt horrendously guilty, because it felt like the right thing to do to atone for all the wrong things I had done. By the early hours of the following morning, I had resolved to do it because I wanted to.

I used to be jealous of Jess having Alan to herself. A tiny bit of me that night grew jealous of Alan for having Jess to himself. If I'm honest – because no one would believe me if I didn't share this — my final, half-smiling thought before losing consciousness was how ironic it would be if, after all this, we had ended up shagging, right there and then, 'victims' both, on Ed the suffragit's second-hand sofa.

*

Somehow we managed to resist the irony, although it amused me that when Ed came downstairs for breakfast and saw the two of us wrapped up for warmth, and lack of anywhere else to go, on the same sofa, he sneered: 'No, Sam, you didn't, did you?'

I didn't reply for a moment, enjoying his look of shock.

'Don't tell me you've let another woman use you,' he continued. 'Have some self-respect, man.'

Fortunately, Jess laughed. 'It would be a pretty effective revenge, wouldn't it, if Alan had cheated on me with Amanda?'

Ed and I laughed, too, desperately hoping Alan hadn't.

'Would you?' I asked Jess, smiling.

'If you were the last man in the world, yes.'

I jumped off the sofa, stealing the covers, and performed a little victory dance.

'It doesn't mean I've forgiven you yet,' laughed Jess, her teeth chattering in the cold.

Still, it was a start and I was glad of the horseplay, for it was the last bit of entertainment I was to have for a while. The highlights of that Saturday morning included a further 587 people joining the Facebook group in my honour, three of them in Honolulu, and a phone call from the director of *Richard II* to sack me because another cast member had alerted her to the group and she was so horrified by my actions that she couldn't bring herself to work with someone like me.

'Aren't second spear-carriers allowed to be cunts?' asked Ed, sympathetically.

'Evidently not,' I said. 'Although I bet it was the third spear-carrier who shopped me.'

I didn't tell Ed how disappointed I really was. That job had meant a lot to me. It also felt like my one of my last surviving links with Rosie. Had it not been for Rosie's encouragement, I would never have come within an inch of being second spear-carrier.

I spent the rest of the afternoon desperately trying to get hold of Rosie on my freshly charged phone, but she clearly didn't want to talk. Mary wouldn't answer her mobile, either. 'I don't care about Mary, but you really have to get hold of Rosie,' urged Jess. 'We can't carry out our plan if you don't.'

All I actually wanted to do was to write a cowardly apology letter to both of them. A letter had worked with Alan. But no, Jess was right. The time for cowardice was over. I resolved to start with Mary, despite what Jess had said. Mary would be easier. Mary could start the ball rolling. I didn't care that much about her, but I did at least owe her an explanation. So I showed up outside the church in Clapham on Sunday in hope of forgiveness.

It came readily, but not in the way I had expected.

'Oh, don't worry about all that,' said Mary, taking my arm and unleashing a stream of consciousness as we strolled around the church grounds. 'I was fairly sure you were faking it, but Lisa said you were quite a laugh so I was willing to go along for the ride to see where it ended up. Not all of us want to get married straight away, you know. Some of us girls just want to enjoy ourselves and have a fling. Plus, you're the kind of guy who would get on well with Daddy so I thought, hell, if I have to marry a Christian eventually to please him then this one is more fun than the rest of them and looks like he might be some use in bed. But then you got all dreary and overly zealous, and so I was going to end it myself.' She broke off to wave at Stock Market Christian, who was revving his Porsche on the other side of the car park. 'Anyway, I'm with Jason now. It's a win-win, really. Either Daddy likes him and he gives up his job to live happily ever after with rich little me, or I give up my job and live happily ever after with fairly rich little him.'

'You're both faking it?' I asked, incredulously.

'Oh, no. I believe it sometimes. It's better than believing nothing, I suppose. And he *really* seems to believe it. Makes him feel better for being so rich, I guess. Either that or he's faking it to get into my pants. Who knows?' Stock Market Christian tooted his horn. 'Anyway, must go. No hard feelings. I hope it works out with that other girl. She seemed nice enough. Sorry about the Facebook group and the fighting and everything.' She kissed me goodbye, somewhere near both ears. 'Oh, but you'd better pay Daddy back at some point or he'll be livid. He's more of the "eye for an eye" school of thought.'

And with that Mary skipped across the car park, her long, elegant legs and glossy mane vanishing into Stock Market Christian's low-slung car, leaving me with the distinct impression that I had indeed been used.

Deciding that that was quite enough for one weekend – the confrontation with Rosie could wait for Monday – I went back to Ed's place, where he, Claire and Jess were sitting on the sofa discussing the only thing any of us discussed at that moment: the engagement party from hell. Jess still hadn't managed to speak properly to Alan and appeared unwilling to return to the flat they used to share and confront its memories. But at least Claire had finally decided to believe us, which I suppose was a start to winning back my friends. We chatted for a while – the same circuitous conversation about whether or not Alan had slept with Amanda – until Claire and Ed grew bored and excused themselves, leaving the two pariahs alone.

'So how did it go with Mary?' asked Jess. I hadn't wanted to share the scene outside church with the others, but I felt Jess had the right to know. We were in this together now.

'Oh, priceless!' She could barely stop laughing after I'd told her. 'You and Mary are as bad as each other. You actually deserve to be together. Oh, I wish I could have been a fly on the wall. Did it dent your pride?'

'Maybe Rosie was using me, too,' I said, ignoring her. I didn't think any of this was at all priceless. It was costing me a lot, in every sense.

'I doubt it somehow. I think Rosie actually loved you More fool her.'

'How do you know?'

'Because it was me who told her that your name isn't Max.'

'You did what?' I could feel the blood rising as, suddenly, it all became so obvious.

'Well, as you know, I read the letter you sent to Alan,' said Jess. 'I was so angry that you'd been rude about me to him, and then I read how you were stringing these poor girls along... Well, it made a mockery of how I see a proper, loving relationship. *How dare you criticise ours,* I thought, and yet treat your own so cavalierly. It made me so livid that I wanted to punish you somehow. I thought about it long and hard, and in the end I just couldn't stop myself. Rosie was clearly the one you actually liked. You mentioned where she worked in your letter. It wasn't very hard for me to track her down and send a warning email. I just didn't expect her to turn up in the middle of my engagement party... '

I wanted to scream at Jess. I wanted to yell in her face and call her a treacherous bitch who had wrecked my life. What right did she have to play moral arbiter? Who had asked her to poke her nose into my relationships? I'd loved Rosie. She'd loved me. It was all going perfectly well until Jess had got involved. I was phasing out the lies. I was slowly killing Max. I was seeing less of Mary...

But then I realised that much of this could apply equally to Jess and Alan. Who had asked me to get involved with their relationship? Who had asked me to complicate everything by turning Alan's boss against him? The difference was that Jess had never lied to Alan, had never given him a false name, had never two-timed him... If Jess could forgive me for what I'd done, surely I could forgive her for what she'd done? Who had she betrayed, ultimately? She'd been confronted with the fiancé's friend she'd loathed and an innocent girl he'd been using. It was an open goal. All things considered, she had actually acted quite honourably.

'I'm very sorry,' said Jess, quietly at last. She had been watching me apprehensively for a while. 'You really loved Rosie, didn't you?'

'You needn't be sorry.' I smiled at her – genuinely, I hoped. 'I would have been found out sooner or later. You probably did the right thing.'

'I always do the right thing.'

We both laughed.

'And as I always do the right thing,' she continued, 'I think I should point out that there is someone else in love with you as well. Someone who actually knows your real name – the real you.' She paused for dramatic effect. There was the sound of banging next door. Jess pointed at the wall with a smile. *What did she mean?* 'You appear to be oblivious to the fact, which is perhaps understandable given everything else on your mind, but two of your best friends are currently simulating wild, consensual sex next door in a bid to make you jealous.'

'Ed?' I said. 'Is Ed gay?'

'Oh, for God's sake, Sam. It's Claire. It's always been Claire. She's been in love with you since the day you met.'

Chapter Nineteen

Much like Christianity, Communism and birdwatching, the main problem with my masculinism campaign was that it attracted the wrong sort of people. I needed real men to join me, men who would put the masculine back into masculinity. Ironically, I needed the very people who were least aware of the campaign's importance. Instead, I attracted wimps, misfits and Neanderthals. The Suffragettes were lucky: they had the strongest of their gender on their side. We had the weakest.

Not that 'we' actually constituted very much. The email from Al in Earls Court, Australia, asking what I was going to do next, had struck a chord but didn't exactly provide any answers. What *was* I going to do next? Al from Earls Court and Ed from Hackney did not constitute a movement. If Al, or any of the others who had sent kind emails, were looking for a leader, I'm not sure they had found one in me. I set up an internet forum for discussion and even, on one disastrous occasion, organised a meeting in the pub. No one would let anyone else buy a round for them, as it was demeaning, so we mainly sat in awkward silence, our grunts occasionally punctuated by an arm wrestle or a rib-eating competition. Then a few people came back to my shoebox and watched porn. It was not a success.

I didn't stop believing what I had written in the article but, ultimately, I was just a dumped teacher with too much time on my hands. The main thing keeping the campaign going was that it was really annoying Tara, which in itself was worth its weight in gold. 'I wish you'd just come out as gay after I'd broken up with you,' she said, a little harshly, when she came round to collect some of her stuff. '*That*, I could have dealt with. *That* would have been much preferable to *this*. My colleagues are teasing me non-stop about what I must have done to you.'

Well, I knew what she meant. One of Matt's exes had become a lesbian after they'd split up, prompting endless mockery from Sam. But it was difficult to feel too much sympathy for Tara's treatment at the hands of her colleagues. Wasn't one of the older, richer ones treating her rather well? Far too well...

'Oh, come on, Ed,' said Tara, scrabbling the rest of her DVD box sets into a bag. 'Let's move on, shall we? There's no need to be such a cock about it.'

I gasped. 'How dare you use such a crude, anatomical term of abuse.' I wiped away a tear as I showed her to the door. 'I find your gender-specific swearing very offensive.'

'What? Co– ?'

'The c-word,' I interrupted. 'Don't say it. Don't even think it. It's the nuclear swear word. It burns my ears. It offends my soul as a man. I can't believe you would use such language. Away. Go. Just get out.'

And that was the last I saw of Tara for a very long while.

With my ex-girlfriend out of sight, if not out of mind – I saw her everywhere: in a walk, a laugh, a gesture, a favourite top – and plenty of time still on my hands before the start of term, I'd found myself persuaded by the others on the online forum to concentrate a bit more on the campaign. The *Guardian* gave me a small weekly column in the back of one of their unread supplements, in which I was able to expound some of my views at greater length. I wasn't sure I really had any views in addition to the ones I had already shared. 'Oh, don't worry,' said my friend on the paper who had got me into all this trouble in the first place. 'Just sit and stare at a blank screen for a few hours and something will come out.' Bizarrely, he was right: in great torrents of bilious prose I found myself espousing all sorts of opinions I'd never known I'd held before. Who would have thought I could be so opinionated? I discovered I had views on extending paternity leave to two months and allowing men to retire with equal pension rights to women at sixty. I proposed a National Prostate Cancer Month and free hair transplants on the NHS for anyone losing their hair before the age of forty. I even put on record my suggestion to create a Minister for Men, whose first act, I opined, should be to ban anyone without a penis from attending football matches.

'I thought you wanted me to be controversial?' I said, plaintively, to my friend when he called to complain about the storm unleashed by my football comment.

'There's controversial and there's controversial,' he explained. 'You were controversial.'

'You mean the kind of controversy that alienates half your readers is the wrong kind of controversy?'

'Precisely.'

The rest of the forum took the news of my sacking very badly. Al wanted to march down Whitehall and hold a rally in Trafalgar Square. I wasn't persuaded. Could a ragamuffin troupe of ten losers really be called a march? No, he argued, but we could burn our boxer shorts outside Downing Street. How would that help, asked someone else. It would be our equivalent of burning our bras, explained Al, provoking an interesting discussion about whether feminists had removed the bras they were wearing in order to torch them or whether they had carried a spare one for the purpose. Their laundry-day bras, perhaps. No one knew. We, of course, would have to carry a pair of boxers with us, as it would be a damned fiddly job taking them off while standing outside Downing Street. We might even get shot by the anti-terrorist police. 'Not if we wore our boxers outside our trousers,' suggested Al. 'That would make it easier.'

Needless to say, the great suffragits march never took place – much to my relief and, I think, that of my headmaster, who had been making increasingly anxious noises about my newspaper columns. 'It just doesn't fit all that well with your role as a teacher,' he'd told me, calling me into his study and peering at me over the top of the *Guardian*. What he'd really meant, of course, was that the kids would destroy me if they got wind of it. It was bad enough teaching a subject like English in a tough school like mine, but writing for a newspaper which wasn't the *Sun* on a topic that wasn't football... Well, it was a death warrant, if I ever succeeded in teaching any of my pupils to read sufficiently well to find out. I was too young – and too old – to die in a playground.

So I came back after the autumn half-term and gave up my part-time job as a journalist to concentrate on the comforting routine of school – a familiar comfort only marred by feeling the absence of Tara even more keenly now that she was no longer there in the evenings. It was the little things I missed most about being in a relationship. We used to laugh together over the illiteracy of the homework I had to mark. Now, every time something silly or interesting happened during the day I would start composing a text about it, before realising I had no one to send it to. That winter I realised that, deep down, I'd been kidding myself that the summer had just been an aberration, a temporary blip. Maybe, I had persuaded myself, Tara had succumbed to a bout of heatstroke and would see the error of her ways in the cool, calm logic of the months that followed.

But of course Tara did not come crawling back, begging for forgiveness and a chance to sit around again in our shoebox swapping jocular tales from my impoverished day. Tara, in fact, seemed quite happy crawling around her rich lawyer's penthouse on all-fours in his hard-earned lingerie, begging for another spanking (or whatever it is that depraved lawyers get up to in the rare moments they're not billing in six-minute slots).

There I go again: anger. But at least the cycle of denial, bargaining and depression appeared to be over. I had nothing left to deny or bargain over. And that, curiously, I found quite uplifting. So instead of drinking angrily in my new-found free time, I spent all my spare moments over the winter writing a play – a series of monologues, in fact – about the crisis of masculinity. I didn't need the *Guardian*, I'd decided. Who reads papers any more, anyway? This play would be my ultimate revenge on Tara: a carefully thought-out diatribe on the new breed of superbitch emasculating our menfolk. I didn't want to arm wrestle or hold rib-eating contests with people I didn't know. I didn't want direct action. I wanted revenge. More revenge. Political, academic, erudite, public revenge. Revenge, revenge, revenge. And that was a dish best served up cold on a stage – a medium for which I'd always wanted to write, but had never had the time.

I didn't have to go too far to do my research. There was my own history with Tara, of course, as well as the experiences of the people I'd met since the forum had begun. I'd also taken a keen interest in the activities of Sam, Matt and Alan. For me, all four of us represented different examples of masculinity in crisis. My plight was obvious: led on and ditched en route to the altar, doomed to spend the rest of my life on the shelf. Matt looked destined to become 'him indoors', the archetypal kept man. Alan, of course, barely had any autonomous decision-making power. Even Sam was unable to behave in the way nature intended, without being universally censured by an increasingly feminised society. I spent most of those long dark winter evenings alone, filling pages and pages with analysis and experience.

It was also during the course of the next few months that I started spending more time with Claire. When she first got in touch after my article came out, I felt a brief, unexpected flutter of excitement that it might be because she fancied me and had heard I was back on the market. Sure, I had vowed to be celibate after Tara left – sex is just another form by which women control men – but still, it's nice to be fancied every now and then. I had always quite fancied Claire. And once you've been single for a while, you begin to wonder if anyone new is ever going to find you attractive.

Sadly, though, Claire's main reason for making contact appeared to be so she could berate me for my deeply-held belief system. 'How on earth could you write such shit?' was, I think, the exact phrase she used. In her (rather blinkered) opinion, women still had a tougher time than men because they were paid less, aged worse, were less likely to be employed while young for fear they would take maternity leave, less likely to break through the corporate glass ceiling later on, and more likely to be a victim of sexual or domestic abuse. Worst, and most unalterably, of all, they had to suffer the agony of childbirth, menopause and period pains, which MEN COULD NEVER UNDERSTAND.

To our surprise, Claire and I actually understood each other very well the more time we spent together. It felt weird initially, because she was Sam's friend first and foremost, but we just hit it off. She had her opinions, I had mine, but we never let them get in the way of our blossoming friendship. She called me an anachronistic misogynist. I called her an anachronistic man-hater. And then we'd go out and watch plays together, argue about them afterwards and get drunk. I think we both respected the fact that the other actually had opinions, however much we enjoyed misrepresenting them. So when she confessed one evening in the new year that she had always been in love with Sam, I must admit that I had mixed emotions. Part of me was delighted for her; I even felt begrudgingly happy for Sam. She was just the sort of girl who would be good for him. But I also felt a twinge of jealousy. What about me? Why couldn't she fall in love with me? I had a job. I owned half the debt on a shoebox. I'd had a steady relationship in the recent past without assuming a false identity or two-timing a born-again trustafarian.

'Why Sam?' I asked, a little bluntly.

'Just because.'

And I knew what she meant. Everyone bloody loved Sam. *Fucker.* Why did he always land on his feet?

The trouble with her and Sam, Claire explained, was that

they were rarely single at the same time. And when it appeared that he was falling for this Rosie girl, Claire decided that this might be her last chance to get together with him before it was too late. Claire and Sam were already firmly in what she called the 'friend zone'. The downside, she explained, of our generation's fondness for having friends of both sexes was that it put a large number of potential relationships off-limits. Either you got together in the first couple of months of your acquaintance, or not at all. There was no romance in friendship, no sexiness. Claire's rather perverse logic, then, was that the best way of stirring the dormant passion in Sam's cynical alpha breast was to make him jealous. Show him that she had got together with one of his friends – one of her own friends – and he would question whether he, too, wanted the same thing.

'So, basically, you want to use me?' I summarised for her.

'Just as men have been using women throughout the ages,' she retorted.

'Just as all women use men now.'

'Well, maybe,' she said, smiling. 'Maybe not. But I bet it would make Tara jealous, too, if she thought you and I had got together.' Claire took me by the hand. 'Let's use each other, eh?'

So it was that I found myself kissing Claire at Alan's engagement party – not because I really thought it had anything to do with Tara, who probably couldn't care less, but because I had, despite myself, fallen completely for Claire. And when, a few days later, Jess and Sam were talking next door while Claire and I banged, screamed and thrashed around in a feigned sexual encounter that would have embarrassed a porn star, I swore to myself that I would not give up, would not let this lie, would not shirk from any tactic – noble, foul or downright illegal – until I was doing this for real with the fully-clad girl currently banging a golf club on my bedroom wall and urging 'big boy', whoever and wherever he was, to give it to her a second time.

Chapter Twenty

I've heard Alan and Jess having sex enough times to recognise the soft, muted sounds of a couple in the throes of passion. What Ed and Claire were doing next door, on the other hand, sounded distinctly like two friends banging a golf club on the wall while giggling a lot.

'Of course that's what they're doing,' said Jess, smiling. 'Claire doesn't fancy Ed or anything. She's just trying to make you jealous.'

'Well, she's not very good at it.'

'The fake sex or the jealousy?'

'The former.' I thought for a bit. *What did that mean, then?* 'Well, mainly the former. But then the two are mutually exclusive, aren't they, now you've told me? It's impossible to be jealous of fake sex. I don't particularly want to be there, in Ed's place, making stupid animal noises while my friend plays with his five wood. But watching her play with my – '

'Woah, Sam, don't even go there.'

I apologised. I'd forgotten that you had to install a filter between your brain and your mouth when talking to girls. Jess and I might have been getting on well, but still, she wasn't Alan.

Jess was a great deal more persistent, though. She kept on firing questions at me about Claire, forcing me to think long and hard. There was no getting away from it: the *idea* of Ed and Claire being together definitely did make me jealous. And I don't mean jealous in a selfish, dog-in-the-manger way. I wasn't worried about losing another friend. I didn't mind if everyone ended up happier than me. No, I was concerned about losing the *possibility* of me and Claire. And if that was the case, where did that leave me?

Well, shit. I swore silently. It left me with a fairly obvious conclusion, didn't it? Perhaps I did have similar feelings for Claire, whatever you wanted to call them. It wasn't the first time they'd surfaced, but maybe it was finally time to do something about them. I might not have 'been in love since the day we met', but I had certainly always adored Claire. I might not have fancied her as much as I did other girls, but I had always cared for her. I might not have wanted to sleep with her, but I had always wanted to spend time with her. And wasn't that more important? We got on. We had similar friends, similar interests. She made me happy. I made her laugh. We already knew each other. There were no surprises. We wouldn't have to go through the tedious cycle of getting to know someone new, followed by the inevitable disappointment after six months when you find out they're weird and then having to start all over again with someone initially more promising but, in retrospect, even worse.

Claire and I? Well, we didn't have to wait until thirty-five, did we? We could have an arranged marriage before then. Marrying Claire would mean that I could finally start thinking with my brain. I'd stop putting sex on such a pedestal. I'd stop screwing everything up. We'd grow old gracefully together. Sam and Claire. It had a nice ring to it, didn't it? I rolled it around my head, played with it, imagined it on artfully embossed dinner invitations. *Oh, yes, we must get Sam and Claire round. What a fun couple Sam and Claire are.* And it wasn't as if Ed would mind, was it? He was in on the joke with Claire. Anyway, he was Tara's for ever. Tara's and his masculinist forum's.

'What are you thinking?' asked Jess, eventually. The noise next door had stopped – hopefully Claire had more stamina when she wasn't using a golf club – and I suddenly realised I'd been sitting in contemplative silence for some time. I was on the point of answering when Claire walked in, looking flushed, and kissed Jess and me goodbye. I had just looked at her in a new light, I realised, as we listened to her drive away. She was really very pretty. She had decided to stand by me, despite everything. How right she was to consider me for a potential relationship! Girls were so much wiser than boys.

I turned to Jess. 'What am I thinking?' I repeated. 'I'm thinking this could all have a very happy ending.'

*

Not just yet, though. It was all far too soon after Rosie. Claire could be postponed until later in the year or maybe the year after that. It was nice to have the idea as a back-up. There was no rush. And in any case, I reminded myself, this wasn't primarily about my happiness any more. There were still mistakes to correct, apologies to make, couples to reunite. Maybe once that was all done, I could think about myself again.

On Monday morning I waited outside Rosie's office. I hadn't wanted to stalk her, but I couldn't see any other way of making proper contact. I had texted, rung, emailed, sent her a message on Facebook… She didn't want anything to do with me. It was time to resort to old-fashioned methods.

Sadly Rosie's methods were equally old-fashioned. When she first saw me, loitering with unmistakable intent outside her office, she shot me a brief, piercing look and continued on her way. She looked more magnificent than ever, I thought: that steely flash of wounded anger complementing the softer side I had known. I went after her and tried to put my hand on her shoulder. She shuddered at the touch. Finally, she stopped and faced me, a tear forming in the corner of one eye.

'Look, I don't want forgiveness.' I spoke very quickly.

'Good. Because you're not getting it.'

'I don't deserve forgiveness,' I admitted. 'I just want to apologise. And explain.' I tried to smile. 'Oh, and I need your help with something.'

Rosie laughed, despite herself. 'You need *my* help with something? After everything you've done?'

'It's not like that. It's about Jess.'

We went for breakfast in a greasy spoon opposite, where neither of us ate or even spoke much for the first few minutes; we just sat in silence, a ketchup-flecked table of issues between us. When, eventually, Rosie started to talk, it tumbled out in a single, violent torrent of cathartic abuse. I listened without interrupting. It felt like the least I could do.

Rosie, I learned, hadn't been after my perceived money, or my relative amusement value in comparison with other, more genuine born-again evangelists. She hadn't been using me to make a friend she fancied jealous. She hadn't done anything nearly as base as everyone else seemed to be up to. She had genuinely and absolutely loved me, in all her vulnerable innocence. She had loved me more as myself than as 'Max'. She'd preferred the unemployed actor to the banker-cum-dreadful-entrepreneur. So I hadn't just messed up something promising; I'd destroyed something great, something potentially very beautiful indeed.

'So, really, I owe Jess one,' she concluded. 'Were it not for her warning, it's possible I would have stayed with you for a very long time.'

'Why?'

'Because I completely fell for you, you stupid prat. I fell for you, and that was the biggest mistake of my life.'

'Why?' I asked again, even though I already knew the answer.

'Because you're obviously an utter shit.'

I winced and got up to leave. I didn't want to hear any more painful truths. I'd reached the door before I stopped. I hadn't come for me, I reminded myself as I sat down again, I'd come for Jess. And Rosie had said she owed her one. There was a glimmer of hope. I bit my tongue and gently prompted Rosie as she went on to say how guilty she felt for wrecking Jess's engagement party. She hadn't known there would be an engagement party there, of course. She'd had a few days off work recently, so Jess's email alerting her to the fact that I was an utter shit had been read at an unfortunate time – on the day of the party itself. Rosie had thought she'd find me in that bar with my new *Richard II* friends. Once there, she hadn't meant to cause a scene; she was so livid that she couldn't help herself. She hadn't meant to interrupt the party. She hadn't meant to throw her drink over Mary's head…

'No, really,' I said, remembering Stock Market Christian's Porsche outside the church. 'That bit was fine. Mary deserved it.'

Rosie laughed, involuntarily, before remembering how cross she was meant to be with me. Her face turned again to its now default expression of withdrawn pain. 'So, anyway, if there's anything I can do to make it up to Jess, just tell me and then you'll never see me again.'

I reminded her how, thanks to Amanda's insinuations, Alan thought I had slept with his fiancée the evening before his engagement party. If Rosie could just tell Alan that it wasn't true, everything would be okay. He would believe it if it came from her. Rosie so obviously hated me that she had no incentive to lie. Rosie would be a very believable alibi.

'Fine,' she agreed.

'You're a wonderful person,' I said, moving my hand across the table to take one of hers.

'I'm not doing it for you.' She withdrew her hand as if it had been stung.

'I know. You're doing it despite me. And that's what makes you wonderful.'

She half-smiled. 'Oh, Sam, you know the tragedy with you?'

I shook my head. Most of my life felt like a tragedy at that point.

'It's that you're so full of good intentions, and yet it all boils down to complete bullshit.'

I murmured a quiet agreement. It was horrible to be found out like this.

'But at least you appear to have realised that fact,' she

continued. 'So I'll do this for Jess. And for your friend, Alan. He sounds a whole lot nicer than you.'

I agreed that Alan was a whole lot nicer than me.

'Then he deserves to be happy,' said Rosie.

I picked up her coat. 'Shall we go then?'

'Now?'

'Yes.'

'Fine,' she said, snatching her coat out of my hands. 'Suits me. I'd like to get this over with as soon as possible. As far as I'm concerned, the moment at which I never have to hear from you again can't come too soon.'

I started to protest then caught myself and stopped. I'd promised Rosie an explanation, as well as an apology, but there wasn't really any explanation, was there? *Darling Rosie, I'm sorry for pretending I was someone else, but you see, I was scared about getting older and being lonely, and also I had a bet with my friends that I could nab a rich girl and I didn't have the confidence to do it on my own merits so I thought I'd stick with the name of Max. Plus, I'm sorry about that other girl, the born-again nut-job, Mary, but I was hoping to use her to finance the lifestyle to which you thought I was already accustomed. That's not to say I didn't really like you…* Well, no, it wouldn't wash. 'Each man kills the thing he loves,' as Oscar Wilde wrote in Reading Gaol. 'The coward does it with a kiss. The brave man with a sword.'

I was a coward.

We spent the journey to Alan's office in silence. 'What now?' asked Rosie, when we emerged from the underground and stood outside the huge, glass-fronted building.

'Now?' I replied, taking a deep breath. 'Now we sort this out.'

We walked into the atrium, our footsteps echoing across the marble floor, and approached the reception counter. 'Would you be good enough to tell Alan Muir that his friend Matt Lewis is downstairs to see him?' I announced, sounding more confident than I felt.

The girl called up his extension while we sat down to wait. 'How many names do you have exactly?' hissed Rosie.

I ignored her. I was composing a text message to Jess: 'Stage one complete.'

Two minutes later, Alan appeared at the security barriers, swiped himself through and looked in vain for our friend.

'Matt?'

His eyes settled on me in a gaze of pure loathing. They flickered briefly at Rosie, registering an equal amount of confusion.

'Sorry, mate. I wasn't sure you'd come down for anyone else.' I grabbed his security pass and pushed him towards Rosie. 'Now, *finally*, I can introduce you: Rosie meet Alan; Alan meet Rosie. She'll explain.' And before Alan or anyone else could stop me, I'd swiped myself through the barriers and lunged into the relative safety of the lift. I sent a second text to Jess.

The lift soared upwards. I knew where I was going: the sixth floor. I'd been there before, to screw Amanda sideways. Now I was going there to undo all the awful consequences of screwing Amanda sideways.

I walked down the long corridor, past the rows of head-bowed workers, past the photocopier I had hidden behind with my trousers around my ankles.

The door to Amanda's office was open. I could see her working through a pile of accounts at high speed with a red pen, another one clenched between her teeth. I took a deep breath and went straight in, closing the door behind me.

'What are you doing here?' Amanda registered a brief flicker of fear before reverting to her more usual sardonic drawl. 'Good engagement party last week, wasn't it? Sorry we didn't get a chance to chat.'

I bit my tongue. It was vital I kept my cool.

'Now, now, Sam,' she continued. 'I'm sorry it got a bit out of hand. I didn't mean it to end like that. But I did warn you last summer not to mess around with me. I warned Alan, too, when he answered back in front of the rest of my team. I warned that fat fiancée of his when she wrote me a threatening letter a few months back. You don't screw with Amanda. I'll always win.'

I threw my arms open in a gesture of surrender. 'Fine, we give up.'

Amanda smiled. I smiled back and decided to take a punt in the dark. 'You know, Amanda, I really wish I'd seen you again after last summer.'

'Really?'

'Yes. It was quite an experience. I'm not sure anything has come close since.'

Amanda leant back in her chair and allowed another self-congratulatory smile to play around the corners of her lips. 'I knew you'd see sense eventually.'

'How do you mean?'

'No one ever sleeps with me just once without trying it again.'

'Even Alan?'

She laughed. 'Alan? Hell, no. He wouldn't even sleep with me once, poor lamb. His loss.'

'Indeed.' I checked again that no one could see us and moved closer. I had the first confession, but I needed more. 'Well, Amanda, to the victor, the spoils. I'll give you what you want, if you promise to stop being nasty to him.'

'I don't get it,' she said.

'No,' I said, within touching distance now. 'But you're about to.'

She laughed raucously. It was not a nice laugh. 'Oh, Sam, you ridiculous little man. Do you really think you can just walk into my office in the middle of the day and seduce me?'

I recoiled, blushing a little. It had been going quite well until then.

Amanda continued: 'You don't really think I was that bothered about you, do you? It was just a fuck at an office party, for God's sake. And not a particularly good one, if I'm honest.'

I pretended to look crestfallen. I didn't have to pretend too hard. It's not very nice being told you're a below-average lover by an Amazonian fortysomething with enough experience to know what below-average means.

Amanda softened a little. 'Oh, Sam, don't look so sad. It wasn't that bad. I mean, I've had worse.' She thought for a moment. 'I don't know when, but I'm sure I have at some point. And if you'd like to give it another go some time, then it might be fun. Maybe don't drink so much this time… You're a nice enough boy, and I suppose you did me a favour by getting rid of my ex for me.'

I stammered: 'So you weren't punishing Alan at work because I hadn't got in touch?'

'Is that what you've been torturing yourself about?' Amanda laughed. 'God, you've got a big ego. And has he really been complaining to you about me being "nasty" to him? *Pathetic.*' Her laugh suddenly turned into a frown. 'Anyway, even if I had been a little harsh on him, why would you want me to stop? Alan hates you, doesn't he? Thanks to me, he thinks you've shagged his fiancée. Why would you want to do something nice for him?'

'Old time's sake. Anyway, I imagine you've been running rings around him, haven't you? Give the poor guy a break.'

Amanda chuckled to herself. 'Well, I admit it has been a lot of fun. And he deserved it. Most of it, anyway. He was getting cocky and needed putting in his place.'

'I'm sure he did. So what kind of things have you been doing to him?'

'Oh, just winding him up, really.'

'Like what?'

She looked at me suspiciously. 'I don't know why you're so interested.'

'Go on, tell me. I like a good, humiliating story as much as the next person. Especially now that you've humiliated me. And it's not as if there's much love lost between me and Alan these days. I'd feel guilty if you were punishing him because of me. But now that I know you're not, it would amuse me to know what you've been doing to him. Alan and I have as good as fallen out over that fat fiancée of his. They hate me even more than they hate you.'

Amanda relaxed back in her seat. 'Well, I suppose there's no harm in telling you, given that you're no longer proper friends. I told him he would get sacked if he didn't sleep with me before his wedding.'

'Sacked?'

'I never really meant it, of course, but it's kept me amused on slow days.'

'Hilarious.' I focused hard on keeping the sarcasm out of my voice. 'It must have been quite a laugh.'

'Oh, yes, you should have seen his scared little face.' Amanda smiled – unpleasantly – at the memory.

I laughed encouragingly. *Keep going,* I thought, *just keep her going.* 'I can't believe he resisted you, though. What did you do to the poor kid?'

'Oh, you know, silly stuff. I'd pinch his arse in client meetings or stare provocatively at his crotch when he got up to go to the toilet.'

I roared with fake laughter. 'Brilliant!'

'And whenever we've been away on business, I've pretended there's been an overbooking and we've had to share a room. We even made him dress up as a Chippendale at the Christmas party.'

'A Chippendale! Priceless!'

Amanda sighed. 'The only shame is that Alan never really rose to the bait. He's too boring, I suppose, to do anything interesting, and I eventually got bored of the game as well. But then I heard him tell someone that his engagement party was just over the road so I thought I'd drop in and call a truce. I thought you might be there, too, and we might even have a little repeat performance to see if you'd improved at all in the meantime. But I didn't expect to find quite so many other women after you… Anyway, I was never going to say anything scandalous and then suddenly Alan started denying everything when there was no need and it all got out of hand… Hang on. Sam? Sam? Where are you going? Shall we do lunch? Am I going to see you again?'

'I'll see you in court' was the answer I wanted to give. I'd been waiting to say a line that good most of my adult life. But most of all, I just wanted to get out of there as quickly as possible. I tore out of Amanda's office, past Alan's startled colleagues, past the photocopier, down the corridor and into the lift. Once the doors were safely closed, I took my phone out to call Jess but there was no need. She had trusted me enough to pre-empt news of the successful completion of stages three and four. As the doors opened into the lobby, I looked through the glass walls of the office, out into the street, and saw Alan on one knee in front of Jess, as Rosie looked on at a discreet distance, smiling faintly. I ran towards them, but Rosie had vanished by the time I'd got there, skidding onto my knees beside Alan and asking Jess if she would, please, for the love of God, marry my best friend.

At some point in the laughing, crying, undignified hug that followed, I caught sight of Amanda, standing in what I later discovered was the same place as, six months previously, she had glimpsed Jess about to propose to the employee she had been harassing ever since. This time, however, we were all on our knees, all asking, all saying yes.

'Just one more thing,' I said to Alan, taking my mobile out of my pocket again and stopping the recording. 'You might find this useful.'

Chapter Twenty-One

For the next few weeks, I bathed in a glow of self-righteous happiness. So *this* was what it felt like to be a good person. *This* was what it felt like to do good. Good things happened to good people. Although Alan was back with Jess, they had both decided it would be better to live apart until they got married, which meant I could live with Alan again in the meantime. It was just like old times, only better in one key respect: I no longer felt the need to vanish every time Jess came round (which was often) to leaf through wedding brochures and argue over which variety of dove to release at the reception. Now Jess and I could barely get enough of each other. We had in-jokes which even Alan didn't get. A lesser man might have minded; Alan just beamed from ear to ear whenever Jess and I made each other laugh, happy that his two best friends had finally hit it off. 'My barrister and my barista' – as he referred to us in one of his wittier moments.

I didn't even feel particularly guilty about duping Amanda in her own office. She had played on Alan's insecurities for her own amusement and almost destroyed him in the process. She had bullied Jess and wrecked their engagement party. Worst of all, she was on record as being under the mistaken impression that I was a below-average lover. So, frankly, she deserved whatever she got – whatever that might end up being. Alan still seemed unsure of his next steps. He had played the recording through a dozen times, chuckling and frowning to himself in equal measures. But that seemed as far as he wanted to take it for the time being. Amanda left him in peace now at the office. Jess had the evidence she needed to believe him. Maybe that was all he had ever wanted.

In any case, it wasn't my business any more. There was a sense of relief that I hadn't been the root cause of *all* the trouble, but I still blamed myself for being the catalyst. It was big of Alan to forgive me – once again – and I didn't want to push him to take any further action. It was his career, not mine.

Talking of which, I felt it was time to address my own non-existent prospects, which took a peculiar turn one day in March when Ed approached me with the script of a one-man play he had written called *The Cock Monologues*.

'*The Cock Monologues*?' asked Matt when I met up with him at Debbie's for the first time in what seemed like ages to share this disquieting news.

'Yes, it's all part of Ed's masculinism nonsense.'

'Ah. And there I was thinking that it was because you're a cock.'

I laughed, almost convincingly. It was good to see my friend – especially as Debbie was out with her youngest, Sarah – and hear his dreadful jokes again. Matt hadn't completely vanished from the radar since the engagement party fiasco, but he'd made his disapproval fairly clear. We had a bit of patching up to do. We also had a lot of catching up to do, especially on the Debbie front, where it appeared that the unemployed doctor who had beaten me on the bet to 'live the dream' was actually stuck in the middle of a waking nightmare.

'Where do I start?' he said, leaning back against Debbie's kitchen counter and wiping a fleck of child vomit off his shirt. 'Where can I possibly start to explain the sheer tedium of being a kept-man house-husband to a working woman you're not married to and a pseudo-father to two young children who are not yours?'

Once he'd got over the difficulty of starting, Matt found it equally difficult to stop his list of complaints. Many of them focused on Debbie herself – I *knew* I was right about her – but it was the more systematic ones that really stuck with me: the sense of shame he felt as the only man waiting outside Tumble

Tots; the boredom of having no one to talk to during the day; the guilt of fancying the Ukrainian cleaner who came round twice a week; the loneliness of knowing no one else in a similar position. Most of all, his lack of tangible achievement made him feel entirely useless. He was a man, dammit. He needed something to measure success by. Frankly, I told him, he needed a job.

'Speak for yourself, mate,' said Matt with a snort.

I didn't really have an answer to that. I've always given expert advice; rarely taken it.

'I mean, where's my sense of worth?' Matt continued. 'On a good day in medicine, I'd send a few people home alive. Some were happier than when they came in.' He rubbed the stubborn vomit stain on his shirt again, making it worse. 'On a good day now, I get through to the evening without changing my clothes more than once. Or opening more than one bottle of wine while doing the ironing.'

There was a sudden piercing scream from next door, where David, Debbie's four-year-old, had been quietly watching cartoons. Matt ran through to see what was the matter. I followed at a discreet distance and observed him valiantly attempting to comfort a howling, terrified little boy, who seemed to have been scared by something he'd just seen on television. Matt was a natural – not that David seemed to appreciate it.

'I hate you,' he wailed. 'Not my daddy. Want Mummy. Hate you. Want Mummy. Not my daddy. Hate you.'

I beat a tactical retreat to the kitchen and waited for Matt to quieten him down. Pre-school nightmares were not my forte.

'Actually, mate, I could do with some help,' called Matt, summoning me back next door.

Between the two of us, we managed to divert David with magic tricks, war games and an indoor game of football, which cracked a window, until he decided he wanted to watch some more cartoons and promptly fell asleep. Quite frankly, I could have done with a sleep myself after all that.

'Jesus, mate, do you do this every day?' I asked, when we flopped back into the kitchen and made another cup of tea.

'Quite a few days, yes. It takes its toll.'

I looked at Matt more closely. He didn't look his best, it was true. His handsome face had lost some of its confidence. He looked bowed, beaten even. 'What about Debbie?' I asked. 'How's it going with her?'

'Oh, I don't know. She's seriously high maintenance.'

I nodded. All blokes know what high maintenance is. High maintenance is bad. We want low maintenance. Low maintenance but high performance. A high maintenance girl is like owning an expensive sports car. She looks great but she knows she looks great. She goes like greased lightning, but you have to polish her ego constantly. She regularly blows a gasket if you don't handle her with care. Leave her out in the cold for too long and she won't even start. Stay with her long-term and her value starts decreasing exponentially. Plus, there's a high chance some other poor sod will come along and nick her without realising just how high maintenance she is.

'Do you love her?' I asked.

'No.'

'Can you imagine that you might love her?'

'I don't think so.'

'Then get out,' I said. 'Get out while you still can.'

'Really?'

'Yes. *Physician, heal thyself.* You don't owe this woman anything. And you owe it to the children not to get too attached to you.'

Matt laughed bitterly. 'That doesn't seem to be a particular danger with David. But still, he's a pretty cool little guy. I'd feel guilty leaving him.'

'Listen, mate. You can't stay with someone you don't love just because you're a nice guy. Maybe you once liked Debbie, but you clearly don't any more. The bet's over. It was a stupid idea. Let's get on with our lives. Anyway, you'd be doing her a favour. Believe me: prolonging the inevitable only makes it worse.'

'I believe you. You're the expert at screwing up relationships.'

I laughed. It was good to know that there were times when it was okay to speak out honestly to your friends. Perhaps Matt and Debbie were still in the window-of-opportunity phase.

'What about you?' he asked.

'Me?'

'Yes. You and Rosie.'

'Sadly, there is no me and Rosie. There was only "Max" and Rosie.'

'She won't forgive you?'

'Nope. I think there are some things you learn to tolerate, forgive even, in a relationship: flatulence, nose-picking, infidelity – '

'You're right, there are worse crimes than infidelity,' agreed Matt. 'Indifference, for example.'

'Yep. I'd rather a girlfriend slept with someone else than didn't bother to make an effort with me. But pretending to be someone else in order to get into a girl's pants? No, I think we've passed the point of no return.' I shrugged. 'Anyway, there's someone else… '

Matt listened while I shared the conclusions I'd reached about Claire: that it was worth giving it a shot, that it was the easy, logical solution to my troubled, wandering heart. He listened carefully, without interrupting, and then told me, very directly, very bluntly, that I was making the biggest mistake of my life. 'You were honest about Debbie,' he said. 'So I'm going to be honest about Claire. You can't just turn a friendship into a relationship at the drop of a hat, especially when you don't even fancy the person in question.'

'I think I might fancy her after all,' I said. 'Anyway, nothing ventured, nothing gained.'

'This is one venture you should not attempt.'

'But now's the perfect moment,' I said. 'Claire's been made redundant so she's going to direct me in *The Cock Monologues*. If I don't mention it to her now, I'll spend the rest of my life thinking of her as the one that got away.'

'Don't say I didn't warn you… ' Matt started to say. But before he could share any more of his dire warnings, his mobile rang and he was summoned to fetch a high-maintenance single mother and her baby from the swimming baths.

*

Ed's play was obviously a rip-off of *The Vagina Monologues*. Or at least it was meant to be. Sadly, it fell between two stools – neither particularly insightful nor particularly funny.

Apart from my evident suitability for the title role, I don't think I was Ed's first choice, to be honest. Of our little group, we've probably been the least close. Plus, I think he mainly wrote it so he could spend more time with Claire. The two of them had become good friends and he wanted to give her something to do while she lived off her redundancy pay and looked around for another way to earn a living. Every other actor had sensibly turned down the script, even the desperate ones who hadn't worked for years. Yes, they would be 'the star' – the only star of a one-man show in an unconfirmed venue with a script penned by an emasculated, campaigning madman… So no, on balance, they'd probably be better off sticking to their day jobs in WH Smith.

I think Ed had only asked me, then, out of polite desperation, and probably in the expectation that I too would say no. If so, he had grossly underestimated my own desperation.

In the end, four things made me accept the part. One was the opportunity to spend time with Claire. To a lesser extent, I also wanted to help out Ed. Another was that I had signed on to a new temping agency, which had reminded me just how horrible office life was. And the fourth? Well, bizarrely, it had something to do with a combination of Mr Money-Barings and Rosie.

Rosie had been surprisingly kind since the day she'd helped me get Alan and Jess back together. We hadn't seen each other again – her promise had stood firm – but she had been generous enough to close down the 'Sam Hunt is a cunt' Facebook group before it gathered any more members from Nepal or Nebraska. She'd also said she'd spoken to her company's accountant who'd agreed to return half the fee for the Max House account, given that the work hadn't actually been carried out for me. They would chase Max for the rest – wherever he was now – and pocket my remaining £2,500 in return for dropping any legal charges against me. What legal charges, I had asked. Don't worry, we'd think of something, Rosie had replied. Like what, I had said. Like impersonating someone richer than oneself and being a dick, Rosie had replied. Oh, I had said.

The upshot was that I still owed Mr Money-Barings £2,500, in addition to my other credit card debts of five times that amount. Mary had kindly forwarded me several of her father's letters, which had left me in no doubt that he was not about to forget his loan. I had written back to apologise, beg even, but sadly his favourite part of Old Testament scripture did indeed appear to be the bit about an eye for an eye, and not the verses in Exodus, Leviticus and Deuteronomy that aren't so hot on money-lending. That money was going to have to be repaid somehow, and the only way I could think of raising any extra cash in a short period of time was to take on Ed's play. A musical about The Prodigal Son it wasn't, but it would have to do. Mr Money-Barings wrote again, agreeing to give me another couple of months.

I had a contact who ran a shabby pub theatre in Islington. I'd helped him get a part in a fairly sought-after production in Edinburgh a few years back and he still owed me a favour; he agreed to rent out his theatre at a slightly reduced rate. If we sold out for three weeks, and Ed was feeling generous, I could just about afford to pay Mr Money-Barings back.

So it was that I found myself sitting in a rehearsal room with Claire on our first read-through of the script of *The Cock Monologues*. I'd got about as far as page four before flinging it down on the floor.

'It's a bit rubbish, isn't it?' agreed Claire.

I nodded glumly. It was a bit hurtful as well. On reading it more closely, I noticed that a lot of the scenes contained thinly veiled references to some of my recent antics. It was as if the author had deliberately tried to make me look bad.

'Hang on,' I said. 'Why did you agree to direct this, if you thought it was rubbish?'

Claire blushed and tried to stutter something about having time on her hands. But I had rumbled her. However much she went on about 'helping Ed out with something he cared about' and – her biggest lie of all – 'feeling guilty after ending their little fling', this was the point at which I knew Jess had been right about Claire's feelings. It certainly explained why she had been so off with me ever since that glorious night at the opera.

'I just thought it would be fun to spend some time working with you,' she said simply. 'Just like the old days.'

And then I had the decency to blush as well.

Claire was right, though: it was a lot of fun, especially after we'd decided that the only way to make the play work was to take the piss out of it. Somewhat stupidly, Ed had left the rehearsal period entirely in our hands. Normally you can't keep writers away from rehearsals. I've worked on a few productions in which the director has deliberately given the writer false times and venues in a bid to stop them making a nuisance of themselves. Ed, however, spouted some rubbish about not wanting to spoil the creative link between the star and the fourth wall, assured us he was looking forward to the first night and went back to school, leaving us to it.

'It', in this instance, turned out to be putting a slightly more comic twist on everything poor Ed had written. *The Cock Monologues* (his working title was *The Penis Monologues*, but that had already been staged, apparently) was meant to be a serious reflection on the state of masculinity today, each monologue mirroring the original vagina-oriented version. So we kicked off with 'My angry cock', in which I was supposed to rant 'humorously' about the injustices wrought against my penis, and indeed 'penii worldwide' (Ed was a finicky teacher and, in this case, a wrong one, as *penis* is a third-declension noun, like *tigris*, and therefore the plural, if you want to be a pedantic cock, is *penes*), such as condoms and the tools used in STD check-ups. Another shamelessly plagiarised monologue was called: 'I was twelve and a half, my big brother caught me at it because I forgot to lock the bathroom door' and was supposed to refer to that charming adolescent moment when you first realise that the function of this strange organ between your legs isn't limited to urination.

It didn't require too much imagination to turn any of this nonsense into something a little more entertaining. The thin line between satire and seriousness is only a question of tone, and Claire and I have never been very good at serious.

While we did indeed have a great deal of fun in those rehearsals, it could never be 'just like the old days', as Claire had promised. The old days were gone for good. These days, Claire banged golf clubs on the wall while simulating sex with Ed in a bid to make me jealous. These days, I told all our mutual friends that I wanted to go out with her and they – and especially Jess – spent the whole time trying to nudge us together. There is nothing like the pressure of trying to live up to the vicarious expectations of your friends.

The new days often conspired to make things very awkward indeed. There would be a moment, an awkward pause in conversation, a flirty comment or glance which, in the old days, Claire and I would have laughed off or ignored, but now had to consider in the new light of what we both knew the other one knew we knew but hadn't yet expressed, either verbally or physically. If Claire had been a new person I'd just met, it would have been easy. We would have gone on a date and it would have been obvious that we were crossing into new territory. But how do you cross into new territory with someone when you have already visited most of the territories together beforehand? Maybe Matt was right: you can't date a friend. You can't leave the friend zone once you're in it. Dinner with Claire wasn't a dinner date. It was a way of replenishing lost calories. Neither could I – or more accurately, neither did I feel I could – simply take her hand one afternoon in the middle of a professional conversation about spot-positioning and stage-left exits and say, 'Sod this. Kiss me now, Claire, or a bit of my soul dies for ever.'

No. What we needed to do was to get uproariously drunk and just 'do it'. Then we'd wake up the next morning like a happy, familiar couple in the eighth year of their relationship, but still with all the exciting novelty value of new sex.

Simple.

In retrospect, I can see that sharing this plan of action with Claire might not have been the most romantic gesture.

Jess, my new sounding board on all things girl-related, was completely against it. 'Do you not understand women at all?' she demanded, somewhat unnecessarily.

At the time, however, my plan made perfect sense – to me, at least. I was frustrated at the rate of change, frustrated by the frustration, to be honest. Claire was my friend. We could talk about this like grown-ups, couldn't we? A conversation would be the catalyst.

So, in the final week of rehearsals, I finally summed up the courage to ask her where we stood.

'Clairewheredowestand?'

'What?'

I didn't normally gabble when I was asking a girl out. I repeated myself, so slowly that I sounded like the talking clock: 'C l a i r e, w h e r e d o w e s t a n d?'

'I know you're the star of this show, but there's no need to start using the royal "we",' she replied in her new director's voice. 'But if you're asking about the first line of the third monologue, then the answer is that you should be standing in the second spot, downstage right.'

'No, no. Where do we stand in general?'

She laughed, nervously. 'Well, if you're on the escalator, you stand on the right. If you're on the platform edge, you stand behind the yellow line. If you're at the post office, you stand in line. If you're – '

'No.' I cut her off. She was gabbling far worse than me. I suppose she must have seen where this was going. 'I mean, where do we stand, you and me?'

'Oh.'

I studied her face for clues, but it betrayed nothing. She said nothing. She wasn't planning on making this easy for me. I took a deep breath and continued: 'Because obviously we've known each other a long time and we get on really well and I like you a lot and I think you're pretty and stuff and maybe you like me too, I don't know I think you do, but there's this great big wall of sexual tension between us making things awkward and neither of us wants to bring it up or spoil it by talking about it and you're probably waiting for me because I'm the man, but the whole friend thing is making me unexpectedly nervous and we're both thinking what if it didn't work out would we still be friends and I think we would and, anyway, it will work out as we get on so well… '

I stopped for another breath and then tried again more slowly: 'What I'm trying to say is that the best thing is probably just to get really drunk one night and see where it takes us.'

Claire's inscrutable features finally broke into a smile. 'My mother always told me I'd be swept off my feet with a big romantic gesture like this,' she said.

'Really?'

'No, you idiot. She didn't.'

After that inauspicious start, the 'big conversation' improved slightly. Claire, it transpired, felt a similar cocktail of emotions to my own, really – confusion, affection, fear. There was 'definitely something there', we agreed. It would be 'a shame not to explore the option further'. It was 'difficult to know how to kick it all off'. We sounded like two bankers discussing an investment opportunity. This semi-excruciating encounter finally concluded with a rather prim peck on the lips and an agreement to go out for dinner after the opening night of *The Cock Monologues*, drink until we could no longer remember our own names, let alone each other's, and then fall into bed, fall in love and live happily ever after.

Simple.

Five minutes before the first curtain, I was crouching backstage, vomiting the single Dutch-courage gin and tonic into the small basin in the corner of what might loosely have been termed my dressing room. I gripped the wall for support and dragged myself slowly back to a standing position, surveying in the mirror the reflected debris of a hundred forgotten productions: a discarded wig, laddered tights, a Sellotaped running order. Outside I could hear the murmur of expectant voices. I looked at myself in the mirror again, checked my make-up and tried to pull myself together. Tonight was important. Tonight was what I did; who I was. I'd forgotten how much I loved and feared and missed the dreadful, toe-curling excitement of going on stage. And then later… Well, we'd come to later, later. That was the right way – the only way – to deal with later.

Claire popped her head round the corner of the dressing room. 'It's a full house,' she said. The tension showed in her smile.

'What? You mean we've sold all fifty-five seats?'

She laughed. 'Yes. And I think we know fifty-four of them between us.'

'Shame. I'd much rather die on my feet in front of strangers.'

'Nonsense. Go knock *them* dead.'

No one died in the first part of that evening – either on stage or off it. It was, Claire assured me afterwards, a triumph. I had to be told, because I could scarcely remember any of it myself. Some actors are acutely aware of an audience. They hear every programme rustle, every cough. They can't help but notice the unsmiling faces of the first row and the great emptiness beyond. But when it's going well for me, I vanish into a kind of trance. And this went very well indeed. I was only truly conscious of where I'd been when the house lights came up and I was standing exhausted in the spotlight, receiving a standing ovation from fifty-four people I knew.

'Just so funny,' declared Matt when I joined the others downstairs afterwards.

'I loved the skit about the perils of going skinny-dipping in cold weather,' said Alan.

'You would,' said Jess.

'Oi,' replied Alan, laughing.

'My favourite was the monologue about male changing rooms,' said Matt.

'You would like that bit, King Kong,' said Claire.

'How would you know?' I said, a little jealously.

'No, seriously, Sam,' said Alan. 'Funniest thing I've ever seen. You were brilliant.'

'Nothing to do with me. I'm just the talking prop. Ed here is the real genius.'

'It's not really supposed to be funny... ' Ed started to say, before shrugging and tailing off. He was enjoying the plaudits as much as I was. We all decided to stay in the pub downstairs to celebrate a successful opening night. The critics were in the following evening and they might not be as generous as fifty-four acquaintances. Painful past experience had taught me that it was best to enjoy the preview period while it lasted.

We settled in at a table downstairs, where I had drink after drink bought for me and basked in the praise. It's surprising, really, that more actors aren't egomaniacal alcoholics. You get up late and spend the evenings as the centre of attention twice over – once on-stage, and again in the pub – as everyone plies you with beer and tells you how wonderful you are.

One person, however, didn't think I was wonderful at all.

'You really are a cock,' said Ed when we found ourselves alone briefly the wrong side of midnight.

'Thank you, Ed. I'm a method actor and I like to inhabit the role I'm portraying.'

'No, I mean it. You *really* are a cock.'

Away from the others at last, Ed went on to nit-pick the bits of the monologues Claire and I had changed. He didn't feel we'd reflected the seriousness of his art; we'd debased the high tone of his campaign, etc. But it was clear there was something else on his mind. He'd seemed happy enough earlier when everyone was praising his artistic genius.

'Come on, Ed,' I said. 'What is it really? Is it Tara?'

He shrugged. 'Yeah, I guess. Partly. I really wanted her to turn up and see this. But she's on holiday or something.' He took another huge swig of his beer. 'But also, it's about Claire.'

'Claire?'

I listened as Ed explained how he had fallen for our friend. How he'd met up with Claire alone in the evenings. How he had felt threatened and overshadowed when the three of us were together.

'So, essentially, you're a cock,' he concluded. 'I only put this stupid play on to spend more time with Claire. And then you went and got in the way by saying yes to my token offer to act in it, when you were supposed to say no.'

Well, perhaps I should have been more understanding, and

told Ed that we shouldn't fight over a girl, let alone a girl who was also a friend to both of us. But Ed had riled me. I'd stopped his bloody play being a complete disaster, hadn't I? He was far more of a cock than me, in fact. At least I'd been straight up about the whole Claire thing. I hadn't been banging golf clubs on walls.

'Cock yourself,' I replied, maturely.

'Cock you.'

'Cock off.'

Ed unleashed a primeval roar and grabbed me by the shirt. Maybe he had run out of cock-based insults.

'Look, what do you expect me to do?' I removed his hands from my shirt. 'Quietly step aside for you? Throw in the towel? You can't just put a "reserved" sign over someone if your friend also likes them.'

'Why not?'

'Because that's not how it works. Anyway, isn't this Claire's decision?'

'I don't see what Claire has to do with it,' said Ed.

I laughed, before realising he wasn't joking. 'Mate, I've already told her how I feel. Plus, she feels the same and we're going to have sex tonight.'

'You what?'

I explained our arrangement.

'Fine,' said Ed. 'In that case, I challenge you to a drinking contest. Last man standing gets Claire.'

'I don't think Claire wants you, Ed, standing or not.'

'Shut up, Sam. A drinking contest.'

'Why not just challenge me to a duel, you cock? Or shall we just get them out and measure them?'

'Shut up. A drinking contest.'

I accepted, if only to shut him up myself. Quite frankly, I couldn't see any other way of getting rid of Ed that evening. And so it was that I found myself standing at the bar, the evening of my first theatrical performance in eighteen months, throwing shot after shot of tequila down my throat with one of my oldest, but least loved, friends in a bid to ascertain who would get to sleep with one of my oldest, and most loved, friends.

Tequila is meant to make you happy, if you believe the song. But it didn't. It made Ed throw up. And it made me horribly, unhappily drunk. The others put Ed in a taxi and went home themselves, leaving me and Claire looking coyly at each other across an empty bar. This was it, then. I had won. Here was my prize. *Congratulations.*

'How are you feeling?' said Claire, moving closer and taking my hand.

I gazed unsteadily into her eyes. 'Ready.'

But I wasn't ready. Far from it. I wasn't ready when Claire started to kiss me, and I felt no more emotion than when we'd done something similar at drama school all those years ago. I wasn't ready when she rubbed up against me like an affectionate cat, purring, nuzzling and occasionally breaking off to scratch my neck in what I think was supposed to be an erotic, feline gesture. And I certainly wasn't ready when she reached into my trousers during the taxi ride back to hers and started quoting lines from the play we had been working on for the past three weeks.

'Is Mr Postlethwaite pleased to see me...? Oh, hello, Mr Postlethwaite... Anyone at home... ? Where is my great big angry cock?'

I played along as much as I could, quoting the lines back at her, laughing as we tumbled semi-naked along her hallway and into her bedroom. Yet even the laughter didn't seem to help Mr Postlethwaite, who was on strike, partly thanks to the tequila I had had to drink to get to this unhappy stage, partly thanks to Claire's bizarre notion of foreplay.

Mr Postlethwaite was finally persuaded to salvage some degree of pride by his owner thinking of his ex-girlfriend Rosie, allowing Claire, who would never be my girlfriend, I now realised, to mount Mr Postlethwaite like a rabid banshee on heat.

'Oh, Sam,' she moaned, gathering steam.

'Oh, Claire,' I moaned, rapidly losing steam.

Oh, Claire, I really meant to say. *What has happened to us?* What has happened to me? Why am I lying here on my back, squinting drunkenly up at my steam-gathering friend whom I don't fancy in the slightest? Why am I so scared of being alone that I thought this would be some kind of solution? The truth was that I was never going to be ready. Not now. Not with Claire. Not with anyone. *I am not a swan.*

'Oh, Sam,' she moaned again.

'Oh, Claire,' I echoed, my eyes tightly closed. Just a few more minutes and we could forget the whole thing.

'Oh, Sam.'

'Oh, Claire.'

'Oh, Sam.'

It was a different sort of moan this time. Not a good moan. 'What's wrong?' she said.

I stopped abruptly. 'Everything. Absolutely everything. I'm so sorry.'

'Don't be,' she said, rolling away and leaving Mr Postlethwaite to die a thousand deaths. 'Everything is wrong for me, too. I'm just a whole lot better at faking it than you.'

We lay companionably in her uncomfortable bed, talking and laughing as couples do, but in every way not a couple. Claire asked if I was gay, because I clearly didn't fancy her. I asked her if she was a lesbian, because she clearly didn't fancy me. She punched me slightly too hard on the arm and we agreed that we would be better friends to each other from then on, even though we both knew it would never be quite the same again. We had crossed a line and there was no coming back, however much both of us wanted to retreat.

At 3am, just as we were falling into an uneasy sleep, my phone rang.

'Ignore it,' mumbled Claire, sleepily.

At 3.01am, hers went. Then mine again. Then hers.

227

I picked hers up.

'It's me,' said Alan, his voice almost unrecognisable with fear. 'I'm at A&E with Ed. Please come right away.'

Chapter Twenty-Two

'Just ignore it, Alan,' muttered Jess, turning in her sleep.

It wasn't the first time that Ed had called us in the middle of the night. When Tara first dumped him, he would often ring at strange times, knowing that I would provide a friendly ear for his drunken angst. Then, as his new campaign gathered pace, the calls dried up and Jess and I enjoyed our sleep uninterrupted again. You cannot indulge your friends for ever, we reasoned. Surely Ed realised that.

So when the phone went this time, at 2am after the first night of his play, Jess and I were probably both thinking 'here we go again'.

But thank God I didn't ignore it. Something made me pick it up – the same instinct which prevented me from drifting back into confused slumber when all I could hear at the other end was heavy, raspy breathing followed by the sound of the phone being dropped and the line going dead. Something told me this was serious.

I flung on some clothes and opened the door to Sam's room. He must have gone back with Claire, because Matt was sleeping in his bed.

'Quick.' I shook his covers. 'Wake up.'

Years, however distant, of night-time practice on medical wards had left their mark. Matt was dressed and in my car within ninety seconds. As we tore across town to Ed's flat, there must have been twice the legal limit of alcohol in my blood, yet I had never felt more sober in my life. Matt called Ed again and again en route, but there was still no answer. Fearing the worst, we double-parked outside, rang the bell, thumped on the door and eventually got in by breaking the same kitchen window as the last two burglars to loot his flat. Ed was lying on the sofa, still fully dressed, his phone in one outstretched arm, a packet of pills in the other. On the table, next to a half-empty bottle of vodka, was a handwritten note: 'To my friends'.

'Bollocks to that,' said Matt, screwing up the note with one hand and checking for Ed's pulse with the other. He nodded grimly, cleared Ed's airway and lifted him as if he were a small child, Ed's limp arms looped round his broad shoulders.

'Get the car,' he commanded, picking up the pills with his spare hand and checking the label. I had never seen anyone so completely in their element. 'We've got about fifteen minutes to get him to a hospital.'

The next day, when Ed felt well enough to talk a little about what had happened, he confided that he had no idea why he'd called me. His mind had been made up; the note written; the pills taken.

'I suppose there must have been a bigger part of my subconscious wanting me to live than wanting me to die,' he reasoned.

But I'm not really sure how much reason came into it. Ed had been trying too hard to *reason* everything. He'd tried to reason how Tara had dumped him; tried to reason how she'd moved on. He'd searched for meaning in Sam and Matt's silly little games and attempted to rationalise everything in a play. But, in truth, there was neither rhyme nor reason in what he had experienced, merely emotions, some understandable, many not. Ed was an emotional man, not a rational one. He had been through a break-up that, for him, had been worse than a divorce, even a bereavement. He needed time to let these emotions run their course. Then he would understand.

He smiled at me as I stuttered my way through some of these thoughts. 'I'm sorry,' he said for the thousandth time. 'I really am. I'm still not sure why I called you, but I'm glad I did.'

But was that enough? Would he still be glad the next week or the week after? We were all very shaken, especially Sam, who was in a terrible state, blaming himself for everything. However much we tried to cheer him up, he knew as well as the rest of us that the catalyst for what had happened was his ill-advised night with Claire. Out of respect, none of us ever read Ed's note, but we knew what it would have said. It was Tara who had destroyed Ed; Sam and Claire, however unwittingly, who had reminded him of just how much damage she'd done. Ed could neither move on, nor backwards, which was where he actually wanted to go.

I was there when Sam and Claire arrived, ashen-faced, at Ed's bedside at 4am the first morning. They were still there three days later, taking it in turns to keep vigil. On the fourth day, I visited after work, interrupting a conversation that appeared to have been a competition over who could apologise the most.

'It was *so* selfish of me,' said Ed.

'So selfish of *me*,' protested Sam.

There was an awkward silence while I hovered by the door, unsure whether or not to join them.

'So, how's the play?' asked Ed at last.

'The play? We're hardly going to carry on with that while you're… ' Sam trailed off, lamely, gesturing at Ed: the hospital bed; the drip still in his arm; the nurse who popped in every twenty minutes to check he wasn't about to do himself any more harm.

Ed sat up bolt upright, pulling one of the drips out of his arm. 'Sam, if you and Claire don't keep on doing that play, I'll bloody well try to kill myself again.'

'Ed – '

'No, don't "Ed" me. You two can't just stop because of this. Listen, I'm going to be all right, okay? I promise. Don't worry about me. Worry about yourself, and what will happen to you if you don't worry about yourself. You've got talent in abundance. We all saw it that night.'

'I thought you hated what we did to it.'

'I was just jealous. Anyway, I barely believe a word of what I wrote any more. Masculinism isn't really in crisis; just some men. A lot of men, perhaps. Me, in particular. But not all of them. You and Claire... Well, you actually turned my drivel into something quite good. Something amusing, occasionally even thought-provoking. So, for God's sake, grab this chance and make something of your fucking life.'

It took a suicidal teacher whom he'd never really liked that much to finally put a stick up Sam Hunt's arse. After a hiatus of five days, *The Cock Monologues* re-opened to triumphant reviews. 'Hilarious', thundered *The Times*. 'Seriously amusing', roared the *Daily Telegraph*. 'Very funny... ', said the *Independent*, although the quote emblazoned across the publicity material forgot to mention that the dot, dot, dot stood for the omitted qualifier: ' if you have an IQ of room temperature and a mental age in single figures.'

Regardless, the play transferred to a bigger theatre and helped make Sam's name, and to a lesser extent, those of Ed and Claire. Sam earned enough to pay back Mr Money-Barings and rediscovered his old belief that happiness had very little to do with money and a lot to do with finding something you enjoyed and doing it well.

Ed, meanwhile, pretended not to mind being upstaged by Sam yet again. 'You can't get much more beta male than this,' he said to me on the night *The Cock Monologues* opened in the West End. 'I write a play to get the girl, and then my friend steals both the girl and the play.'

'Ed, you do realise that the girl at least is still up for grabs?'

He stopped re-reading the programme and swung round to face me. 'Then why the hell didn't someone tell me?'

'Dunno.' I shrugged. 'We thought – '

'You thought I was still hung up on Tara and preoccupied with trying to kill myself?'

I shrugged again. That was exactly what we'd all thought. It was exactly what we all continued to think, to be honest, however much Ed protested that he was all right and we shouldn't fret about him. He seemed to cheer up as the days got longer and warmer, but of course we still worried as he continued to live alone in the flat he'd bought with Tara, and which she refused to let him sell because of its rapidly mounting negative equity. We worried about him because he was our friend. And if we didn't, who else would?

In the end, it was Ed's continuing instability that gave me the idea to revisit the situation with Amanda. My first instinct had been to let sleeping dogs lie. I'd enjoyed her comeuppance as much as Sam had appeared to (her amusingly withering critique of his technique aside). It certainly gave me useful leverage over her in the office, as she had been nothing but cordial to me ever since. But most of all, the incident made me happy because it meant I had Jess back. I didn't want to dredge up a miserable period of my life.

But then in April my company announced that there would be another round of redundancies in our department and Amanda turned vicious, back-stabbing anyone and everyone in a bid to shore up her own position. The rumour was that she would keep her job while the other two directors – one male, one female, both with children and both a great deal more able, and more pleasant, than her – would lose theirs. They didn't deserve that, and I wasn't enjoying my own job very much any more. Suddenly, I had a plan.

'What do you think?' I asked Jess, after explaining it over breakfast one morning. I sat back and braced myself for the response.

'What do I think?' she replied, disarmingly softly. 'I think it's a very brave decision. And if it's what you really want, I will support you every step of the way.'

I choked on my cornflakes. I wasn't sure when I had last made a decision, let alone a brave decision, or one that Jess had actually supported. That morning I walked to work for the final time with my head held as high as a prizefighter.

*

Three remarkable, stressful, glorious months later, I eventually got what I wanted out of Amanda and my old firm. Thus emboldened, I summoned up the courage to discuss with Jess the rest of the idea I'd been slowly formulating. Again, I had been expecting a huge row, but she was surprisingly supportive, all things considered, and only queried a few of the details. My life had become a whole lot easier, I reflected, since Jess had come round to my friends, a date had been set for our wedding and I had finally found the right moment to present her with an engagement ring of her own, on a holiday in Istanbul in May. I suppose she thought she'd got me now, not that she'd ever not had me. A ring. A date. A dress. A pliant best man. A boss who's no longer sexually harassing you. It's funny the little details it can take to convince some women.

Just one thing, then, still left me in any doubt: would this crazy notion actually work? Would the four of us actually get on after all these years? I decided that my stag weekend would be the test.

'I just want to do something simple,' I told Sam, whom Jess had finally agreed could be my best man – slightly to Ed's disappointment, I think. 'Not too many people. Nothing too expensive. No strippers. No shaving. No paintballing. No go-karting. No forced drinking. No nightclubs with hen parties. No Easyjet flights. No kidnapping. No shooting sheep with grenade launchers. No elaborate games. No video evidence. And absolutely no karaoke.'

'Don't worry, Mr Yes-Man,' said Sam. 'I'm sure you'll like it.'

'You better look after him,' Jess warned him. 'Or I'll hunt you down and kill you.'

Sam laughed. He knew Jess had forgiven him long ago. 'Don't worry,' he retorted. 'I'm sure we'll be much better behaved than your hen weekend.'

'That's what worries me,' said Jess. She turned to me. 'And, darling, if they do take you to a strip club, for God's sake, man-up and enjoy yourself.'

Not every groom takes well to being told to 'man-up' by his fiancée, but it was nice to know Jess had my back.

In the end, we didn't take an Easyjet flight anywhere. Sam's organisation was a great deal more imaginative than that. I was woken by three masked men in dinner jackets at 6am, dressed, blindfolded and bundled into a taxi. When I was allowed to look, I found myself at St Pancras station, about to board the Eurostar to Paris for a weekend loosely themed around James Bond. After checking in to the most central hotel we could afford, we spent one hour in the Louvre and fourteen hours in nightclubs and casinos. We drank and partied and laughed and argued. We ate good food and drank good wine; we hired fast cars and argued and laughed all over again, twenty-five years of history behind us and, I believed, for the first time in a while, a fairly good future ahead of us, too. I was getting married to a girl I loved. Matt was retraining as an A&E nurse while working locum shifts. Sam and Ed were beginning to find their feet, if not their hearts. A new chapter, then, was opening in all our lives, but we didn't need to close the old ones quite yet, either.

The second day of our long weekend also happened to be Sam's thirtieth birthday – a landmark he had been dreading reaching before the rest of us. Yet the day itself found him in remarkably good humour, bouncing fresh-faced into the hotel breakfast room, full of wise saws and modern instances.

'Thank you, children,' he said after we had finished our hungover chorus of 'Happy Birthday'. 'In view of my new-found maturity, I'd be grateful if you could address me as Mr Hunt from now on.'

'*What a cunt*, more like,' said Ed, pouring him some coffee. 'That's what we call you behind your back, anyway.'

'No one ever calls me Dr Lewis,' complained Matt.

'That's because you're only twenty-nine,' said Sam. 'And also because you're now a big gay nurse.'

Matt threw a burnt sausage at him, which Sam caught and stuffed in his mouth.

'Mr Hunt,' I said, taking advantage of the lull. 'Didn't you tell us at Lisa's wedding last summer that age wasn't linear? Yes, I distinctly remember you saying that Ed had a long-term girlfriend and a mortgage, making him at least thirty-three.'

'True,' replied Sam, spooning more food onto his plate. 'But now Ed has neither, making him twenty-three once again. On the other hand, he is balding worse than ever, which puts him back up at twenty-nine. I, by contrast, have the physique of a twenty-five-year-old, the liver of a forty-year-old, the wisdom of a tribal elder and the let's-pretend job of a toddler, all of which averages out at a nice, round, contented thirty.' He pointed at me. 'Although on reflection, Mr Muir, that is approximately half your actual age, now that you're on the verge of getting married and therefore never having sex again in your life.'

'And when did you last have any action, Sam?' I said.

Sam blushed momentarily. I tried not to show how much I enjoyed noticing it. It was rare for me to get one over him.

'Last night,' he blustered, regaining his composure.

'Liar. Who with?'

'Christine. The waitress in the last bar we went to.' He took out his mobile and showed us a picture of him with his arm around a girl who looked like a Gallic version of Rosie. '*La fille est belle, n'est-ce pas? Comme les fraises des champs.*'

'Is that actually what you said to her?' asked Ed scornfully.

'Nope.'

'So what did you say?' asked Matt.

'I said, *Je voudrais un Barcardi and Coke.*'

'And what did she say?' I asked.

'*Dix euros, s'il vous plait.*'

'And that was it?'

'No, then Ed took a picture of us.'

'And then?'

'She went to serve someone else.'

'And is her name Christine?'

'I'm not sure.'

I let the silence hang for a moment, savouring the victory.

'Not exactly what I'd call action,' I concluded.

'No.'

'There's probably no need for Ed to buy a new map of the world and stick a big, pink Sam-action pin in the middle of Paris.'

'No.'

'Anyway, happy thirtieth birthday, mate.'

And then we all burst out laughing, and Sam laughed, too, clapping me just a little bit too hard on the back. What I like – love – about Sam is that he always enjoys laughing at himself more than at other people. There are few greater qualities in a friend.

'So anyway, children, and Alan,' he said, retaking control of the group. 'What are we doing tonight?'

'Anything except a strip club,' I said.

'Come on,' implored Sam. 'What would Bond do?'

'Bond would kill you several times over.'

'But it's my birthday.'

'It's my stag.'

'I'm organising it.'

'I'm paying for it.'

'But I'm the best man.'

'And I'm the groom.'

'The groom's outvoted,' said Ed.

'Yes,' agreed Matt.

'Three to one,' said Sam. 'Four to one, if we count Jess's advice. So do man-up and have a good time.'

At the end of the previous year, I'd thought that a relationship was between two people, not an entire group. On that sunny July weekend in Paris, I realised again that I'd been wrong. A relationship is always about more than the two people at the centre of it. It's about the relationships you form with others, as individuals and as a couple, the friends you bring together around you, the whole more than the sum of its parts.

So, yes, I thought that evening, as I surveyed three of my best four friends in one of Paris's filthiest strip clubs, *I am manning-up, I am enjoying myself. My plan will work. And they are in for one heck of a surprise in my wedding speech.*

Chapter Twenty-Three

It all finished, appropriately enough, at a wedding.

Like most people between the age of twenty-eight and thirty-five, the rhythm of my calendar year is ruled by the predictability of the marrying classes. In late summer, the girl tends to get down on one knee in front of her boyfriend's boss and emasculate him by proffering a hideously naff male engagement ring. Over the winter, they generally fall out because the girl accuses the guy of sleeping with his boss and he accuses her of sleeping with his best friend she's always disliked, and then the following summer... But no, not this time. Alan's wedding wouldn't be the same as all the rest. This time, I was going to suspend my cynicism. These two actually *were* meant to be together.

Some things, however, didn't change. I still had to use the hastily assembled Hotmail address to reply to the invitation – surely they knew I was coming? *I* was the best man – because I didn't have any writing paper. The traditional row about the date still took place, in all its filthy glory, because it clashed with Alan's mum's niece's wedding, and Jess's staggeringly posh mum had already booked an expensive marquee. Various peripheral friends still lobbied transparently for an invitation. And to my shame, I still had to resort to the traditional set of £3.99 tablemats from the list because I was too slow off the mark and all the better presents had gone.

There was even a certain symmetry to the way in which Alan's wedding day itself started.

'Wake up, you dozy tosser.'

'Go away, fuck face.'

'Big day today.'

I groaned and pulled the duvet a little higher. 'Not as big as your big, disappointed mother, who's about to lose you for ever.'

But it was a big day, for me as well as Alan, not least because I was allowed to drive him to the ceremony in his new sports car: the one luxury he had allowed himself since the record-breaking payout from his old firm for sexual harassment. It had been an extraordinary three months, all things considered. We'd guessed that Alan might take voluntary redundancy and move on to a new job he preferred. Matt had even wondered whether he might use the dirt he had on Amanda to secure a slightly better severance package. But none of us had expected him to take the company to an employment tribunal, sue them for sexual harassment and win a landmark out-of-court settlement that made the front pages of most newspapers.

Alan had been hailed as a pathetic loser and derided as a pioneering hero in fairly equal measures. 'What red-blooded male wouldn't want to be sexually harassed by this woman?' demanded one tabloid above an attractive picture of Amanda. 'A new hero for men's rights,' declared an opinion piece by the familiar-sounding Ed O'Brien, jumping back on the broadsheet bandwagon for one last bit of extra holiday money.

For his part, Alan didn't seem to care that much. 'It was just the right thing to do,' he said, and none of us had any real response except to marvel privately at his courage. It was one thing to be bullied by a woman in the workplace. It was quite another to turn it so magnificently to one's advantage. He had painstakingly collected evidence – emails, eye-witness accounts from colleagues, my testimony, even the footage taken by his dad with an old camcorder at his engagement party – and given Amanda the shock of her life that she had always deserved. We all knew who the real alpha of our group was.

Not that you would have known it to observe Alan on the morning of his wedding. Once fully conscious, I was the only one capable of thinking straight. Having helped him find his clothes, I had to help him get dressed. Having helped him get dressed, I had to help him find his car keys. Having found his car keys, he couldn't remember where he had parked the car. All the while he babbled incomprehensibly, fretting about everything from last-minute changes in the seating plan to how rude I was planning on being in my speech.

'Shut up!' I yelled, my patience finally exhausted as he started to drone on about the organist's choice of music. I banged my head against the kitchen door until the drone stopped. 'Just shut up! Shut up! Shut up! Shut –'

'Sorry.' He fell quiet at last, surprised by my outburst. When he spoke again, it was in a whisper. 'It's just that I'm not sure if I can go through with this.'

We sat down on the sofa while Alan stared at the floor in agonised silence. Eventually he continued, his gaze barely rising above his freshly polished shoes: 'It's just that it's all so scary. So grown-up. I mean, look at me, Sam. I'm about to be a married man, but most of the time I still feel like the nervous five-year-old you threw pebbles at all those years ago. Maybe you were right when you said that growing-up was overrated, because a large bit of me just wants to crawl back under the covers and not face today.' He ran his hand over his tidy hair and turned to look at me directly. 'I'm about to make a public promise to stay with one woman for the rest of my life. And although Jess is the woman I love, the only woman I've ever loved or ever will, and although I don't want to be with anyone else, I know that, when I'm there in that church, about to say that vow, there's going to be a voice in the back of my head whispering: "Don't do it, Alan. Don't trap yourself. This is not what you want. Be free. Be selfish. Be a man."'

Alan took his expensive new handkerchief out of his button-hole and blew his nose, loudly and messily. I offered him mine as a replacement and looked again at my friend. There was no doubt that I knew what he meant. I was well acquainted with that voice in the back of one's head, even if mine tended to shout instead of whisper. It was another good reason why I was unlikely ever to get married. I could, therefore, have indulged Alan. I could easily have said that I shared his concerns, that he was right to panic, that it was only natural for bridegrooms to have last-minute doubts. But something told me that, after almost nine years of dating Jess, Alan would respond better to a bit of tough love. So I read him the riot act, toughly and lovingly. I told him he was being a tit – a great big sexually harassed tit of a former accountant – and that Jess was the best thing that had ever happened to him. If he didn't pull himself together, I concluded, I would go and marry her myself.

'Thanks, Sam,' said Alan, at last, getting up from the sofa and brushing himself down. 'That was just what I needed to hear.'

We hugged – a good, solid hug without any awkwardness – while I looked over the top of his head at the flat that had been my home for so many years. Alan had said he'd have a word with his uncle about my staying on there. But it wouldn't be the same, would it? Alan wouldn't be there; he'd be living somewhere else with Jess. And when would we get to see him, anyway? Friends get married and then they vanish, however much they protest they won't, into Marriage-Land, a small country like Lichtenstein or Andorra, which no one who isn't married can ever find. I stifled a small sob of my own – so small that Alan wouldn't have noticed. This was his day and I was there to make it go smoothly. I led him to his new car.

For once, it appeared that the course of true love would run smooth. All the things that have to happen at church passed without mishap. Alan choked just enough on his vows for the women in the congregation to think he was sweet but not so much that the men would think him a wimp. Jess looked prettier and thinner than usual, and didn't fall over her dress, while her bridesmaids were sufficiently attractive to give the relatives a bit of eye candy, but not so beautiful that they upstaged the bride. Amanda didn't turn up and demand to be screwed sideways before Alan got married. The vicar didn't even bother to allude to God, but did manage a weak joke when no one said anything after the 'hold your peace' bit. I fumbled with the ring, but caught it before it hit the floor. Alan's mother managed a fixed smile when she congratulated Jess outside. Claire dropped the bouquet.

After the service, we walked along well-tended Home Counties hedgerows to the huge marquee provided by Jess's parents and I started to get nervous. Everyone assumes that actors are great at giving speeches. They forget that the words are normally provided for us. Even that is nerve-wracking enough.

'I'm on top table.' I turned to Ed, who was also studying the seating plan and looked pleased to have been placed next to Claire.

'Of course you're on the bloody top table. You're best bloody man.'

'Yes, mate, I know.' I patted him on the shoulder. 'Bad luck.'

However, life on the top table, I soon discovered, was a great deal less fun than on the lower rungs of the wedding pecking order. No one drank properly. Everyone faced outwards. And the only person to flirt with was Jess's ninety-three-year-old grandmother.

The first course came and went, mainly untouched by me. Pudding. Coffee. Unidentifiable chocolates. And then, just as the shadows were beginning to lengthen outside, someone tapped a glass and Jess's father, 'unaccustomed as he was to public speaking', was on his feet. He stayed there for half an hour, a feat of heroic, epic dullness which he started with a somnolent anecdote about where he was when Jess's mother went into labour (work, I think), continued through Jess's first words ('I want', probably), her Grade 2 cello exam (in which she achieved a merit) and her GCSE results ('more A-stars than

I could count'), and ended, tearfully, by welcoming Alan ('my new son') into the family.

As this was Jess's wedding, she decided that the traditional mute role of the bride was not for her. She followed her father and spoke eloquently, briefly and from the heart, leaving no one in any doubt of her love for Alan. I admonished myself, quietly and for the final time, for ever having doubted that fact.

It was a tough act to follow such a sweet speech with a string of puerile jokes about Alan's boyhood and early adult life, but I think I rose acceptably to the occasion. Once I was on my feet and the first laugh had tumbled out, I actually began to enjoy myself. When I got to the nice part at the end about how much I had always loved Alan, and how I had grown to love Jess as well, I noticed a rather pretty girl on a distant table wiping a tear from her eye. I wiped away an imaginary tear of my own and made a mental note to share my top-table magic with her as soon as my duties were over.

'And so,' I concluded, 'I used to be a little cynical about marriage. I used to think it was what you did when you turned thirty and the music stopped. I used to think weddings were simply an endless round of hymns and in-laws and seating plans and first dances and speeches and cakes and bands that think they can play The Beatles and "champagne" that's not quite champagne. I used to think all that applied to everyone. And I was wrong. It was Alan and Jess who made me realise I was wrong. They're perfect for each other. They're perfect for marriage. Always have been. Always will be. And I will always be a friend to both of them.'

I sat down again, to enthusiastic, smiling applause, making way for Alan. 'On behalf of his wife and himself' – to a huge and predictable roar of approval – he thanked the bridesmaids, the organist, the friends of Jess's mother who had arranged the church flowers, the ushers, the designer who had helped with the Order of Service, the vicar, the choir, the caterers, the waitresses, everyone who'd come, from far and wide, near and narrow, everyone who hadn't been able to come... By the time he'd showered the entire room, many of them twice over, with heartfelt gratitude, I was starting to fidget impatiently. This was why I'd always thought weddings were one big sham. What had we learned about Alan and Jess as a couple?

Get a bloody move on, mate, so I can go and chat up pretty, weepy girl on Table 11.

But then Alan put down his notes, took off his glasses and started talking about Jess. I stopped fidgeting and everyone else woke up as he described how they'd met, how he'd felt when he'd first seen her, how he hadn't slept for a week between asking her out and their first date. 'And you know what?' he added. 'I still feel that sense of excitement every day.'

And if I really thought about it, I think I did know that. It was obvious in the way he spoke about her, the way he acted around her. It had always been obvious. I had just chosen to ignore it because I was jealous. Alan could have inconsequential last-minute doubts like any normal man, but his love for Jess was evident to everyone. I'd said it in my speech, but now I actually believed it. Maybe soulmates did exist after all. Maybe some people were actually lucky enough to find them. And keep them.

I looked across at Ed and Claire, as he performed a nervous cinema-yawn and draped his arm over her shoulder. She gave him a half-smile and allowed him to leave it there. Matt, who was sitting on the same table, caught my eye and gave a thumbs-up. I returned it. We were one-down then – maybe even one or two more on the way – two to go. Matt and I would be all right, though. We were copers. Maybe we were still too immature to find someone for life. Or perhaps we never would. Matt had finally ditched Debbie. Claire wasn't my soulmate, nor Lisa nor Mary Money-Barings nor Christine. And if Rosie was,

I didn't deserve her. But we still had our mates, didn't we? Just as long as I didn't end up like Amanda.

And then Alan did something quite remarkable.

We thought he had finished. He'd wound up the anecdote about proposing to Jess in Istanbul. There were no dry eyes left in the marquee, just as everyone had shed tears of mirth when he'd described her pre-emptive proposal to him outside his office. He was a much better speaker than anyone had imagined. But then he paused, the room in his hand, and whispered something in Jess's ear. She smiled and handed him something unidentifiable and made of metal. Alan straightened up again and continued.

'There is one final thank-you I'd like to say, if you'll forgive me, and that is to my best and oldest friends, Sam, Ed and Matt. They have stood by me for over twenty-five years, through thick and thin, good times and bad, and I love them all like brothers. I want to say a very personal thank-you to all of them and also, I hope, a practical one.'

I looked across at Ed and Matt who both looked as confused as I did. None of us had any idea what he was talking about.

Alan went on: 'My wife and I have talked this over at length, and we are agreed that marriage can be an isolating experience while you're still young. We don't want to live alone in a small, cocooned flat. We don't want to lose touch with some of our oldest friends. We're not convinced that two is enough these days. Now, as most of you know, I recently came into a rather large sum of money in somewhat unfortunate circumstances.' A knowing murmur went up around the room. Alan continued: 'While Jess and I are moving into our new marital home in Camden, I hope Ed, Sam and Matt won't think it too presumptuous that I have also invested in the three-bedroom house next door.'

There was a long, stunned silence while Ed stared at Matt, who stared at me, who stared at Alan, who was, I now noticed, dangling a front-door key and staring anxiously into the void. Everyone stared at all of us. And then Matt smiled, and Ed grinned, and I beamed from ear to ear. Alan and Jess looked at each other and laughed, allowing the rest of the wedding party to break into spontaneous applause at the sheer, contagious joy of it all.

Did I think it was presumptuous? No, I thought it was bloody marvellous. I'd given Alan a set of tablemats; he'd given me one third of a house.

Not that it would work long-term, of course. We'd argue, and fight, and maybe even meet other people ourselves with whom we wanted to organise a £20,000 party with a forty per cent chance of ending up in divorce. And in the meantime, it would be difficult to moan to the landlord about the leaking boiler when the landlord was your best friend. Plus, no doubt we'd get on Jess's nerves if we popped round the whole time. But until we were absolutely sure Ed was okay, until Matt had finished retraining and had a secure job, until I'd properly found my feet as an actor… Until then, whenever, and if ever, that might be, what was wrong with growing older in small steps?

Jess and Alan made their way out onto an empty dance floor. The lights dimmed, the band started and Alan slipped an arm round her waist. She let him lead and they moved as one fluent whole, spinning away from each other and drawing back close again. They had clearly been practising. A circle formed around them, the music gathered tempo and Jess beckoned the rest of the party to join them. Matt needed no second invitation; he'd grabbed pretty, weepy girl from Table 11 before I was even out of the starting blocks. Ed was close behind with Claire. I turned left. I turned right. *No one.* And so I went up to Jess's grandmother and asked if she would do me the honour. She gripped me tight with the hand that wasn't holding her stick and we cleared a path out to the middle of the floor.

'It has been the most wonderful wedding, hasn't it?' My voice sounded alien, but I meant it nonetheless.

Jess's grandmother looked up at me and smiled. 'You have no idea how happy it makes an old lady to see her granddaughter on a day like this.'

I looked around at all the people who had been brought together by Alan and Jess. I looked at Alan's mother, laughing as Jess's father twirled her across the floor. Behind her, Jess's mother was helping Alan's father remove his jacket as he prepared for the dad-at-a-wedding dance to end all dads-at-a-wedding dances. I looked at all these people and thought, well, maybe, just maybe, I did have a little bit of an idea after all.

'It's all about the family, isn't it?' I replied, spinning Jess's grandmother in a very gentle celebratory arc as the drummer rolled out the final bars of the first song.

'Yes,' she said, as I bumped clumsily into Ed and Claire, locked in a passionate embrace. 'It's all about the family. And the friends.'

There was a tap on my shoulder as the next song started up. I looked round.

'Excuse me,' said Alan. 'Do you mind if I cut in?'

'Really, mate, this is taking the love-in too far. I don't want to dance with you.'

'No, you idiot. I want to dance with Jess's grandmother. In the meantime, perhaps you'd do me the honour of dancing with my wife.'

Alan let go of Jess's hand and I took it instead. We started to dance.

'Mrs Muir,' I said. 'You look absolutely ravishing.'

'Thank you, Sam. And thank you for your speech.'

'Thank you for the house.'

'I'm looking forward to being neighbours.'

'Me, too. Until death do us part.'

Jess let out a small, ambiguous noise. It might have been a sigh of pleasure. It might have been a muted howl of despair.

'Until death do us part.'

Acknowledgments

I'd like to thank:

My wonderful parents, and the rest of my family, for not disowning me after my first book

Diana, Matt and Ali, for their helpful suggestions and invaluable encouragement

Charlie Campbell, my ever-supportive agent at Ed Victor Ltd

Mary Morris, my excellent editor at Duckworth, and her brilliant colleagues

Michael McManus, for saving me from the wrong career path all those years ago

Christopher Howse, for generously finding me a new one while I wrote this book

Jimmy Ellis, the ur-alpha male, for unwittingly giving me the idea

Ed A-B, for his entrepreneurial good humour

Gaby's lovely book club, even if they didn't get their way on the colour of Rosie's hair

Literary Review, for teaching me, very gently, that I can't write about sex

I'd like to apologise to:

My delightful evangelical Christian friends, especially if they turn out to be right

3/11